Shadows of the Past

by

Sherry Moore

PublishAmerica
Baltimore

© 2004 by Sherry Moore.

First printing

ISBN: 1-4137-2988-6
PUBLISHED BY PUBLISHAMERICA, LLLP
www.publishamerica.com
Baltimore

Printed in the United States of America

This is dedicated to my family –

For my husband and children, who are my everything – I love you!

For my parents, who never lost faith in me and set the foundation which I have learned to follow;

For my sisters, who told me I could do anything and always stayed by my side;

And to my friends, who have shown me that there are angels on earth!

PART 1
In The
Beginning

CHAPTER 1

Samantha Higgins opened the main door of the police station, relieved to be finally going home. As she stepped outside, a warm breeze touched her face and she let out a sigh. *It is finally over,* she thought to herself. For the hundredth time, Samantha thought back to when the terror had first begun four and a half years ago. As she did each time she would think about the past, she thought about how she might have avoided everything that had happened.

* * *

Samantha quickly stepped into the warm house. She shivered slightly as she dusted the snow off of her jacket. She shook her head as she threw her jacket on the floor.

"Figures that it would snow on a Friday night."

She ran down the stairs to her room and turned on the stereo. As she pulled off her boots she glanced at the backpack, which she knew was completely filled with homework.

"If my teachers think that I am going to spend my weekend reading a bunch of textbooks, they have another thing coming." It was the middle of January and Sam was in her senior year of high school. At seventeen, Samantha Higgins was the princess of manipulation. Everywhere she went, she put on an image that best suited her environment. When she was at her job, for example, people saw a very mature, hard-working young woman who looked to be at least twenty-three. At school, she had always been at the top of her class. None of her teachers knew about the beer that she hid in her locker or ever suspected anything bad when she missed class from time to time. She was good at coming up with believable stories that would have the teachers feeling sorry for her in a minute. She knew that she did not deserve some of the grades that she received, but she was not about to complain.

Sam's appearance helped her above everything else. She was petite and had long, wavy blonde hair and amazing green eyes. She looked innocent and trusting, and yet very mature. She was a beautiful young lady and people always seemed to be drawn to her. It amazed and amused Sam to know that she could be whatever people expected her to be – and she took full advantage of it.

Sam walked over to the window and watched the snow that was falling hard outside. She picked up the telephone and, as she dialed her friend's number, she ran her finger along the frost on the window. The phone was answered on the first ring.

"Hello?"

"Hey Laura, what are you doing?" Sam walked back over to her bed and sat down.

"Oh, not much. Have you looked outside? As hard as it is snowing, how are we supposed to go out tonight? If we take that old junker of a truck of yours, we will either freeze to death or end up in a ditch somewhere."

Sam laughed as she pictured her friend acting in complete panic. "Ha ha, very funny. Don't worry, I was thinking of asking my mom if I can borrow her car tonight."

Laura laughed. "You do not actually think that she will let you use her car, do you?"

"I am going to do everything that I can to try to convince her." Sam heard someone coming in the front door. "Hey, I think my mom is home. Let me call you back in just a little bit, ok?"

"Sure, Sami. Good luck."

Sam hung up the phone and waited for a moment to think about what she was going to say to her mother. All of a sudden Sam's bedroom door flew open and her mother was standing there holding out Sam's wet jacket.

"Samantha, how many times have I told you not to leave your jacket on the floor by the front door?"

"Here we go again," Sam mumbled to herself.

"What was that, young lady?"

"Nothing, Mom. Look, I'm sorry, ok, but my coat was soaking wet from the snow." She grabbed her coat from her mother and, as she turned away she rolled her eyes. "Give me a break," she mouthed.

"I don't know how many times I have told you to hang your coat up over a chair when it gets wet. I'm really getting tired of seeing it lying on the floor like that." Her mother walked over to the stereo and turned it off. "I'd swear you must be going deaf. How can you listen to that awful music as loud as you do? I just don't get it."

Sam rolled her eyes again. "So how was your day, Mom?"

Her mother looked at her for a moment and took a deep breath. "Oh, it was ok, I guess. The roads are starting to get pretty icy and you know how much I hate driving in this stuff."

"Yeah well, now that you happen to mention it, would you mind if I borrowed your car tonight? I had made some plans to go out on a double date with Laura and you know how awful my truck is in this weather. Besides, could you see my friends huddled in the back of the truck? Plus, my heater is still not working." Sam started to twirl her hair around her fingers as she waited for her mother's response.

"You have got to be kidding me!" She looked at Sam in surprise. "You aren't actually planning to go out in this weather, are you?

"I had already made the plans and there is no way to break them at the last minute like this. Everyone is relying on me to pick them up. Besides, this weather doesn't bother me at all, you know that."

"I really don't care if this weather bothers you or not. I am not going to risk you getting yourself and your friends killed, not to mention what might happen to my car." Her mother walked over and sat down next to her. She touched Sam's hair lightly with her fingers. "That is my only way of getting to work, and I just can't take the risk. You will just have to make other plans." Her mother stood up and started to walk out of the room.

Sam jumped up off of the bed and followed her up the stairs.

"Come on, Mom, you can't do this to me. I promise that I won't do anything to your car. Please?"

Her mother looked at her seriously for a moment. She shook her head in frustration. "Ok, fine, but if anything happens…"

"Nothing will happen, I promise. Thanks, Mom." Sam ran back down the stairs and called Laura back.

"How did it go?

"I'll tell you, Laura, trying to change my mother's mind about something is like trying to pry a bone out of a dog's mouth. With a little work though, I finally got her to agree to let me use her car."

"Alright Sami! So what time are you going to pick me up?"

"Let me just get changed and I will be over in a little while."

"Sounds great, see you in a bit."

Sam hung up the phone and started to get ready for the night ahead of her.

CHAPTER 2

As Sam drove to Laura's house, she thought about her mother. She loved her in a way that no words could ever describe and yet she also felt very intimidated by her. In a way, she wanted her mother to think that she was perfect and that she could never do anything wrong. She could fool her most of the time, but parents always seem to have a way of finding out the truth about the trouble that their children have gotten into. When Sam got into trouble, it was her mother's words that were always the worst punishment. She could always make her cry.

Sam shook her head. If only her father had not abandoned them. He had left when Sam was only four, and Sam's mom had to bring up Sam and her older sister Jessica by herself. Although Sam and Jessie were too young to remember his leaving, they could always see the pain in their mother's eyes when they asked about their father. They had both learned at a very early age not to bother asking.

Sam heard a loud noise and blinked hard as she realized that someone had honked at her. She had been drifting towards the center of the road. She shook her head and tried to concentrate on the snow-packed roads the rest of the way to her friend's house.

Sam picked up Laura and then they drove a couple of blocks to where they were picking up their dates. The girls watched as the two young men ran through the snow and then jumped into the car. Sam had just met Josh recently and, as she watched him now, she wondered what she saw in him. He did not own a car and he would probably never work a day in his life.

Laura's date, Greg, was not a whole lot better. He was six foot two inches tall and had long, scraggly hair. Although they were both tall, her sophisticated looks strongly contrasted his unkempt appearance. Sam realized that these boys were a lot of fun to party with, but that was about all.

Sam looked at Josh, who was now sitting in the passenger side of the car.

"So Josh, did you get the directions to the party?"

"Yeah babe, I sure did. Hey, where did you get the car?"

"It's my mom's, so try not to get anything on the seats, ok?"

Josh shrugged and Sam shook her head.

They had only been driving for about ten minutes and Sam was starting to have a difficult time seeing where she was going. They had the radio turned up high and everyone was singing and talking loudly which was fogging up all of the windows. She was trying to make her way onto the highway when she noticed that a pickup truck was in front of her. The truck was going so slow that Sam started to get annoyed.

"Where do these stupid people get their drivers' licenses, anyway?" She mumbled to herself. "I'm just going to pass this idiot."

Sam started to pull around the truck when suddenly she saw the edge of the road. She hit her foot hard on the break pedal but the back tires started to slide on the icy road. As the car slid closer to the edge, Sam saw that the side of the road dropped off down a steep incline and they were heading right for it.

"We can't do this," she shouted. "Oh man, we're going to do it anyway. Hold on everyone."

She could hear Laura scream as the car went off the side of the road. It felt to Sam as though the car was going to roll over onto its side. She grabbed onto the steering wheel and closed her eyes, not quite sure what to expect.

The car bounced hard to the left and then hard to the right. It felt like the car would never stop bouncing when suddenly the car was rolling smoothly on the highway again. Everyone was silent for a moment and then three of the tires went flat.

"Is everyone alright?" She turned around and saw that they had not been wearing their seat belts. Greg was lying on top of Laura, holding her down and it took them another moment before they sat up. Laura immediately started to rub the side of her head.

"My head hurts a little bit, but I think I am alright. How about you guys?"

Sam looked at Josh and was surprised to see him smiling.

"Man, that was great! What a ride. What did we drive through anyway? Man, I bet you totaled this car out."

Sam sighed again and then got out of the car to see what damage had been done. As soon as she stood up she got a sharp pain in her abdomen. She put one hand over her stomach and leaned against the car. It was such a sharp pain that it took her breath away. No one had noticed her standing there and by the time everyone had gotten out of the car, the pain had stopped.

She turned and saw that the car had come down a steep embankment and had landed on the highway below. She was surprised to see that, from what she could tell, there was not a scratch or dent anywhere on the body of the car. She looked at Josh in surprise.

"I don't understand it. After what just happened you'd think that the car would be a mess."

Josh laughed. "Silly girl. The way we bounced around, you probably bent the sub-carriage. The under-carriage of this car has to be fried. Let's see if we can get these tires back up at all."

Josh and Greg opened the trunk to look for the spare tire and also found a can of fix-a-flat . They changed one tire and managed to get air in the others. They all got back in the car, but within a couple hundred feet the tires were all flat again.

"We are going to have to leave the car here. Why don't we see if we can find a phone. We better call someone to come and get us," Greg suggested.

"Why don't you and Josh run down to those homes down there and see if someone will let you use their phone," Sam instructed. "Laura and I will wait here by the car in case the police show up."

Sam and Laura waited and watched as the snow lightened to just flurries. The boys returned and within twenty minutes Josh's dad had arrived. They explained to him what had happened and he walked behind the car and glanced up at the on ramp above them.

"You can see the tire tracks in the snow," he said. "Man, oh man, I can't believe you kids are still alive. You must have bounced around on those rocks and ice, and Lord only knows how you ended up back on the road again. By all rights, the car should have flipped and you kids should have all been killed or at least seriously injured. Well, come on, let me take you back to my place so you can call your folks."

Once they were back at Josh's house, Sam started to get nervous. How was she going to possibly explain what happened to her mother?

"What are you thinking, Sami?"

Sam turned to see Laura standing next to her. She was worried about how pale her friend looked.

"I am trying to figure out how I am going to tell my mom what happened."

"Well, don't worry about it too much. She will probably be so worried about you, that she hopefully won't even think about the car right away."

Sam smiled at her friend. "I sure hope you're right."

CHAPTER 3

"You what?"

Sam blinked hard as she listened to her mother screaming in the phone.

"I told you not to drive my car in this weather. Where is my car now?"

Sam took a deep breath. "It is on the side of the road on Highway 6. I can't remember which exit we were by. Hold on while I get Josh's dad."

Sam set the phone down without even waiting for a response. She looked up at Josh's father. "Could you please tell my mother where the car is?" He nodded and Sam walked out of the room into the living room. Laura followed her and put her hand on Sam's shoulder.

"What happened, Sam?"

Sam looked down and started to cry. "She just blew up. She never even asked if we were hurt. All she cared about was her stupid car." Sam pulled away from Laura and walked back to one of the bathrooms. It was then that she found out that she was bleeding. She did not know why she had not thought about it before when she had been cramping so badly. She subconsciously put her hand on her stomach and felt guilty for having ignored the baby inside of her. Suddenly she realized what the cramping and bleeding must have meant and she started sobbing uncontrollably. She tried to pull herself together when a sharp pain shot across her midsection again, knocking her to the floor. She felt as though she could not breathe and she was doubled over on the floor.

"Sami, are you alright in there?" Laura was knocking on the door. "Sam?" She started to open the door when saw her friend lying on the floor in a pool of blood. "Oh my God! Don't move, Sami! I'm calling for help."

Laura ran into the living room just as Josh's father was hanging up the phone. "Samantha's mother is having her neighbor drive her and she will be here in just a few minutes. Laura, what is wrong?" He could see she was flushed and very scared.

"It's Sam. Please, call an ambulance. Hurry, I think she is having a miscarriage." As she said the words, Josh and Greg looked at her in surprise. Neither one had known that Sam was pregnant.

13

The emergency room waiting area was fairly busy as Sam's mother waited to find out what was happening to her daughter. She jumped to her feet when she heard her name being called.

"Mrs. Higgins? This way please."

She followed the nurse to where a doctor was hastily writing notes on a board. He smiled when he saw her. "Hi, Mrs. Higgins, I'm Dr. Martin. Your daughter is fine. She has lost some blood, but not enough to cause any worry." He paused and then looked at her seriously. "Unfortunately, she has lost the baby."

"Baby, what baby? My daughter is not pregnant." She looked confused and was shaking her head. They must have had her confused with someone else.

"She didn't tell you? Well, this is definitely not the way to find out. Your daughter was about four months pregnant. From the way your daughter described the car accident, the bouncing around must have caused her to lose the baby. I'm sorry you had to find out this way. She is in bed four if you would like to see her."

When her mother walked up to her, Sam did not look at her. She had been surprised at how much it had upset her that she had lost the baby. It had been a horrible night and she did not have the courage to face her mother.

"You were pregnant? How could you hide this from me?" There was a look of shock and then anger as she sat on the edge of the bed. "Who's the father? Was it one of the boys you went out with tonight?"

Sam looked down and felt the sting of tears touch her cheek. "No. His name is Dave and I go to school with him. I just got so tired of everyone teasing me that I was still a virgin and I just didn't want to say no anymore. I didn't know I was going to get pregnant."

"God, Sam. The least you could have done was use birth control. Did that not occur to you? How long were you planning on hiding this from me?" She was almost shouting and she had stood up and had her back to Sam.

Sam tried to sit up but the pain was too much. She looked pleadingly at her mother's back. "Dave was so mad when I told him, Mom, that he said he was going to kill himself if I told anyone. I knew you would be furious and I just didn't know what to do. I just figured I would deal with it when I had to." She did not want to admit to her mother that it had never occurred to her to use birth control.

"Well this is just great. Not only do I not have a car now, but I can't even trust you anymore either. You are going to be paying for whatever has to be done to that car, as well as whatever this is going to cost," she said as she pointed around the room. "And don't bother to make any more plans with your friends. You won't be going anywhere except school and work for a long time." Her mother turned and stormed past the nurses' station just as the doctor was approaching. Everyone at the nurses' station had heard her and suspected correctly what she had been so upset about. Dr. Martin just shook his head and went to get Sam's release papers.

CHAPTER 4

"Poetry is like a diary of one's life," Mrs. Johnson stated as she began to pace back and forth in front of the class. "Now there are many different forms of poetry that can be used…"

Sam looked out the window next to her seat and watched as two squirrels chased each other around a tree. It had been a couple of weeks since the incident with her mother's car, and it seemed like her relationship with her mother was only getting worse.

Whenever they were in the family room together and a commercial about a car would come on the television, Sam's mom had to say something. Sam laughed to herself as she thought about what had been said the night before.

A commercial came on about a local auto dealership and it showed a woman who loved her new car. Sam's mom had turned to Sam and said, "I bet she doesn't let her daughter use her car."

Sam shook her head. *I am getting really tired of this*, she thought to herself. She looked down at the empty page of her notebook and shook her head as she closed the book. *I am so miserable living at home – I wish that there were some way that I could get away from there. Mom will obviously never understand me. I hate my life right now.*

Sam leaned her head down on the desk and just gazed out the window when suddenly she realized that Mrs. Johnson was calling out her name.

"Samantha? Thank you for joining us again. It seems that you have found something much more important than my class. Why don't you share it with the rest of the class?"

"You have got to be kidding," Sam said as she stared at her teacher.

"No, I am not. Go ahead Samantha, we are waiting."

Sam stood up and grabbed her books. "I don't need this crap. I get enough of that at home." A few of the students laughed and others were whispering to each other as she rushed past her teacher and went out into the hallway, where she stopped and leaned against a locker. Mrs. Johnson came out and stared at her for a moment.

"I just heard about your car accident. I'm sorry that you lost your baby, Samantha."

Sam looked surprised and than she flushed with embarrassment.

"I know you are having a tough time, Samantha, but you need to concentrate on your studies while you are in the classroom. If you need to see the school counselor, I will excuse you this time, but I expect more mature behavior in the future. Do you understand me, young lady?"

Sam bit the inside of her mouth and nodded. As soon as her teacher had returned to the classroom, Sam released the tears she had been fighting back.

"Great, now my teacher even makes me cry." Sam heard the bell ring and she quickly tried to pull herself together. Suddenly she felt someone's hand on her shoulder and she jumped. She turned around and was surprised to see Tammy, a girl that she had known since elementary school. They had once been very close, but this last year of high school their interests had changed and they had stopped spending time together. Sam looked at her now, surprised that she had stopped her.

"Sami, are you alright?"

Sam laughed sarcastically. "Yeah, just great." Sam turned and saw Laura walking down the hallway and she ran to catch up with her. "Hey, Laura, wait up," she yelled as she left Tammy standing alone behind her.

Tammy shook her head and then she headed off in the opposite direction.

CHAPTER 5

The card slid easily in the security slot and the door clicked open loudly as Sam entered the building. She walked the short distance to the Human Resources Department and quickly sat down at her desk. Her mind had been going in so many different directions lately that she was glad that she had her work to retreat to.

Thanks to one of her business teachers, the Brewery had hired Sam during the end of her junior year. She had quickly taken on the writing, publishing, and distributing of the plant's monthly publication and she was good at what she did. The certificates she was proudly looking at now proved that.

"How are you feeling today, Samantha?"

Sam jumped as she turned and saw her supervisor, Julie, standing next to her. Sam leaned back in her chair and smiled. She loved her job and she adored Julie.

"Hey, Julie. Guess what? I am working on this great article for our publication. I think you'll like it. If it's ok with you, I would like to interview the guys in department eight upstairs. Those guys don't get enough credit for all their hard..."

"Sam. I'm sorry to interrupt you, but Jodi from Personnel needs to see you. Do you want me to come with you?"

Sam looked at her in surprise. "What would Jodi want to see me for? She can't be wanting to transfer me to a different department; we are so busy here." Sam shrugged. "Do you mind coming with me?" Julie nodded but there was a strange look in her eyes.

They walked down the long hallway and when they entered the Personnel office, Jodi immediately stood up to greet them. "Hi, Ms. Higgins. Julie, it is a surprise to see you here this morning as well." She walked up to Sami and gave her a long, serious look. "Samantha, you have been a hard worker and have done some really wonderful things here. It has come to my attention, however, that you are pregnant. Is that true?"

Sam tried to keep her composure as she spoke. "No, ma'am." She glanced down at the floor. "Well, I was pregnant, but had a car accident and lost the baby." She glanced back up and Jodi smiled warmly at her.

"I like you, Samantha, but my loyalty is to this company. We have an important reputation in this community as well as all over the United States. In this division, you are the only minor we have ever hired. We hired you because of the high praise we received from your business teachers." Jodi took a long sigh, almost as if she was inhaling a cigarette. "I'm sorry to have to tell you that we cannot have our only minor being pregnant. We are going to have to lay you off, Samantha. You can call it a reduction in work force, if you would like. I will even give you a full month to look for another job. Actually, we have hired someone from another department to replace you, and we will need you to use this month to train her. You can take any time you need for interviews and we will give you a positive report to anyone you need us to. Do you have any questions?" Sam shook her head as her upper lip quivered slightly. "Good. Thank you for coming by, Miss Higgins. Julie. Have a nice day."

Sam and Julie left her office and Julie put her hand around Sam's shoulders. "You handled that beautifully, Sam. I'm proud of you."

Sam was numb as she walked back to her desk. She sat down and rubbed her temple. "Julie, would you mind if I just go home?"

Julie nodded and Sam grabbed her backpack and headed for the exit. The security guard smiled as she approached him. He was a large man and was intimidating to most people, except Sam. She always joked around with him before leaving work.

"Leaving so soon, darlin'?"

Sam tried to smile as she approached him. "Hi, Ben. You wouldn't believe the day I have had. It is one of those Calgon take me away kind of days."

Ben chuckled and held the door open for her. "Don't you go lettin' this place get to you now," he ordered. "I expect to see you back to your ole self again tomorrow, you hear, young lady?"

Sam just nodded and quietly went outside. It was raining and Sam ran through the parking lot to her small truck. Her tears were mixed with the raindrops on her cheeks as she made her way home.

Once home, Sam felt like she was going to go crazy. She started to pace around her bedroom.

"I can't stand this any longer," she cried out loud. "I lose my job just to come home and be grounded. Give me a break." She stopped pacing and stared at her car keys for a moment. "To heck with it. What Mom doesn't know won't hurt her."

Sam grabbed her keys and headed out to her truck. As soon as she stepped outside she smiled to herself.

"Why didn't I think about this before?" She laughed and then got in to her truck and drove over to Laura's house. When she knocked on Laura's door, she laughed at the shocked expression on her friend's face when she opened the door.

"Sami, what are you doing here? Your mom will kill you if she finds out that you aren't home."

Sam smiled. "Let me in, you goof. My mom will never know that I ever left."

"But what if she tries to call you?"

"Simple. She'll get a busy signal. I took the phone off the hook, of course. She thinks I live on the phone anyway."

"Sweet! Come up to my room; I want to show you these new tunes that I just got."

Sam followed Laura up to her room and they listened to music and talked about some of the boys in their classes. Sam had stopped seeing Josh and Laura was trying to figure out how to get rid of Greg so that she could go after someone else.

"Laura, has there ever been a time in your life when you weren't seeing at least two men? Why would you possibly want to get rid of Greg? It really isn't your style."

"Oh shut up," Laura said as she threw a pillow at Sam.

Sam laughed and grabbed the pillow. She held the pillow close to her and looked up at her friend. "Hey, is your mom out of town again?"

Laura nodded. "Yep. Pretty awesome, huh?"

"Yeah. You are so lucky. I would do anything to get away from my mom right now. Ever since the accident, things have been pretty rough. I don't think she will ever stop being mad at me. I think the pregnancy was just the icing on the cake, you know. If she has it her way, I will be grounded for the rest of my life."

"Why don't you just move in here with me, Sami? I really don't have to follow any rules and we could do whatever we wanted to. I have always been pretty lucky that way. Maybe it is because Mom is gone so much she feels she has no choice but to trust me." Laura shrugged and then smiled at Sam. "All I know is that it would be great if you were living here too! What do you think?"

"I don't know how I would get my mom to agree to it. I am not eighteen yet and I would probably have to run away from home to move in with you." Sam looked down at her watch. "Oh shoot. Speaking of my mom, I better get out of here before she gets home and catches me. I'll call you later, ok?"

"Yeah, see ya."

Sam ran out to her truck and drove as fast as she could back to her house. When she got there, she ran into the house and down to her room. She flipped on her music and sat back on her bed with a smile on her face. Suddenly she jumped back up.

"Oh shoot, the phone," she said as she ran back down the hall and put the phone back on the hook. She could hear the front door opening and she sighed with relief.

"Man, that was too close. That would have been a lot easier if Mom hadn't taken the phone out of my room, too."

She went back to her room and turned down her music so that she could listen to what her mother was doing. She could hear her footsteps going up the stairs. She got off her bed and walked over to the bottom of the stairs. She was going to turn around and go back to her room when her mother called out to her.

"Dinner will be ready in about twenty minutes," she said sternly and then Sam could hear her go into the kitchen.

Sam shook her head and walked back to her room. She really did not know what to say to her anymore, and it seemed to Sam that her mother really did not want anything to do with her, either. That night Sam told her mother that she had a lot of homework to do and she locked herself in her room. As she sat on the floor next to her bed, she leaned back and thought about what Laura had said to her earlier. As far back as she could remember Sam had fantasized about running away from home. Each time, however, she would picture her mom crying hysterically when she realized Sam was gone.

"Boy, now that really is a dream," Sam mumbled to herself. She laughed sarcastically as she sat down on the floor and rested her feet up on the bed, her homework long forgotten.

"Shoot, I'd be surprised if Mom even noticed that I was gone."

For the next hour, Sam thought about all of the ways that she could escape her mom and live with her friend Laura. She finally gave up and went to bed.

The next day Sam stopped by her office and told Julie that she was too humiliated to work there for another month. She gathered up her things and, after saying goodbye to a few people and hugging Julie and Ben, she calmly walked out of the building. She stopped by her house after that and dropped off her things. She took the phone off the hook and then left to go to Laura's house again.

They were laughing and talking until Sam happened to look down at her watch and realized that she should have already left to go back home. She jumped to her feet in a panic and started to quickly gather up her things.

"Oh man, I better get out of here or my mom will beat me home. Where the heck did I put my keys?" Sam looked everywhere and then she started to panic again. "Laura, you have to help me find my keys. Have you seen them?"

Laura shook her head and watched as Sam frantically searched for her keys. Suddenly Sam stopped and sat down on Laura's bed.

"There is no way I'm going to beat my mom home now." She took a deep breath. "What the hell am I going to tell her this time?" Sam leaned her head back and shut her eyes. "I can't even call her because I took the phone off the hook."

Sam waited for a short while and then dialed her house. It was not very long before it was ringing.

"Hello," her mother answered.

"Uh, hi, Mom."

"Samantha, where the hell are you?"

Sam cringed at the tone in her mother's voice. "Well, Mom, I know I wasn't supposed to have left the house, but Laura was really upset and she need to talk to me."

"So what was wrong with using the phone? Oh, I know. You couldn't use it because it was off the hook."

Sam looked down. She knew that she was in a lot of trouble. She couldn't even answer her mother, but her mother had plenty to say to her.

"Sam, if you are not back here in ten minutes, I am going to deadbolt the lock and you can find somewhere else to sleep tonight."

"But Mom, I can't find my keys. Could you at least give me a chance to figure out where I put them?"

"You have got to be kidding me. You expect me to believe that you lost your keys? Yeah, right. Like I said, either be home in ten minutes or don't bother coming home at all."

"Fine, then I just won't bother to come home at all," Sam screamed into the phone as she started to cry and then she slammed the phone down. She turned to look at Laura. "I can't believe she doesn't believe me." She shook her head and wiped her eyes with her shirt. "She is locking me out. Now what am I supposed to do?"

"Uh, Sami? Here are your keys." Laura reached out her hand to give her the keys. Sam looked at her strangely.

"Where did you find them?"

"Oh, they were right over there," she said as she pointed towards her dresser.

"Laura, I had already looked there twice. What did you do? Hide my keys from me?"

"I was just playing around, Sami."

"Oh great. Thanks a lot. Your playing around just got me kicked out of my house." Sam shook her head. "How could you do this to me?"

"What's the big deal? In case you forgot, yesterday you were wishing that you could get away from your mother. I just helped you do it. You should be thanking me, not getting mad at me."

Sam looked at her, not quite sure how to respond.

The next day Sam skipped her classes and went home to get her clothes. She had filled one suitcase when she realized that her mother had been standing behind her, watching her pack.

"I knew you would be here today to get your clothes," she said to Sam.

Sam stared at her for a moment and then turned back to the suitcase in front of her. "Yeah, well, you seem to know everything, don't you? This is probably for the best anyway. You obviously don't want me here any more than I want to be here."

"So you think that you are just going to pack your bags and leave, huh?"

"That's right. You said it yourself last night. I had no way of getting home within your time limit so you told me not to bother coming home at all."

"So where is it you are planning to live? How are you going to support yourself?"

Sam glanced back at her mother, wondering if she knew that she had been fired. "Laura and I had been talking a lot lately about living together. This just sets it into motion a little earlier than we planned," she said quietly as she walked over to her closet.

"Oh, I see. So this was just another one of your little plans. You just wanted to leave home before you were eighteen and this is how you planned to do it. Well, congratulations, you got what you wanted."

"Give me a break, Mom. You think that I planned this whole thing? I wish I could have! You have been cold to me ever since I had the accident. It was an accident, you know. I didn't do it on purpose. Yeah, so I didn't tell you I was pregnant. Do you think it was fun for me to lose the baby? What if I had wanted to keep it? Either way, I didn't plan for any of this to happen, so just lay off me." Sam turned away from her mom so she would not see that she was crying again. *Damn her for always making me cry.*

"Don't you dare use that tone of voice with me, young lady."

"Why, Mom? What are you going to do about it? Ground me? Kick me out?"

Her mom stood there silently for a moment. "Sam, the world is not as easy as you seem to think. When you have to learn to survive by yourself, well, let's just say it can be very difficult out there. Trust me, I have been there. I am still there. I really don't think that you are ready for what is out there."

Sam turned and glared at her mother. "Oh, so now you suddenly care about what happens to me? Isn't it a little late for that? I swear I feel like a bird locked in a cage. I need to be set free and that is exactly what I am doing now. I am getting free."

"Samantha, I wish you could just take a step back and think about what you are doing here. Mark my words, you are not ready!"

"Yeah, well I guess we will just have to see about that, won't we. Goodbye, Mother." Sam grabbed her bags and walked as fast as she could back to her car. She looked back at the house and saw her mother standing in the window crying. She once again tried to hold back her own tears as she put her bags in the car and headed back to Laura's house.

CHAPTER 6

Graduation came and went and Sam was still living with Laura. It had been almost six months and she had not spoken to her mother at all since the day that she had left home.

Laura's mother has been surprised to see Sam, but did not mind her staying with them. All she had asked was that they keep the house clean and not have any wild parties in her house. She had hoped that Sam would work things out with her mother, but she was too busy with her job to get involved. She was out of town so often, in fact, that the girls did not pay a lot of attention to the so-called rules that she had set.

It was a Friday night and the two girls were at a party that was only a couple of blocks away from Laura's house.

It was four-fifteen in the morning and Sam and Laura were staggering arm-in-arm down the sidewalk towards Laura's house. They both had drunk a lot of alcohol and they were laughing at how silly the other was acting. Both were afraid that if they let go of the other's arm that they both might fall to the ground. They had just walked into Laura's kitchen when suddenly Laura's mother appeared before them, screaming hysterically.

"Do you girls know what time it is? I have been worried sick! You are both supposed to be at home. What in the world possessed you two to go out drinking and then decide to come staggering home at four o'clock in the morning? This is it! This has happened one too many times." Sam and Laura looked at each other in surprise.

"Ever since I arrived home and found you girls missing, I have thought about all of the other times that you two have pulled stunts like this. Don't look so surprised, I am not stupid. Samantha, you may think you are mature enough to be away from your home, but you're not. I have had several talks recently with your mom and I don't like the way you have changed and I definitely don't like the way that you have changed my daughter."

"Oh, Mom…" Laura tried to interrupt, but her mother waved a hand to silence her.

"Just let me finish, please. Samantha, your mother and I had thought that this time away would be good for you, to give you a chance to get your life back on track. I have overlooked a lot of things you have been doing, but I am not going to do that anymore. I want you to move out." She could see the look of shock on the girls' faces and she continued on. "I won't just throw you out on the street. You have until next weekend to find somewhere else to go. If you haven't left by Saturday night, I will put your things out on the front lawn and someone can come and haul them away. I suggest you start packing now." With that she turned and left the kitchen. As the girls stood there speechless, they heard the front door being opened and then slammed shut.

"Oh great, what am I supposed to do now," Sam said as she shook her head. She looked at Laura and then left the room.

Sam used that week to locate her high school friend Tammy. She and Tammy had spent a lot of time together at one time, but they had hardly seen each other in several months. Sam remembered that she had been fairly rude to her in their last semester of school and she hoped that she could reconcile enough to get her help. After several tries, she finally reached Tammy on the phone. It was already Thursday afternoon.

"Hey Tammy! This is Sam. Sorry I haven't talked to you in a while but you know how it is. Hey girl, I need a favor. Can I stay at your house for a few days? I just need a place to stay until I can find an apartment." *And a job*, she thought to herself.

Tammy sounded annoyed. "Sam? How nice of you to call me. Gee, how many months has it been?

"Look, I said that I was sorry that I haven't called you. I have been going through some really bad problems at home. My mom kicked me out, you know. Is there any way I can stay with you for a while? I really have no where else to go." Sam tried to sound convincing.

She heard Tammy sigh. "You know darn well that my parents wouldn't let you in this house if you paid them. Who are you kidding?"

"Hey look, I have to find a place to stay. I'm desperate. Would you help me, or what? Like I said, I know I have been a jerk, but I have been going through so much stuff, you wouldn't believe it." Sam tried to sound like she was going to cry.

"Well, you can't stay here. That is just out of the question and you know it." Tammy paused for a minute. "Well, I am working as a nanny during the day. If you can find a place to sleep at night, maybe I can sneak you in over there during the day so that you can at least take a shower and eat something."

"Where am I supposed to sleep at night? In my truck?"

"If you have to. Be thankful that you will at least be able to take a shower and maybe eat a little something. Lucky for you it is summertime and not the middle of winter." Tammy sounded annoyed again, but that didn't bother Sam at all. She had always been able to get her friends to do whatever she wanted them to, and Tammy was no different. It took her a little more work this time, but Tammy had taken the bait.

"Thanks, Tammy, I really do appreciate it. I promise I will find a place as soon as possible."

"I sure hope so, Sam, because it can be a very dangerous world out there sometimes."

Sam shook her head. "Yeah, yeah, thanks for the advice. I'll see you soon." Sam hung up the phone and laughed. *Dangerous world,* she thought to herself. *How could the world be dangerous when you can always find someone to help you?*

CHAPTER 7

Samantha was unable to find a place to stay at night and ended up sleeping in the back of her truck. After a month, she started to hear her mother's words ringing in her ears. "*...The world is not as easy as you seem to think. When you have to learn to survive by yourself... it can be very difficult,*" she had said. Sam started to wonder if she had made a mistake, however, as crazy as her life was now, be it pride or stupidity, she would not go back to her mother and admit that she had been wrong. Instead, she was even more determined to somehow make it work. There was nothing worse than hearing your own mother saying, "I told you so," and Sam was not about to hear it again.

That night Sam was listening to the rain and thinking about her mother. "I wonder what you are doing right now, Mom," she said out loud to herself. "Do you ever think about me?" Sam closed her eyes for a moment and then she started to laugh to herself. "Who am I kidding? Mom is probably having the time of her life now that I am gone."

Sam leaned back as she continued to watch the rain fall around her. *It is strange sometimes what life dishes out to you, but things have got to get better*, she thought. Suddenly Sam sat up straight, almost hitting her head, and laughed as she wiped a tear off her cheek.

"What am I doing? Why am I sitting back here feeling sorry for myself? Give me a break. I have a freedom that a lot of people my age don't have. I mean, that was the whole point of leaving home; to be on my own with no rules and no mother to drive me crazy. And that is exactly what I have."

Content with her thoughts, Sam leaned back down, pulled her sweater tighter around her shoulders, and drifted off into a deep and yet troubled sleep.

The next night Sam went out with her friend Laura. Laura's mom had of course warned her not to see Sam anymore, saying that Sam was only trouble, but Laura was not about to abandon her friend. Her mom was out of town again and the way Laura saw it, what her mother did not know would not hurt her.

Laura and Sam had been driving around for hours looking for a good party to go to, but this particular night they were just not having any luck.

They were stopped at a traffic light and Laura decided to confront her friend with her concerns about the way that Sam was living. That was one thing that she did have to agree with her mother about.

"You know, Sam, you have got to straighten up your life. Everyone knows you have been living in your truck. Get with it, girl! I thought you had a job, why haven't you gotten an apartment?"

"Laura, don't start on me now. I got fired from my job a while ago, remember? I have been putting up with the lectures from Tammy for the last two weeks and I don't need to hear it from you, too. Can you believe that she's tired of letting me use her employer's shower and she says I have to stop eating their food, too? She's the one that offered to help me in the first place." Sam looked annoyed as she lit up a cigarette. Smoking was a new habit that Sam had decided to take on and of course, Laura had also started to smoke. Laura always mimicked Sam, and besides that, they both thought it made them look cool at parties.

"She did not offer you anything," Laura said, looking at Sam and shaking her head. "Sam, have you forgotten that you talked Tammy into letting you use her employer's house? She should not have to risk getting fired for you!"

"Look, I said I didn't want to discuss it right now so lay off, ok? Hey, stop here at this gas station, I need to get some more smokes."

Laura pulled the car over into the gas station parking area. Sam opened the car door and glanced at Laura.

"I'll be right back," she said as she got out of the car. As soon as Sam stood up she stretched her arms up and clasped her hands above her head. She was so tense that she felt stiff. Maybe part of it was from sleeping in the back of the truck for so long. Lord only knows that it could not possibly be very good for your back. Or maybe it was from the stress that she felt from hearing all of the lectures from everyone about how she was living her life. She was so tired of hearing how wrong it was for her to be living out of her car and how her life was going nowhere. No one seemed to understand just how hard it had been for her. Luckily she had found a small newspaper route and that at least gave her enough money to feed herself for now.

Sam stretched again and then headed for the door of the convenience store. It was a warm night and the smell of gasoline was strong in the air. Sam rubbed her nose annoyingly as she entered into the store.

As soon as she walked into the small store, Sam immediately noticed a very attractive young man standing behind the counter. She smiled to herself as she noticed that he had obviously noticed her as well.

Sam casually walked up to the counter and tilted her head slightly as she ran her finger along the counter. She loved to flirt. She lowered her eyes in a teasing way and asked him for a pack of cigarettes. The man behind the counter was enjoying this game as much as Sam was.

"So, what is a beautiful young lady like yourself doing wandering around on a dark night like tonight?" he asked Sam as he set the cigarettes down on the counter.

Sam smiled. "Oh, my friend Laura and I just thought we would wander around and see what we could find to do tonight," she said as she pulled out her wallet.

"Can I please see some ID?" he asked casually.

Sam looked at him in surprise and then nervously handed him her driver's license. She knew that legally she should not have been buying cigarettes, but she had gotten away with it so far. She held her breath and watched as he looked intently at her license.

"This picture just does not do you justice, Samantha."

Sam tried not to look too relieved as she smiled and then leaned onto the counter. "Ok, so you cheated. So what is your name?"

"Greg, and it is very nice to meet you." He held out his hand to her and when she put her hand in his, he just held onto it tightly for a moment.

Sam glanced out the store window and saw that Laura was shaking her head disapprovingly. Sam laughed to herself.

"What's so funny?" Greg asked her.

"Oh nothing. I'm sorry, but I need to get going. My friend is waiting for me."

Greg glanced out the window and then slowly let go of Sam's hand. He wrote down his phone number on a piece of paper and as he handed it to her he smiled, his eyes showing the full desire he felt for her.

"Call me, Samantha, and I can guarantee you will have a great time. Drive carefully, beautiful."

Sam smiled and waved goodbye to him and she quickly walked back to the car. As soon as she opened the door, she could not help herself from gloating about what had just happened.

"Did you see that hunk? Wasn't he just gorgeous? And look, he gave me his phone number!" Sam was holding the piece of paper like it was a check from the state lottery.

Laura shook her head. "You better be careful, Sami. The way you flirt with men you don't even know, you are going to get yourself in trouble one of these days!"

"Hey, lay off me already!" Sam looked annoyed and then lit a cigarette. "Let's find us another party!"

CHAPTER 8

Samantha had not called the man from the gas station right away. It was three weeks later that she came across the piece of paper where he had written down his phone number. She unfolded it and stared at it for a moment. It read, "Greg 555-2273." Greg. At first Sam did not feel right about calling a man she did not even know, but as she looked back down at this phone number again, she remembered how handsome he had been.

"Oh, what the heck. It can't hurt anything," she said out loud to herself. She had still been sleeping in her truck and it took her a while to find a pay phone. She dialed the number and he immediately answered.

"Um, I don't know if you will remember me, but I, um, met you one night a while ago at the gas station that you work at. You had given me your number." Sam stumbled on her words, not quite sure what to say.

"This must be the cute little blonde. Samantha wasn't it? How could I ever forget that smile? What took you so long to call me?"

Sam relaxed. They talked for an hour and a half and finally she agreed to meet him for dinner the following evening. It was his day off and he said that he could not think of anyone better to spend it with.

The next night Sam was scared again. What if this guy turned out to be a weird person, like a murderer or a rapist? *Nah*, she thought to herself, not the way he was talking to her last night. She figured that murderers and rapists would probably say really strange things, whether it was in person or over the phone, and this guy always seemed to say the nicest things to her.

Greg was six feet tall with brown hair and blue eyes and he was built like a football player. She had agreed to meet him at the gas station where they had originally met, and then they drove to the restaurant in his car. He was a perfect gentleman at dinner – opening doors, holding out Sam's chair, and he even ordered her food for her. The evening went so well that she did not think anything of it when he asked if she would mind if they stopped by his house for a moment. He thought a late-night stroll at a nearby lake would be nice and he just needed to stop by his house for a flashlight. Sam agreed nonchalantly. *What a wonderful evening*, she thought to herself.

When they arrived at this house, Sam noticed there were lights on inside.

"I have a roommate," Greg explained casually as he opened the car door for her. He escorted her up the walkway to the front door and into the house. As they walked into the living room, Sam noticed a man sitting in a recliner. He had black hair and, as he glanced up at them walking in, she saw that he also had the deepest, most amazing blue eyes she had ever seen. He had one leg lazily draped over the side of the chair and he was holding a book in his hand. He looked up at Sam and smiled a very warm and almost sensual smile up at her. Greg cleared his voice and then introduced them.

"Samantha, this is my roommate, Kyle. Kyle, my date, Sam," he said, as he stressed the fact that Sam was his date.

Kyle stood up and looked down at Sam. "It is very nice to meet you, Samantha," he said in a very soft but masculine voice.

Greg started looking around and seemed to be getting very annoyed. "Sam," he said in a somewhat demanding voice, "why don't you come back here to my room and wait while I look for the flashlight."

Sam pulled her eyes away from Kyle's and followed Greg down a long hallway. He stopped when they reached the doorway to what she guessed was his room. "Wait here," he said.

Sam looked around the room. It was definitely a man's room. There were pictures of women, mostly nude, all over the walls. Sam shrugged disgustingly. "Typical man," she mumbled. She had been waiting for about five minutes when Greg came back. She was shocked to see that he was wearing a towel and more than likely, nothing underneath it.

"I decided I wanted to take a quick shower before we left. Want to join me?" As he spoke he held his hand out to her in an inviting way.

"Are you crazy?" Sam shouted

"Oh, come on, Samantha. You know you want me. You were sending off vibes all evening."

"You think that just because I had dinner with you that I should sleep with you? How dare you! Please take me back to my truck. No, better yet, you go take a cold shower and I will walk back to my truck!" Sam brushed past him and ran back down the hallway to the living room. Her heart was racing as she expected Greg to come running after her. Kyle was not in the living room and she was not sure if she was relieved or not. She stormed out the front door, making sure to slam the door hard. She started marching up the street and suddenly realized that she had no idea which direction she needed to go. Tears of frustration started to stream down her cheeks, as she looked to her right and then to her left. She stood there for just a moment when she heard someone honking a horn behind her. She jumped at the sound and then turned around embarrassed and flustered.

"I'm sorry I startled you. I thought you might need a ride." It was Kyle. He looked at her so tenderly that she felt that he had shown up to save her. With a sigh of relief she got in his truck. It was a large pickup and he leaned over and extended his hand to her to help her step up into it.

"Thank you. Is your roommate always that crude?"

Kyle laughed. "I can only imagine what happened. You have to excuse Greg. He seems to think that women worship the ground he walks on. I'm sorry if he did something to upset you. Are you ok?" Kyle looked genuinely worried and it touched Sam's heart.

"Yes. Mad, but ok. I was sure that he was going to come after me when I left. Thank you for coming to my rescue. I probably would have walked all night if you had not shown up."

"No problem. As for Greg, I think he is mostly talk." Kyle looked down at his watch and then looked directly into Sam's eyes. "It is getting kind of late, would you like me to take you home now?"

Sam was mesmerized by the color of his eyes. Even in the darkness of the night, with just the streetlights illuminating them, she found herself captivated. She suddenly realized that she had been staring at him and she blushed and quickly looked away. "Actually, I am parked at the gas station where Greg works. If you wouldn't mind dropping me off there, that would be great."

Kyle looked concerned. "Are you sure you don't want me to drive you home? I can help you get your car tomorrow."

Sam looked at him and blushed again. "Actually I have been sleeping in my truck lately. I know that sounds crazy, but I just don't have enough money to get into an apartment right now." Sam shrugged. "Sometimes things just don't seem to go your way, you know? But you have to do what you have to do to survive in this world."

Kyle looked horrified. "You are sleeping in your truck? How horrible. Would you like some money for a hotel? I hate the idea of you sleeping in your car by yourself in this day and age."

Sam laughed. *What a nice gesture*, she thought to herself. *Why hadn't she met Kyle first?* Sam leaned back into the seat, exhausted. "Thank you for the sweet offer, but no. I'll be ok. Believe it or not, I have been doing this for a while now."

"Ok," he said reluctantly, "if you insist." He was just pulling into the gas station parking lot as Sam looked to see if her truck was still there. Her truck looked very old and small compared to Kyle's and she was embarrassed for him to see it. She thanked him again for his help and quickly got out. She waved goodbye and wearily walked over to her truck.

SHERRY MOORE

After he dropped her off at the gas station, he drove around the building and then watched as she pulled out of the parking lot. He waited for a moment and then he pulled out onto the street heading in the direction he had watched her go. After only a few miles he saw Sam pull off of the main road onto a small gravel road. He drove slowly as he watched her drive into an empty parking lot. There was a small deserted building and Sam had driven slowly around to the back of it. He parked his truck and walked behind some trees where he could get a closer look at her. He watched her climb into the back of the truck and grab what looked like a pillow. When she lay back he could no longer see her, yet he still stood there for a long time, mesmerized by her presence – so close and yet out of reach. He closed his eyes and pictured her in his mind; her long blonde hair softly flowing around her delicate face as she slept. The gentle rhythm of her body echoing her lonely slumber. After what felt like hours, he could no longer resist the temptation to see her. He quietly walked over to her truck and carefully glanced in the back window. He could see her shadowy form underneath a light blanket and he smiled. Feeling complete, he slowly turned and walked back to his truck.

CHAPTER 9

"I'm telling you, Laura, it is really weird how I keep running into Kyle. It is like he is everywhere. First the coffee shop and then, get this, I ran into him at this little hot dog stand downtown."

"What were you doing at a hot dog stand downtown?" Laura asked with a disgusted look on her face.

"Laura, come on." Sam looked frustrated as she looked at Laura.

"Well maybe it is meant to be. Maybe he is your Prince Charming and he is going to take you away from all of your troubles." Laura laughed and Sam threw a crumpled napkin at her. They were sitting in the park, not far from where Sam had been parking at nights, eating a hamburger.

"I'm serious, Laura."

"Well, don't be so serious. Has he actually asked you out or anything?"

"No, that is what's so weird about it. We just talk and that's about it. Maybe he doesn't like me at all."

Laura stretched. "I don't know, Sami, but next time you see him just ask him." She looked down at her watch. "We better get going. The party should just about be wild and kick'n by now."

The girls cleaned up their mess and got into Laura's car. Laura noticed the serious look on Sami's face and nudged her with her elbow.

"Thinking about Prince Charming again?"

"No, actually I was thinking about Tammy. She is totally refusing to let me come over now. In fact, she doesn't seem to want to be around me at all anymore. She said that she felt like I was using her. Imagine that. Well, maybe it's for the best."

Laura shook her head and stayed quiet until they arrived at the party. Sam and Laura had decided on a party that was being held by a friend of Laura's. When they arrived, the girls immediately realized that they did not know anyone else there. Sam was still down and did not feel like mingling with anyone, so they headed for the couch and, while they sipped their drinks, they sat and watched the crowd of people around them.

"I don't believe it," Sam blurted out.

"What? Do you know someone here? I sure hope so, because I am really starting to get bored." Laura looked over in the direction that Sam was staring at so intently.

"It's Kyle. I told you that I keep running into him," she said loudly as she hit Laura's arm.

"Ok, ok, I believe you. You don't have to hit me. Well, at least I finally get to meet your Prince Charming," Laura said looking around.

Sam glared at Laura and then she walked over to where Kyle was standing. He was talking to a couple of guys when she approached him. He saw her and smiled.

"Hi, Samantha," he said and then he turned back to the group he was talking to. "Hey, I'll see you guys later on tonight." He turned his attention back to Sam and smiled as he looked down at her. "My, my, Samantha. We meet again."

Sam smiled. "It's good to see you again, Kyle. My friend Laura is waiting for me over by the couch," she said as she pointed in the direction that she had just come from. "Would you like to meet her?"

"Of course." Kyle took her arm and she led him over to where Laura was standing. As soon as they reached her, Sam introduced them.

"It is nice to finally meet you. I have definitely heard a lot about you," Laura said as she accepted his hand.

"It is nice to meet you as well."

The rest of the evening the three were inseparable. Laura seemed to like being with Sam and Kyle more than seeking out her own companion. Sam did not really mind though because she was a lot more comfortable with Laura there too. It was a few minutes past midnight when Kyle offered to take the two girls out for coffee. Laura immediately declined.

"I better get home. Unfortunately I have to work tomorrow. Kyle, would you mind giving Sami a ride back to her truck for me?" Laura said, ignoring the look of panic on Sam's face. She stretched her arms above her as if she was trying to emphasize how tired she felt.

"Of course not. That is, if you don't mind, Samantha."

"I guess that's ok. Drive carefully, Laura," she said as she glared at her friend.

Laura laughed and then whispered, "Be good" in Sam's ear as she hugged her goodbye. Then they make their way through the crowd to the front door.

Kyle and Sam stood outside the house for a while and talked. The clean air and soft breeze felt good after being stuffed among all of the people that were inside the house. Kyle was telling her about something that Greg had done when Sam looked curiously up at him.

"You know, you look like you are a little older than Greg. How old are you anyway?"

Kyle smiled humorously. "How old do you think I am?"

Sam shrugged. "I don't know, maybe early twenties."

Kyle threw his head back and laughed. "Thank you, little one, for the compliment, but I am actually thirty-two. So, how old are you?"

Sam looked away for a moment and watched some people who were leaving the party. After hearing how old he was, she was not sure if she should tell him her own age. She looked back at him and saw that he was waiting for her answer.

"Would you believe that I am seventeen?" she said, afraid of his response.

Kyle only smiled and lightly touched her cheek. "Ah, just a baby," he said.

Kyle lit a cigarette and then offered Sam one, which she accepted. After he lit hers, he looked at her with a serious frown on his face.

"I don't suppose that you are still living in your truck?" Sam looked down at the ground and shuffled her feet. Kyle put his hands on his hips and gave her a look that reminded her of a disappointed parent. "Alright Samantha, it is almost the end of summer and you are still living in your truck?" He shook his head. "Look, I have to move out of Greg's house because his brother is moving back in. I know you don't have enough money to get an apartment by yourself, so why don't we get a place together? I have enough for the deposit and the first month's rent already. We could be roommates, nothing more. It could be the ideal solution to both of our problems. What do you say?" Sam was in shock. This man whom she barely knew and, as it turned out, was quite a bit older than her, was already asking her to move in with him. *Of course, just as roommates,* she thought disappointingly to herself. If he wasn't thinking of her in any kind of romantic or sexual way, then what harm could possibly come of it? She definitely needed to find a place to live. In fact, just a few nights before a policeman had found her sleeping in her car and had told her to move on. She had spent the rest of that night sitting alone in a booth in an all-night coffee shop.

"A penny for your thoughts, Samantha."

Sam looked up at the concerned look on Kyle's face.

"You looked as though you were a hundred miles away; what were you thinking?" he asked.

Sam sighed. "I was just thinking that I can't go wrong by moving in with you." She looked up into Kyle's eyes and smiled. "Oh, what the heck. Let's do it."

CHAPTER 10

On September first, after two long months of living in her car, Sam moved into an apartment with Kyle. He seemed to have everything they needed - furniture, dishes, pots and pans. All Sam had were her clothes. Sam looked around at her new home and laughed.

"Gee, now that I can take a shower, I guess I better find a new job."

Immediately after she had made the comment, she noticed a strange, almost icy look come across Kyle's face. It was the first time she had ever seen anything negative about him. He did not say a word, but just left the room. Sam frowned and hoped very seriously that she had not just made a big mistake by moving in with him.

She walked around the small living room and looked around. It was small, but it was home. From the living room she could see the kitchen and dining area. She walked down the hall towards the bedrooms and saw that there was only one bathroom for her and Kyle to share.

"I put my extra bed and dresser in this other bedroom for you," Kyle said as he walked out of one of the bedrooms. He was smiling again and Sam relaxed. "I hope you don't mind, but I already put my things in this room. I like the fact that it has an extra window." He stretched and glanced around them. "Did you get all of your clothes out of your truck already?"

Sam smiled. "What there is of it, yes. I just need to put them away." Sam went back into the living room and walked up to the small pile of clothing she had set next to the front door. She carried her things to her room and then collapsed on her bed. Oh, how nice it felt to be on a bed again. She was resting on the bed, not wanting to move, when she heard the front door open and then close. She got up and walked into the living room. Kyle had left. She wondered where he might have run off to, but figured it was none of her business. Besides, she was too tired to care anyway.

Two months passed and Kyle and Sam were getting along so wonderfully that her previous fears had disappeared. They spent a lot of time together; going to the movies, to dinner, out for walks, and Sam even brought him to one of the parties she had gone to with Laura. Kyle's friend Greg started to come by a lot but he never bothered Sam about what had happened when

SHADOWS OF THE PAST

they first had met. She eventually decided that the past was the past.

The only thing that bothered Sam was that Kyle always left in the evening and never mentioned where he was going. Finally one Saturday morning, Sam decided to ask him about his nightly ventures. Kyle was sitting at the kitchen table, reading the comics in the newspaper. Sam sat down on the chair next to him and gazed over at him.

"Kyle, can I ask you something?"

"Hmm?" He mumbled and then laughed at one of the comics he was reading.

"If you don't mind my asking, where do you go at nights? You are so mysterious about it."

Kyle stopped laughing and looked up. His eyes had clouded over and his smile was gone. "Do not concern yourself with my business, Samantha. That was the deal, remember? If you are jealous, don't be. I am not seeing anyone else." With that last comment he stood up and, without looking at Sam, he left the room. She heard him slam his door loudly. *What kind of comment was that,* she thought to herself. It made her mad that he thought she was jealous, especially because he was not "seeing" her, but they were only roommates. His behavior made her even more curious about his nightly outings, but she did not dare mention it again.

December fourteenth Sam turned eighteen years old. Kyle was surprised to see that as the day progressed, she was acting more and more depressed.

"I am not sure why, but I would swear that you are probably the first person to turn eighteen and actually be depressed about it."

Sam laughed. "I am not depressed because I just turned eighteen." She let out a sigh. "I am just down because my mom hasn't called to wish me a happy birthday. I mean, this is supposed to be the best birthday ever, you know?"

"I didn't even realize that you had given her our number."

"Well, I had not actually talked to her directly, but I had left it on her answering machine."

Kyle smiled. "Well, I have a surprise for you. Go get changed into something really nice."

"Why? What did you do, Kyle?"

"Now don't you worry your pretty little head about it, just go and get ready. And that's an order. Go!" He demanded as he swatted her behind playfully.

Sam smiled and went to change her clothes.

Sam was indeed surprised. Kyle, Greg and Greg's newest girlfriend all took her out dancing to celebrate her birthday. Kyle whirled her around the dance floor for hours. Everyone was laughing and having a wonderful time. Finally, when it was announced that the club would be closing for the night, they reluctantly headed back out to Greg's car.

"I have had the least to drink, so I'm driving," Kyle yelled out.

"Fine with me, buddy. We get the back seat!" Greg said as his girlfriend giggled and they jumped anxiously into the back of the car. Sam laughed and got into the passenger side.

"Some things never change," she said to Kyle.

For the first twenty minutes of the ride home, nobody spoke. The radio was playing softly and every now and then Sam could hear a giggle come from the back seat.

All of a sudden Kyle slammed on the brakes, throwing Sam forward. "That son-of-a-bitch. Who does he think he is, riding my ass. I'll show him who owns the road."

Sam was shocked. She had never seen this side of Kyle before. "Kyle, calm down," she said but she immediately got quiet as she saw the look of fire in his eyes. Sam sank back against the seat and dug her fingers into the door handle as Kyle chased after the car that had made him mad. He was yelling and cursing as if the stranger in the other car could hear him. He drove this way for over an hour until the frightened driver ahead of him ran a red light and lost him. Kyle was furious.

When they arrived at their apartment building, Kyle parked next to Sam's truck. He jumped out of the car and slammed his fist into the side of her truck. Sam jumped. She was already unnerved from his driving and the sound of him hitting her truck only added to her timidness.

What is he doing, she thought to herself.

"Give me your keys," he demanded as he held out his hand to Sam. She was shaking as she pulled her keys out of her purse and handed them to him. Everyone was quiet as Kyle burned rubber as he left the parking lot in Sam's truck. Sam held her shaky hands up to her mouth as she stood in the parking lot, horrified, watching Kyle drive off like a madman. *Why would he take my truck and not his own?* she thought to herself. *What if he wrecks my car, or worse yet, gets himself or someone else killed?* Greg noticed the look on her face and, putting his hand on her shoulder, he quietly spoke to her.

"Let him be, Sam. He'll work it out and come home." Greg turned and escorted his girlfriend back into his car.

In addition to Kyle scaring Sam half to death, she realized that she now had a large dent on the side of her truck. Frustrated, Sam shook her head and turned to walk back to her apartment.

Kyle did not come home until the next afternoon, and he acted as if nothing had happened the night before. Sam had learned before that it was best not to say anything about any of Kyle's actions and she was forced to just let the day before remain in the past. Secretly in her own mind, however, she was scared about what might happen next.

CHAPTER 11

Christmas was only two weeks away when Kyle announced to Sam that he was going out of town to see his mother for the holidays. Sam decided that maybe it was time to call her own mother. She knew that she should have done it a lot sooner, but she just didn't know what to say to her. She picked up the phone and dialed.

"Hello," her mother answered.

"Hi, Mom," she said quietly.

"Samantha? Is that you? How are you?" Her voice sounded cold, and yet Sam could still tell that she was worried.

"I'm ok. I know that we haven't talked for a long time, but I wanted to ask you if I could come home for Christmas. I'm sure that it sounds strange, but I would like to see you and Jessica, if it's ok."

"Well, your sister will be here tomorrow and she is planning on staying through the holidays. I'm surprised that you would want to come home, but I suppose it would be ok. At least we would have the whole family together for Christmas."

"Thanks, Mom. I'll come over a couple of days before Christmas so I can help with the tree, ok?"

"Whatever is convenient for you, Samantha. I'll see you then."

Sam hung up the phone and felt as though she had just had a conversation with a stranger instead of her own mother.

Sam was nervous and yet she was excited at the same time. She had not seen her sister for so long that she just could not wait. Her older sister Jessica was in her second year of school at a private Christian college in Missouri and in a way Sam envied her. She had always done well in school and she had gone right to college after high school. She seemed almost too perfect to Sam because she never seemed to do anything wrong and she knew that her mom was closer to Jessie than she would probably ever be to herself.

The day that Sam arrived at her mother's house, she was a nervous wreck. She almost cried when she walked through the front door of her childhood home. Her mother had put up Christmas decorations and lights all over the house and the smell of freshly baked breads and cookies filled the air. She just stood in the doorway for a moment, taking it all in.

"Samantha, is that you?" She heard her sister cry out.

"The one and only," she said laughing. Out of nowhere her sister Jessica came running down the stairs, almost knocking Sam over.

"You bum! Why haven't you written me? Man, it is good to see you! Have you lost weight? You look great!"

Sam laughed and hugged her sister. "You haven't written me either, Jess! Man, have I missed you!" Sam and Jessica walked up the stairs together and then Sam stopped and smiled nervously at her mother. Her mother surprised her when she grabbed her in her arms and held her tight.

"I've missed you, you little troublemaker," she said as tears fell down her cheek.

"I've missed you a lot too, Mom."

They hugged for a long time and then they all walked into the kitchen together.

"I'll tell you, Samantha, it just hasn't been the same around here without you. It's just been too quiet. I miss your blaring music and having six thousand of your friends running through the house calling me 'Mom'!" They all laughed. It seemed that the Christmas spirit had taken away all of the hurtful feelings that Sam and her mother shared, or at least that was what she thought. Sam could not help but wonder what was going to happen after the holidays were over.

That night, they worked together to put up the Christmas tree. As they did every year, they sang Christmas carols, drank eggnog and ate everything that had been baked. Sam's mom always baked some things before Christmas, and then the rest on Christmas Eve. There was never anything left from the first batch.

Sam went into the kitchen to get some more eggnog. When she came back to the living room, she stopped and smiled as she watched her family. Her mom was holding onto a stepstool as Jessica was standing on it trying desperately to put some decorations at the top of the tree.

Sam definitely took after her mother in build and looks. Her mother was petite and had the same blonde hair. The only difference was that she now wore it shorter. Her sister's features were a lot different – she took more after their father's side. Jessica stood about five feet six inches, had light brown hair and brown eyes. She always seemed to glow. She had a softness to her even though she always tried to hide it. She never seemed to be worried about anything and Sam was always amazed.

Jessica climbed down off the stepstool and turned to see Sam standing in the doorway.

"Don't think you are getting off that easy, Sami! Get your butt over here; we still have a million ornaments to put on the tree." Sam happily rejoined her family.

After they had finished the tree, Sam went to her old room and sat on her bed. As she ran her finger along the blanket, she hummed Christmas carols and smiled. Suddenly she heard a light knock on the door and was surprised to see her mother come into the room. Sam did not say anything but just watched her mother for a moment as she walked over and sat down next to Sam

"I just wanted you to know that the holidays have not changed my feelings about what you pulled. You were very irresponsible and you could have gotten other people hurt. I love you because you are my daughter, but I have not liked you very much lately. Let's try to keep the holiday spirit around here, for your sister's sake."

Sam was silent as she watched her mother get up and leave the room. As soon as she had closed the door, Sam buried her face in her pillow and cried.

The next night, Sam and her family were sitting around the living room reading. Occasionally Sam would stop and glance at the Christmas tree, but she avoided looking at her mom.

It was quiet for a long time until Sam's mother laid her magazine down next to her and looked over to where Sam was sitting.

"So Sam, how have you been doing lately?"

Sam looked up in surprise. She was still trying to hide the hurt from the night before. "Fine, Mom. Why?"

"Well, I was just wondering how things were going with this man that you are living with."

Sam looked annoyed. "Well, let me tell you, it is a lot better than my previous living arrangements."

Jessica looked up from her book and glanced at Sam. "For you to be living with some man you don't even know, well, he must be great in bed or something." She looked at her sister to see how she responded to her accusation.

"Give me a break." Sam stood up and looked from her mother to her sister. "Kyle and I are just roommates. In fact, we have become pretty good friends. He has his room and I have mine. Sorry if I don't have anything juicy for you two to get worked up about."

Jessica shook her head and laughed. She loved her sister, but she also knew just how naive she could be.

"Just be careful, ok?"

"Please," her mother added.

"Don't worry, guys. I know what I am doing. Really." Sam looked over at the tree. "You know, I think I saw some more decorations downstairs." Sam walked quickly out of the room. *Some things never change,* she thought.

Her mother and sister looked at one another and shook their heads. They both knew that the conversation was over and went back to reading their books.

Sam lay in bed that night and thought about how worried her family had been. She realized now that she could not tell them about her own fears, for they would surely insist that she come back home. Despite her fears, she sure loved the freedom of being independent, and even living in her car had beat living at home with her mother.

Sam turned onto her back and put her hands behind her head. She realized that she would just have to work out her problems herself. So what if Kyle had a temper sometimes; didn't we all? Everything would be ok. With that thought on her mind, Sam drifted off to sleep.

CHAPTER 12

Christmas at home, for the most part, had been nice. Her mother did not mention what had happened again and both her mother and her sister had stopped harassing her about Kyle. Sam actually had started to really enjoy being around her family again. Spirits seemed to be high and everyone had loved their gifts. Jessica begged Sam to stay through New Year's and, of course, she stayed.

It was the morning of New Year's Eve and they were discussing which channel on the television they wanted to watch to bring in the new year. The telephone rang and Jessica jumped up to answer it.

"Sam, it's for you." She yelled from the kitchen.

Sam went into the kitchen and grabbed the phone. It was Kyle. She had given him her mother's phone number in case of an emergency.

"Hi, Samantha, how was your Christmas?" He sounded in high spirits.

"Great, how was your mother?"

Kyle was silent for a moment and then he cleared his voice. "She was ok. We had a disagreement so I came back home. He cleared his voice again. "Would you mind if I came over and celebrated New Year's with you and your family?" He sounded almost like a child and her heart went out to him.

"Let me ask them. I'm sure they will love having you here." At least she hoped so anyway. Sam set the phone down and went into the living room. She cleared her throat and started to twirl her hair with her fingers. Both her mother and Jessica looked up at her.

"Hey, would you guys mind if Kyle joined us tonight? He had to come back home and he is by himself. It would be a great opportunity for you both to meet him."

Jessica and her mother looked at each other. Indeed it was time they met Sam's so-called roommate. Her mother smiled.

"Invite him over."

He followed the instructions that Sam had given him and was at the house within an hour. When he pulled up to the house he just sat in the car, watching the shadows of Sam's family moving around the living room on the

46

other side of the closed drapes. He smiled as he ran his hand along the flowers he had brought for her mother and the teddy bear for her sister. He knew exactly what everyone wanted and exactly what everyone would want to hear.

From the moment Kyle had walked thorough the front door he had charmed everyone. Sam was relieved to see that Jessica had immediately liked him, although she still teased Sam about their relationship.

"No one that cute can possibly just be your roommate," she had whispered to Sam. Sam just shook her head.

They all decided that they would help pass the time before midnight by playing cards. Kyle had immediately offered to teach the group a card game that he had learned several years ago.

"You guys will love this game," he said excitedly. He explained all of the rules and dealt out the first hand.

Sam was a little confused, but when it was her turn to play, she carefully placed down the card that she thought was the right one. Kyle was quick to correct her.

"You can't play a Jack there, Samantha. Now I don't want to have to tell you the rules again, so try to pay attention, ok? You are going to hold everyone up. We would like to be finished before midnight, so do you think you can get it right this time?"

Sam stared at Kyle and rolled her eyes. "Give me a break, Kyle. It's just a stupid card game." Sam looked back at her cards as did Jessica, but her mother was watching Kyle, who was now glaring at Sam. He noticed her watching him and he smiled at her and then looked seriously down at his own cards.

Keep your cool, Kyle. Just keep your cool.

Sam noticed that her mother kept staring at Kyle and when the card game was finally finished, she asked her mother to help her get some drinks from the kitchen.

"Mom, what is your problem?" Sam asked as she grabbed some glasses. "Why are you sitting there staring at Kyle? He is supposed to be our guest, so why don't you make him feel just a little welcome."

"Samantha, I don't like the way he looks at you. Something about that man scares me."

"Oh come on, Mom. It was just a stupid little card game. Have you ever known a man to not be a little crazy during a card game? Shoot, most men are majorly sore losers. You should just be lucky he didn't lose. Actually, maybe I should be the one who feels lucky, because then you probably would have thrown him out of the house."

"Samantha, you don't need to talk to me like that. I have been around long enough to know a bad apple when I see one."

"Oh great, here we go again," Sam mumbled.

"Fine, you just do what you want, but don't come running back to me when you have realized that you made a big mistake. I guarantee that I will be the first to tell you 'I told you so.' "

Sam's mom rushed from the kitchen and left Sam standing there alone. "I hate when she gets in that 'I know everything' mode," she mumbled and then she grabbed the glasses, the champagne, and the apple cider and headed back into the living room.

Sam noticed that her mother was watching Kyle for most of the night and it annoyed her to see her mother so suspicious of him. Her mother made it obvious that, for some reason, she did not approve of Kyle, and that created a strange tension in the air that kept everyone quiet until it was close to midnight.

Jessica finally jumped up with her glass in her hand and tried desperately to get everyone a little more excited.

"Come on you guys, it's almost time to count down."

Everyone finally stood up and with glasses held high, they all counted down to the New Year; a year that was to unravel a frightening truth.

CHAPTER 13

It was the middle of February and, as was typical for this time of the year, it was snowing fairly hard. Sam opened the front door of the apartment and walked in. She had left work early because she had not been feeling very well. She brushed the snow off of her jacket and threw her keys and purse on the couch, and then went into the kitchen for a glass of water. The card and rose that Kyle had given her for Valentine's Day were still sitting on the counter. Sam leaned forward to smell the rose and then picked up the card to read it again. "To a good friend," he had written, "May our friendship blossom as the rosebud, and may we never wither and die." It was strange, but sweet. Sam set the card back down and then stretched her arms back behind her. All of a sudden she heard a loud noise outside. Sam ran to the living room window and looked out. Kyle had slammed his truck into a telephone pole right outside the complex. Sam grabbed her jacket and ran outside to see if he was ok.

"Kyle, Kyle, are you ok? Did you slide on the ice? What happened?" Sam asked as she tried to catch her breath. It was not only snowing hard, but there was a wind so cold it felt like it went right through her clothing.

Kyle was sitting behind the wheel of his truck. He slowly turned his head towards Sam and the look on his face sent more chills down her spine than did the cold. He had an evil look in his eyes and a smile so demonic that it gave his face a mask-like appearance.

"What happened? What happened, you ask." He let out a laugh that made Sam take a step back. *What was wrong with him,* she thought to herself. She wanted to ask him if he was alright, but something inside of her kept her from speaking.

"Do you want to know what happened, Sam-an-tha?" He said as he slowly stepped out of his truck and then, without warning, he slammed his fist into the driver's side door. He then turned back to her and smiled that wicked smile again.

"Well, let's see now. First I got fired from my job. Why, you ask? I was fired for sexually harassing a customer." He laughed again. "Sexually harassing a customer. Can you believe it? All I did was open her damn car door for her, and that is sexually harassing her. I'll show you what sexual harassment is." Kyle grabbed Sam's hair with his fist and yanked so hard that it immediately brought tears to Sam's eyes.

"Kyle, please, you are hurting me!" Sam cried out as he half dragged her and half pushed her towards their front door. Her feet were sliding on the ice on the ground, which only added to the pain she was feeling. Sam had never been so scared in her life.

"Yeah, I'll show you what sexual harassment really is." Kyle opened the door, let go of Sam's hair and then pushed her hard through the doorway. Sam barely had time to breathe before he was on top of her, hitting her hard in the face. She tried to block the blows, crying hysterically, but he just held her down with one hand and kept hitting her. Suddenly, he stopped. He stood up and looked around the room and then walked over to the counter where the rose sat. He stood there silently for a moment, staring at the rose and then he picked up the vase and threw it against the wall, shattering the glass everywhere. He turned back to look at Samantha, who was curled up like a child, sobbing uncontrollably.

"You're lucky today, Samantha. I'm just not in the mood," he said calmly and then walked back outside, slamming the door behind him. She could hear him moving his truck and she only hoped he was not coming back.

Sam was hurting so badly that she was afraid to move. Kyle had hit her in the face, stomach and chest. As soon as she tried to get up, she let out a loud cry of pain. *He must have broken my ribs*, she thought to herself. She just stayed on the floor and helplessly cried until the pain became so unbearable that she fainted.

CHAPTER 14

Sam was dreaming. She was running in slow motion yet she was not moving. Someone was following her. She tried to scream but there was no sound. She was alone.

"Samantha, can you hear me?" Sam heard the voice, but did not know where it was coming from.

"Samantha, this is Dr. Kaimen. You are at Colorado General Hospital. Samantha? Can you hear me?"

Sam started to slowly open her eyes. At first she could not see anything, but then her eyes started to focus. There was a doctor and a nurse standing over her. They were both smiling.

"I'm glad you decided to wake up. I am Dr. Kaimen and this is your nurse, Jane. You were in a pretty bad car accident, young lady, and you are pretty banged up. Luckily someone saw your truck off the side of the road and stopped to help you." He waited to see Sam's response.

"Car accident?" Sam shook her head in confusion. "What car accident? Where is Kyle?" *What is going on,* she thought.

"Your roommate Kyle? He is on his way here. We called the phone number listed on the identification card in your wallet and he answered the phone. He is very worried about you and he said that he would be here as soon as possible. How do you feel, Samantha?"

"Doctor, was I the only one in the truck?"

"Why yes, you were. Do you remember someone else being in the truck with you?"

Sam looked down and sighed. She remembered that Kyle wrecked his truck and then she remembered how Kyle had attacked her. She knew that Kyle would never have let her or anyone else ever drive his truck. He was almost obsessive about it. He must have set it up to look like she had been out driving in the bad weather and had been in an accident. Sam shook her head in disbelief.

"How bad am I, doctor?"

"Well, you are lucky," Dr. Kaimen said as he opened her chart. "You have two fractured ribs and a lot of bruises. You are going to be hurting for a very long time."

"How long do I have to stay here?"

"We still need to run some more tests, but you should be able to go home soon." The doctor smiled at Sam. "You just relax and we will take good care of you." The doctor and nurse turned and, as they opened the door to leave, Kyle appeared in the doorway. He smiled at the doctor and came into the room.

Sam looked at him in shock and then quickly looked away, fearing that he might try to hurt her again. A single tear started to flow down her cheek.

"Samantha, I am so sorry. You needed medical attention so, as you have probably already figured out by now, I had to stage an accident to explain your injuries. It was the best thing to do for both of us. You know that I didn't mean to hit you like I did. Please, please forgive me." He looked at Sam to see her reaction. Sam only blinked and continued to keep her eyes turned toward the other direction.

"Samantha, honey, you know how much our relationship means to me. I didn't mean to hurt you, please believe me. I was just having a really bad day. Besides, you know what they say, you always hurt the one that you love." Kyle sounded so pitiful that it made Sam sick to her stomach. She turned slowly to look up at him. She could not stop the tears that began to flow down her cheeks.

"How could you... How could you do this to me? Do you go around beating all of your so-called friends?"

"Samantha," Kyle leaned down and took her hand. He smiled at her. "I promise that this will never, ever happen again. Like I said before, I just had a really bad day, that's all. Please say you will forgive me."

Sam looked into his eyes and she thought he looked sincere. *Maybe he really did not mean it. After all, we all make mistakes,* she thought.

Sam sank down deeper into the hospital bed, feeling defeated. She looked up at Kyle, whose eyes were pleading with her. She sighed deeply. "Please don't ever do this to me again, Kyle."

"You just hurry up and get better so that I can take you home," he said smiling. "Oh, and Samantha, let's just keep what really happened between you and me. We wouldn't want to cause any embarrassing problems, now would we?" He stood up, smiled down at her one last time, and then left her room.

Sam sighed loudly. She had never felt more alone than she did at that moment. If she tried to tell anyone about what Kyle had done to her, especially her mother, she was sure that she would be mocked for being so naive as to get herself into this situation in the first place.

Sam slept for a while and then the doctor came back in to see her. He sat down next to her bed and smiled at her for a moment. The way he was watching her made her feel like a little girl.

"Hi, doc," she said smiling.

"Hi, Samantha. I wanted to stop by and see how you are feeling."

Sam painfully inched herself up a little bit and looked down at the floor. "Well, it's like you said yourself earlier. It's painful but I'll get over it."

"Samantha, I need to ask you something personal, if you don't mind."

Sam looked up at the doctor, expecting to be questioned about her medical history.

The doctor stood up and walked over to the window and then turned around to face her again. "I don't know quite how to say this, but I don't believe that your injuries are from a car accident." He noticed the look on Sam's face and smiled as he sat back down again. "Don't get me wrong; I'm not trying to pry in to your personal life. Well, ok, so maybe I am. I have just been a doctor for a long time and I know the difference between injuries from a car accident and what looks like a pretty severe beating. You know that I can help you, Samantha, but you have to be honest with me."

Sam looked away from the doctor and tried desperately to hold back her tears. *Kyle said that he would not hurt me again,* she thought, *and maybe he was right about keeping this to ourselves.* She looked back up to the doctor.

"You know, Dr. Kaimen, I really can't remember the car accident very well. It all happened so fast. Kyle keeps a lot of junk in his truck and I'm sure that when I went off of the road something must have hit me."

Sighing loudly, the doctor ran his hand over his chin. "Well, yes, I suppose that could be what happened, but I hope for your sake that if that is not what happened, that you will talk to me. If you need me, just have one of the nurses page me, alright?"

Sam smiled and rested her head back against the pillow again. As soon as the doctor left the room, her smile disappeared.

CHAPTER 15

Sam's stay in the hospital had not been very long. No one in her family had found out about the "accident" and she felt that it would be best that way. If she had talked to her mother, she would have had to lie about what had happened, and she knew that her mother would have seen right through those lies.

Sam's injuries healed over the next few months and Kyle seemed to be acting like his old self again. He was constantly in good spirits and he had found a new job as a mechanic almost immediately. His insurance company was still trying to decide if they were going to cover the damages to his truck after the "unfortunate accident," so Kyle was forced to take the bus to and from work. At first he did not seem to mind.

One evening after both Sam and Kyle had come home from work, Kyle asked Sam to sit down in the living room.

"Samantha, I have thought a lot about something and I really believe that what I am about to say is for the best. I am sure once you understand where I am coming from, you will agree."

"What are you talking about, Kyle?"

"My insurance company has decided to cover the damages to my truck, but my deductible is so high that it is not worth it for me to bother fixing it right now. I now make enough money at this new job to pay all of our living expenses and I have decided that you will quit your job immediately and I will start driving your truck to work."

Sam looked at Kyle in shock as what he had said hit her hard. He was trying to take away her only means of transportation and in a larger sense, her security. She felt her heart start to beat faster as she spoke to him. "Kyle, you are crazy if you think I am going to quit my job and give you my truck. If you make so much money, buy another car."

Unfortunately, that was not the response Kyle had wanted to hear.

"Samantha," he said as he started to pace in front of her. He was wringing his hands, which made her start to feel very nervous. "Samantha, you do not seem to understand what I am saying. You are going to quit your job and I will be taking your truck from here on out. Do you understand?" He continued without waiting for her response. "In fact, you will stay here during the day and you will never leave this house. Do not think you can fool me, either; I have my ways of knowing if you are not obeying my orders." Kyle leaned forward and put his face close to Sam's. "And don't think that you are going to run back to mommy, either. If you ever try to leave this house, I will kill you. I will kill you and I will kill your family. Do you understand? DO YOU UNDERSTAND?" he yelled into her face.

Sam was too shocked to speak. She was afraid that if she gave him the wrong answer, he would start to hit her again.

"Samantha, it is in your best interest to agree to what I have said. Again I am asking you, do you understand the rules I have set for you?"

Sam nodded her head yes. What else could she do? She was suddenly a prisoner in her own home. Kyle had her right where he wanted her to be and he knew it. He smiled and walked back into his room.

Sam was shaking all over. She went into her bedroom and softly closed the door. She frantically looked around the room, as if she could possibly find something that could help her. Suddenly she heard Kyle's footsteps coming towards her room; his steps were heavy and fast. Sam stepped back as he swung open her door. He walked up to her and she closed her eyes, expecting him to hit her, but instead he just laughed and roughly grabbed her by the shoulders.

"I just wanted to make sure that you knew that I was serious."

Sam shook her head and widened her eyes. "Yes, Kyle, I know that you are serious. Please, just don't hit me again."

Kyle laughed again and then he let go of her shoulders. He turned and walked out of her room. It was at that moment that she realized just how fast and hard her breathing had become and she was shaking all over. She tried to calm down her breathing and then she wrapped her arms around herself and desperately looked around her room. Frightened that Kyle might return, Sam dropped to the floor and crawled towards her closet. At first she just looked into the darkness as if there was something there that could protect her. She sighed and then slowly crawled into the small space. She curled her legs up to her chest and softly hummed a lullaby to herself until she drifted into sleep.

That night Kyle left the apartment again. Sam had awakened long enough to hear him leave and then she had crawled out of the closet and gotten back into her bed. Sam figured that he was probably going to his secret place that he usually went to in the evenings and she knew better than to ever ask him where that happened to be.

Several times during the following day Sam had looked at the telephone, wishing that she could get the courage to call her mother. She kept pacing back and forth trying to decide what to do. *What if what he had said was true,* she thought to herself. She would never let him hurt her family. But then again, if she called her mom maybe she could get her out of the mess she was in. Sam remembered their conversation at Christmas time. "Don't come running back to me when you realize that you made a mistake," she had said, and Sam had hardly spoken a word to her mother since then. Not only would her mother not help her now, but she would probably not even believe her.

Sam suddenly remembered the threats that Kyle had made towards her family. She could not possibly take the chance that he might hurt them, too. No, instead she would remain Kyle's prisoner, doing whatever he wanted her to do. She realized that she really did not have a choice.

The next day Kyle had the phone disconnected. Now there was no possibility of escape. Sam thought back to the argument that she had had with her mom the day that she had grabbed her clothes and left. "I am like a bird locked in a cage," she had told her mother. As tears started rolling down her cheeks, she said out loud to herself, "No. Now I am a bird locked in a cage. And no one can ever set me free."

CHAPTER 16

Sam was lying in bed with her arms propped under her head. It was September first, exactly one year from when Sam and Kyle had first moved in together. In the last year, Sam had gone from being free and independent, to being a puppet. She had long ago given up having any hope of getting away from Kyle. She had learned quickly that if she did what he said, and only spoke when he spoke to her first, Kyle would treat her like gold. He had hit her several more times since the hospital incident, but of course, it was her fault.

"You know, if you only did what I asked, I would never have to hurt you," he always would say.

Suddenly there was a light knock on her door, which forced Sam back to reality. She grabbed the blankets and held them tight as Kyle opened her door. He was holding a bottle of champagne and something else which she could not see and he had a strange smile on his face. Sam was too frightened to ask him what he wanted.

"You didn't think I had forgotten, did you?" He asked as she smiled down at her. Sam grabbed the blankets even tighter as he sat down on the edge of the bed.

"What's wrong, Sam? You didn't forget, did you? This is our one-year anniversary of being together. I thought it was only right that we should celebrate properly."

Kyle quickly grabbed Sam's hands before she could fight him and he tied them to her headboard. He then tied her feet together. Sam tried to scream and Kyle slapped her hard across her face.

"You want to play rough, eh? Well, that's just fine with me. I love it rough!" Kyle laughed and then grabbed a rag which he stuffed into Sam's mouth. Sam started to gag as she cried uncontrollably.

"Baby, don't try to fight me, it will only make it hurt more."

Kyle ripped Sam's clothes off. He had the look of a wild beast on his face – a look Sam would never forget. Sam closed her eyes and bit hard into the rag that was in her mouth. She tried not to feel the way he was roughly grabbing at her body. She tried not to hear the nasty words that he was saying or the animal-like growling sounds that came from somewhere deep inside of him. All she could do was pray to herself that somehow, someway she would get away from him.

CHAPTER 17

After Kyle had raped Sam, he popped the cork on the champagne bottle and laughed. He was happy with himself because he was in control. He took the rag out of Sam's mouth, knowing she would not bother to scream.

Sam lay on the bed completely motionless. Her body and soul had been invaded and abused. What was possibly left for her to fight for?

"Get yourself cleaned up, I am taking you somewhere special tonight," Kyle said as he grabbed the bottle and started to leave her room. "Be ready in ten minutes."

Sam felt herself rise off of the bed and go into the bathroom. Once she was in the shower everything that Kyle had done to her hit her and she started to cry again. She was trying to keep quiet, afraid he would come at her again. She tried as hard as she could to wipe off the filth that she felt he had laid upon her. She scrubbed and scrubbed, but the harder she tried, the dirtier she felt.

Suddenly she heard the bathroom door open and she felt her heart start to race. *Please, God,* she thought, *not again.* She put her hand across her mouth to muffle her cries.

"Samantha, we are going to be late. I am not going to tell you again to hurry it up, so you better get with it." Kyle closed the door again.

Sam tried to catch her breath. She was crying so hard that her chest hurt. She tried to hurry so that Kyle would not get mad at her again. When she had finished dressing, Kyle grabbed her arm and led her outside.

The cool night air felt good on Sam's raw skin as they walked out to her truck. There were a couple of new dents on the passenger side, but Sam did not ask Kyle what had happened. She just did not care anymore and she did not even want to know what trouble he had caused, anyway. Sam knew how bad his temper could be and she just hoped that no one else had gotten hurt.

They drove for about forty-five minutes and then Kyle pulled the truck into a parking lot by what looked to be an old warehouse. Sam did not say anything, but merely got out of the truck. As they approached an old metal door, Sam could hear a strange pumping sound from a machine somewhere out in the distance. Sam could not see any moonlight to guide her and when she glanced out into the vastness around her, all she could see was darkness. There was an eerie feel to the air around her; almost as if she were being watched. She could feel goosebumps on her arms and legs and subconsciously moved closer to Kyle as they walked.

As soon as they walked into the building, Sam knew what Kyle was involved in. As she looked around, her heart started to pound with fear. It was dark inside except for several candles that were spread out in a large circle. There were about twenty men and women dressed in black robes standing outside of the circle of candles. Sam looked down at the floor and saw a large upside-down star. Fear gripped her even harder as she confirmed what she had originally thought – Kyle was part of some sort of satanic cult.

Suddenly everyone looked up towards Kyle and Sam. Kyle gave Sam a push until she was standing in front of everyone. He then walked up to her and, using a knife, swiftly cut her clothing from her body. Sam gasped as the crowd around her started to move closer to her and she tried desperately to cover herself with her hands. She was so scared she was shaking, but she knew that there was no one here that would help her.

Sam felt as if her feet were cemented to the floor. She tried to think quickly – what should she do? Could she run? No, there were too many people. *The chanting was so loud.* She couldn't think. *So many faces.* She looked around at the people as they inched slowly closer to her. Were the lights playing tricks on her mind? Their eyes – their eyes seemed to glow red. Was this real?

The machine in the darkness outside seemed to grow louder. *Chhhh chhhhh, chhhh chhhh.*

"Nooooo!" she screamed as Kyle held the knife above his head.

"You belong to me know!" he screamed at Sam.

Sam dropped to her knees and threw up. Kyle slammed something against the back of her head and then darkness overcame her.

When Sam awoke, she was back in her bed again. *Had this all been just a bad dream?* she thought to herself. She tried to sit up and immediately felt an intense pain shooting through her head, paralyzing her for a moment.

"How did I get myself into this mess? How could I let myself...." Sam turned her face into her pillow and cried herself back to sleep.

CHAPTER 18

The young mother pushed the stroller past Sam's building as she did every day around the same time. The children ran to catch the bus, and the man in the business suit waited impatiently for the car that always picked him up late. Sam watched them all from the window in her room, just as she had every day for as long as she could remember. This was all she had to look forward to. She rarely left her bedroom and she was eating less and less every day. She was also scared to sleep, afraid Kyle would come into her room and hurt her again. It had only been a couple of months since the first time he had raped her and he had forced himself on her several more times after that. Sometimes he was so rough with her that she could not walk the next day. He had not taken her back to the warehouse, but Sam figured that he had probably just wanted to show off his new possession to the other cult members.

Sam's mind felt like it had broken down. She was only eighteen years old and yet in her mind she had already died. If anyone had seen her now, they would have thought that she had some kind of horrible disease and that she had little time left to live. To Sam, her life now was diseased and she had given up on any cure.

One afternoon Sam was sitting on her bed daydreaming when her door flew open. Kyle grabbed her and forced her to lie back on her bed.

"How many times do I have to tell you to leave your door open?" he screamed as he pulled her arms over her head.

"Oh Kyle, please, not again," Sam pleaded.

He tied her hands and feet to the bed and then he climbed on top of her and sat there looking down at her. He ran his finger along the buttons of her blouse and laughed as he watched her close her eyes and turn her face away.

"You look so pitiful when you do that, Samantha." He grabbed her face and forced her to face him. "Look at me when I'm talking to you, whore."

A tear slowly slid down her cheek and Kyle laughed.

"Oh, look at poor little Samantha," he whined. "What's wrong, aren't you having fun yet? You know," he said matter-of-factly, "you should be lucky that I took you off of the streets. I mean, look at you. You never take care of yourself anymore. Who in their right mind would possibly want you?" He leaned down and put his face besides hers. "The only reason I keep you around is because it's such great sex," he whispered and than he ran his tongue along her ear.

Sam was crying so hard that her entire body was making small jerking motions. Kyle sat back up and looked annoyed.

"Well, it's obvious that it won't be great this time. You really know how to spoil a good time." He pulled himself off of her and stood beside her bed and watched her. He shook his head in disappointment and threw his hands up in the air.

"I think I'm going to leave you here for awhile so that you can think about what you could have had. If I have to suffer, well then, so do you."

As soon as Kyle left the room Sam tried to pull her hands free but the more she struggled, the more the rope dug into her wrists. She fought against the ropes for over an hour until Kyle finally came back into her room, quietly untied her hands and feet, and then left again. Sam started to rub her sore wrists but saw that they were bleeding. She grabbed her pillow and held it against her chest as she stared blankly at the wall next to her bed. She felt numb inside and although Kyle had not raped her physically this time, she felt as though she had been mentally raped. She lay motionless in her bed for a long time until Kyle came back in her room again.

"Get dressed," he said and, without another word, turned and left her room.

She got dressed and silently followed him out to her truck. It did not take long for her to recognize where they were going. Her pulse quickened and she gripped the door handle as they drove closer to the old warehouse. As they got out of the truck, Kyle motioned for her to stay by the truck and he walked up to a group of people standing to the side of the building. He glanced back at Sam and then turned and led the group up the hill behind them.

It was strangely quiet and Sam looked nervously around. She looked back in the direction of the hillside and thought she saw a glitter of light. She looked harder and as she stared at the darkened hillside, she started to see small red lights. She blinked hard and watched as more and more of the light seemed to appear. They were dim, and yet she could still see them – and she would swear they seemed to be coming down the hillside towards her. She could hear the voices of Kyle and his followers starting to come back from the top of the hill and the small red lights seemed to respond as well. The lights seem to stop and then move away. She was pondering what she saw when suddenly someone from the group yelled out.

"What the…" she heard him yell.

"What is it?" someone else shouted out.

"Oh, man! It's a skunk! Run guys!"

Sam laughed as she watched Kyle and the others scrambling down the hillside. She could smell the horrible stench of the skunk's defensive and volatile spray and wondered if it had gotten anyone directly.

"Calm down you guys," she heard Kyle ordering. "Did anyone get sprayed?"

Sam watched as the group got settled down and she tried not to show any emotions. In her mind, she felt that they had only gotten what they deserved. As Kyle silently drove her back to the apartment, Sam looked out her window and smiled.

CHAPTER 19

As time went on, Sam began to think a lot about her mother. Thinking about her family seemed to be the only refuge she could seek. The thought that Kyle would never allow her to see them devastated her. It was almost as if, by taking away the chance to be with her family, he was also taking away the one part of her that gave her any hope of being safe and secure again.

So many mornings she had woken up in her closet, huddled like a child. For some reason she felt safe there. Kyle had found her there once, but much to Sam's surprise and relief, he had not bothered her. Instead he had laughed at her, calling her a baby, but Sam did not care. Somehow, when she was in her closet, the darkness that surrounded her always seemed to give her a feeling of safety and security.

One night Sam could hear Kyle getting ready for his night at the warehouse. She sat close to the door, listening to him move around the apartment. She always looked forward to these nights because it gave her time away from him. She was sitting there quietly waiting to hear the front door open when she could hear him heading towards her room. She quickly sat on her bed and fiddled with the blanket as he entered her room. She looked up at him and almost lost her composure when she saw his outrageous attire. He was wearing the black robe like the others had worn, but this time he was also wearing a black cape with red satin on the inside. He looked like he was dressed for Halloween and, as hard as it was for Sam not to laugh, she tried desperately not to show any emotion.

He watched her face for a moment and Sam almost wondered if he could read her thoughts. "Come on," he said to her, "you are coming with me tonight." He saw the look on her face change. "Don't look so disappointed," he sneered. "Besides, I need you with me tonight."

Sam quietly followed Kyle out to the truck. The drive seemed to take less time than she remembered and she had looked down at the floor the entire time.

"Stay here," he instructed as he got out of the truck and walked over to the building.

Sam looked around again and rubbed her arm with her hand. She felt a chill even though she was inside the vehicle. She glanced in the direction of the hillside but this time she could not see anything but darkness. *Where did the moon go?* she thought. It was as if everything just disappeared in the darkness of this place. She could hear that strange pumping noise that she had heard the very first time she had been there and wondered if it was some kind of oil pump. The noise just made this place seem even spookier to her.

Sam sat there alone for a long time and suddenly she thought she could hear a voice. She concentrated, but what she heard didn't make any sense. It wasn't like someone was speaking English but something else and it was barely audible. She could not understand what she was hearing and yet she felt like it was telling her that she would be safe – that she would not be hurt here again. Was there someone else out there with her or was it an animal she was hearing – or maybe it was just her imagination. She felt the hair on her arm standing up and she rubbed her arm with her hand again. She shifted her weight and started looking around again.

Suddenly Kyle was next to her window and she jumped. She had not seen or heard him leave the warehouse and it startled her to see him. Her heart was racing madly when he opened her door.

"Get out, you are driving," he said as he handed her the keys. She walked quickly around the truck and rushed to get in the driver's side as fast as she could.

"Kyle, were you talking to someone outside?" Sam asked him as she started up the truck.

"No. There is no one else out here tonight. Why?"

"I thought I heard something, that's all." Her hands were shaking as she started up the truck.

"You experienced something tonight, didn't you?" Kyle asked calmly.

"Yes, I did," Sam said, surprising herself when she answered him.

"What happened?"

"I don't know how to explain it. I heard something, like a voice, I don't know. It scared me and yet it was almost reassuring at the same time, if that makes any sense." Sam wasn't sure why she was telling Kyle about what had happened. He was being so nice to her at that moment and it reminded her of when she had first met him.

"This place is very special. A lot of us believe that there is a doorway here to another dimension, or something like it. I am pretty sure I know right where it is, too. There is something that lives here, but no one has ever known exactly what. There have been strange things that have happened here, things that have never been explained. Most of the time it has to do with some high school students playing a prank or hazing." He paused for a moment. "You know a cop died here several years ago. When they found his body, he looked like he had been mauled to death."

Sam got chills thinking about it. There was something spooky and yet intriguing about the place. All she knew was that she hoped to never go back there again. They were both quiet again as Sam drove the truck onto the highway. She glanced over at Kyle and saw that he was deep in thought.

"Kyle?" she said cautiously.

"Yeah?" he said as he turned to look at her.

"Why do you believe what you believe in? I mean that satanic stuff."

Kyle leaned back and smiled. Sam could tell he was pleased that she seemed interested. "I believe in what I do because it is the truth."

"How do you know it is the truth?"

"I don't. There are so many different religions and beliefs out there. One group out there has it right about life, our creation, and even death. There is going to come a time, maybe when we die, when we will find out the truth. The group that has it right will be glad they did and everyone else will be in big trouble," he said smugly.

Sam watched the road and thought about what he was saying.

"What do you believe in, Sam?" he asked her.

"I don't know. I haven't known for a long time," she answered honestly.

"Then how do you know that my way isn't the right why?"

Sam didn't answer him but kept on driving. She realized that she was confused about everything she had ever believed in. At that exact moment, she was not sure what was real and what wasn't. They were both deep in their own thoughts the rest of the way back to the apartment. Kyle made sure to get the keys from Sam and they went to their separate bedrooms for the night.

The next morning Sam was sitting in her room, looking out the window and thinking about what had happened the night before. The voice she had heard scared her, but at the same time she had felt almost as if someone was there looking out for her. She wasn't sure how to explain it – even to herself. She wondered why Kyle had been dressed so strangely, especially when no one else was supposedly out there with them. She was still sitting by the window thinking about the night before when she heard the front door open. She could hear Kyle coming down the hallway with fast and heavy steps and almost immediately her heart started to pound. She did not know what could have possibly provoked his anger this time, but she did not have time to ponder it. She started to run for the safety of her closet but before she could reach it Kyle was there, grabbing her by her hair.

"I am really getting sick of you hiding away in your closet," he said as he dragged her over to the bed. Fear gripped her and she closed her eyes as she expected him to tear off her clothes and hurt her again.

Instead he just stood over her shaking his head. "You are such a joke. You are stupid and ugly and, well, basically a total loser. Did you know that? You know, if you ever tried to get away from me, no one would want you. Look at you cowering like a stupid baby. You are just so pitiful that you make me sick." Kyle turned and left the room, leaving Sam emotionally shaken.

She walked over to the mirror and looked at her reflection. She had to turn away from what she saw. "He's right," she said to herself. "No one will ever want me. I hate him for what he has done to me!"

Sam walked back to her bed and sat down. She thought about what he had said and looked down. She started to think about her family again and she wondered if they would even want anything to do with her anymore. Suddenly she looked up. Why was she so upset with Kyle when she had gotten herself into this situation? She thought back to everything that had happened up to this point and then she realized who was really to blame. It was her mother. If her mother had not been so overprotective of Sam, maybe Sam would not be in the position she was in right now.

"It's not my fault, it's Mom's fault," she sneered. Sam stood up and started to pace. If her mother had not treated her the way she had, Sam would never have left home in the first place.

"If only you had believed me, Mom. If only you could have believed that I really couldn't find my keys that day, then I never would have had a reason to leave home. It's all your fault," she said as if she were talking to her mother. She shook her head and smiled. It made her feel better to know that it really wasn't her fault that Kyle was treating her so bad.

That night when Kyle came into her room and once again grabbed roughly at her body, Sam silently cursed her mother.

CHAPTER 20

Sam stood in front of the mirror in her room and saw how tired and worn out she looked. She decided to put her hair up in a ponytail, and while she searched for a rubber band she found her pocket calendar. She shook her head as she realized that Christmas had come and gone. Sam thought about the last Christmas that she had spent with her family – her mother and sister putting decorations on the tree, all of them singing. Even though she and her mother were having problems, they had still had a great time. If only Sam had known then what was going to happen. If only she had not been so stubborn about asking her mother to take her back in again.

"Get with it, Sam, you know darn well that you would not have asked Mom to take you back in," she mumbled to herself as she realized how crazy her thoughts were. Sam knew that she had to stop dwelling upon all of the things that she should have done. It seemed as though she was never quite sure what she felt towards her mother anymore. Some days it was just easier to blame her, and yet other days she took comfort in thinking about when she was a child and her mother would hold her close in her arms.

Sam walked out of her room and went into the living room. She was getting tired of just staying around the apartment all of the time. She started walking down the hallway when she heard the front door open. She stopped and Kyle immediately walked up to her.

"What are you doing?" he asked as he eyed her suspiciously.

Sam did not answer but instead walked into the bathroom. He followed her and leaned against the doorway, blocking the door with his body.

"You look horrible, you know. I think it is time for you to start taking better care of yourself. You haven't eaten in who knows how long, and you don't even wear any makeup anymore."

Sam backed herself into a corner and pressed her body into the counter as if hoping that it would swallow her up and take her away from this evil man.

Kyle saw the look in her eyes and he smiled. He loved the power he had over her. He eyed her the way a warden would look at his prisoner, or the way a lion would watch his prey.

"I think you better take a shower and make yourself look pretty for me."

When she did not move he started to get angry. "Didn't you hear what I said, Samantha? Don't play games with me. Go on now, go do yourself up for me."

Sam could not move. Looking at Kyle standing before her suddenly brought up all of the fear, anger and hatred that had been building up inside of her and she exploded. She lunged forward towards him and let out a scream that came from within the depths of her soul. She started hitting him with what little strength she had left.

Kyle easily grabbed Sam's arms and looked down into her face with a brief look of surprise, but then his eyes changed to fury. He took a deep breath and slammed Sam into the wall. "You are so stupid, Samantha," he said as he looked deep into her dazed eyes. He picked her up off the floor and dragged her into the living room. He dropped her back onto the floor and then left for a moment. When he came back, he came at Samantha with his arm up in the air. He was holding one of his leather belts in his hand. He slammed the belt across her face and body over and over again until her screams stopped and her eyes rolled up into the back of her head.

He looked down at her as she lay on the floor bleeding and unconscious. "You better hope the neighbors didn't hear you, you stupid bitch. You are so stupid. I can't believe you actually thought that you could fight me. I guess we both know who won though, eh. I hope you have learned your lesson, because if not, you will die."

That night Sam woke up dazed and in a lot of pain. She was still on the living room floor. She tried to move but Kyle had beaten her so badly that she could not move without pain searing through her entire body. She did not know how long she had been unconscious, but she guessed by how dark it was that it must have been for several hours. She thought about what had happened and she realized that she had been really stupid to go after him the way she did. After all, she weighed ninety-five pounds to his one hundred and eighty. *At this point*, she thought to herself, *I really don't care anyway.* In fact, she wished that he would have finished her off so that she could finally be in peace.

Sam heard Kyle's footsteps in the back of the apartment. She could hear him humming to himself.

"Bastard," she mumbled as the hatred burned in her eyes and then she cringed in pain.

Sam heard him moving closer to the living room and instinctively she closed her eyes and tried to calm her breathing. He stopped above her and watched her closely for a moment. He then went over to the couch and sat down.

"Boy, Samantha, you have really disappointed me," he said softly, more as if he were talking to himself than to her. "I just don't know what to do with you now. I could take a pillow and smother you – it would be quick and you would never even know what hit you. Or I could cut you up in a bunch of pieces and hide them all over the state so that no one could ever identify you." He laughed softly to himself. He seemed to find that last idea amusing.

"Nah. I think I'll wait and see if you change this time. Maybe now you have learned your lesson and will do as I say. I really do hope so for your sake. I guarantee I won't be giving you another chance."

Sam heard him walk back to his room and close his door. She took a deep breath, trying to calm her heart, which was racing madly. She was relieved that he had not touched her, but his words had cut her like a knife. She knew that, if she wanted to survive, she would have no choice but to do whatever he told her to do. She had no idea where that small will to live had come from, but she decided not to question it. She just hoped that she could keep Kyle from getting upset with her again.

CHAPTER 21

The next few months Sam did everything that Kyle told her to do. She dressed nicely and put on makeup and perfume to please him, as well. He was so relieved to see that she had finally "learned her lesson," that he stopped hitting her. That alone gave Sam a new strength and will to live.

Kyle had also surprised Sam by hooking up the phone again, although it was under the condition that she could not use it and no one was to know that it was there. He made it clear that it was for his use only.

"Don't think you can outsmart me either, Samantha," he had told her. "I will know if you have tried to use the phone."

Sam started to eat again and had regained some of her strength. The stronger she got, the more determined she got to find a way to get away from Kyle. The nights that Kyle left, Sam would sit in her closet, formulating different plans of escape. Most of her ideas seemed impossible to implement, but she knew that she just could not give up.

One day Kyle surprised her. He told her that he had gotten in touch with her friend Laura and that she was coming to visit her.

"Now, I told her that you have been very sick and that you have been in bed for months. You stick to that story. What has happened between you and me is our business. You do not tell her anything. Do you understand?"

Sam nodded. "Of course, Kyle."

He smiled. "Good."

A couple of hours later Laura came over, just as Kyle had said she would. The two girls hugged and looked hard at each other.

"It has been too long, Sami! I must say you look great for having been really sick. You have lost some weight, though. I hope you are feeling better now," Laura said, looking concerned.

"I'm much better now. I'm slowly regaining my strength and I anticipate being my old self again very soon." Sam glanced over towards Kyle and smiled sweetly, but he did not notice the sarcasm in her voice.

The girls talked and laughed for hours. They mainly talked about high school and all of the crazy things that they had done together. It scared Sam to realize just how much, she, herself, had changed in the last year and a half.

She really was a totally different person. In fact, she really did not know who she was anymore.

Kyle stayed with the girls the entire time and that intimidated Sam more than anything else did. Her best friend was sitting right next to her and yet Sam had no way of letting her know that she was in trouble and desperately needed her friend's help. Sam knew that Kyle wanted to make sure that she did not say anything to Laura about the abuse and that he would not take any chances. After what seemed to be too short of a visit, Kyle glanced at his watch and stood up.

"I better take you back home Laura, it's getting late."

Laura did not argue but jumped up and gave Sam a big hug.

"I wish you had a phone, but maybe we can get together again soon! It was great seeing you."

Kyle glared at Sam to make sure that she did not say anything about the phone being hooked up again. He had even gone as far as to hide the phone in the closet during Laura's visit. Sam did not say anything, but just smiled.

Sam waited until Kyle and Laura had walked out the front door and then she walked over to the living room window. She watched as he opened the passenger door for her. *My truck*, Sam realized. *They are taking my truck. It should be me driving away, not them.*

Sam watched Laura smiling up at Kyle. He said something to her and then they both laughed and she got into the truck. Sam shook her head. If only Laura knew the truth. As she watched them leave the parking lot, Sam thought about how lonely and unhappy she had been. She missed her family tremendously, and she would do anything just to go to a movie or get a burger somewhere. It was so unfair that she was trapped in her own home.

Kyle did not come home that night. Sam wondered if he was at one of his cult meetings. Sam stayed awake and thought back to that first horrible night when Kyle had taken her to that old warehouse. She could not remember what happened after she walked into the building except for what she saw in her nightmares. They were always the same; there were flashes of lights all around her and people with strange, distorted faces laughing at her. She was naked and a shadow behind her seemed to close in around her. That is when she always woke up. Every time she thought about it, it made her fear Kyle that much more. He believed that he had powers and that he was capable of doing things supernaturally. He had told her several times that he could use those powers to find Sam if she ever tried to leave him.

"I have ways of tracking you down that you will never understand or be able to fight," he always told her. "There was another girl who thought she could get away," he told her once, "but she didn't get far. I found her and she had to be punished. I caused her to have a horrible car accident that killed her. She died because of me," he had said smugly. "So don't even think of trying to get away from me, because I will always find you, just like I did her, no matter where you go."

He also always stressed what horrible things he could do to Sam's family. Laura and everyone else were being deceived and Sam knew that Kyle would never be left for a fool.

Kyle finally came home around two o'clock in the afternoon the next day. When he walked in the door, he seemed to be in high spirits. Sam started to follow him into the kitchen, but then stopped and went into the living room instead. Kyle seemed to sense that Sam was nervous about something, so he followed her into the living room and sat down in the recliner across from where she sat.

"Did you enjoy your visit with Laura yesterday, Samantha?"

"Yes, Kyle, I did. Thank you for bringing her here for me."

"You're welcome. If you continue to behave, I may even let you see her again sometime soon." He was watching her carefully. "I have to go out for a while. Can I trust you to behave while I am gone?"

"Of course, Kyle. When do you think you will be back?"

Kyle looked annoyed. "Why? Do I have a curfew now?" Then he looked at her suspiciously. "Or maybe you had something planned that you did not want me to know about?"

Sam shook her head. "No, Kyle. I was just asking."

He looked at her for a moment and then his face lightened up again. "Well, don't have too much fun while I'm gone."

Sam waited until he left and then sighed. She walked into her room and sat down. He was only gone for a short time when the doorbell rang, but Sam did not move. The doorbell rang again and Sam finally got up and walked into the hallway. She stood there and stared at the front door, unsure whether to answer it or not. No one had come to the door except when Kyle was home and she was not sure if he would want her to open it. What if it was Kyle testing her again.

The doorbell rang again and there was a loud banging as the person on the other side was impatiently waiting for someone to answer the door. Sam slowly made her way to the door and cautiously peered through the peephole. She could see Greg pacing impatiently and looking at his watch. From what Sam could tell, he was alone. She slowly turned the lock and opened the door.

"Geez, finally. Why didn't you answer the door, Sam?" he said as he pushed his way past her into the apartment. "Is Kyle here or what?"

"No, Kyle isn't here. Sorry I didn't answer the door, I was just about to take a shower." She wasn't sure what else to say as Greg stopped and looked her over. He shrugged and plopped himself on the couch.

Sam moved over by the kitchen and just watched Greg. Neither of them spoke when Sam heard keys outside the front door. Kyle opened the door and immediately saw Greg sitting in the living room. He looked from Greg to Sam and then back to Greg again.

"What's going on here?"

"Oh settle down, Kyle. I just got here," Greg said.

Kyle glared at Sam and walked into the living room. Sam was not sure if she should leave so she just stayed where she was standing.

"What's up, Greg?"

"Check this out," Greg said as he turned towards Kyle. "I have this new business venture and it can make us a ton of money."

"What are you talking about?"

Greg looked like an excited child as he explained his plan. "I found a couple of girls who would be willing to do anything we want them to do and we make the money. I'm talking hookers, man. Don't look so shocked. I'm serious."

Kyle laughed as he leaned back. "You are nuts, Greg."

"Just hear me out. These girls have done this before. They left their pimp or something and they are on their own and they are willing to work for us. Think about it, Kyle. We can have some fun whenever we want and make money off them, too. It's a win-win situation. We can't lose."

Kyle laughed again and then started to stand up. "Greg, I think you have lost it this time."

"Wait, just hold on a second. Just meet them and then decide, ok? Hang on, I'll go get them," Greg said as he stood up and headed towards the door.

"You have them here?"

"They are out in the car. I'll be right back." Greg ran out the door and Kyle laughed. He glanced over at Sam but she was afraid to say anything.

"Hookers. Where does he come up with these ideas of his?" He looked at Sam and smiled. "Although a foursome could be interesting. What do you think, Sam?" Sam flinched as he ran his finger along her face.

Sam could hear voices outside the door and then Greg came back in with two girls. Sam watched as Greg introduced the girls to Kyle.

"This is Trina and this is Bridget. What do you think?" Greg watched excitedly as Kyle inspected the girls. He walked up to Bridget and looked her over. Sam thought she looked so young. She wondered if she was even eighteen years old. She had short brown hair and pretty blue eyes. Kyle looked disinterested as he moved next to Trina. Sam watched as his eyes changed. He was looking at Trina with pure lust and it made Sam sick to watch. Trina looked just as young as the other girl but had blonde hair and a flirtatious smile. Both girls were short and thin and looked to Sam as if they hadn't had a shower for days. Kyle did not seem to notice though as he gently touched Trina's hair. She swayed her body slightly and Kyle smiled.

"Well, did I tell you they were great or what?" Greg asked excitedly.

Kyle shrugged. "There might be potential."

"Good, because I need them to stay here for a couple of days until I get some things taken care of."

"What?" Kyle turned to Greg. "You want these hookers to stay here?"

Sam shook her head as she watched what was happening. She could not believe what was going on.

"It's just for a couple of days! I promise. They'll be no trouble, right girls? Well, I have to run. Take care of the merchandise now!" Greg smiled and patted Bridget's behind and then he walked out the door.

Kyle stood in front of the girls watching them for a moment. "Well, I guess you are staying for a couple of days. Bridget can have the couch and Trina can stay in Sam's room." Sam looked up in surprise and Kyle smiled. "Make her feel at home, Sam," he said and then he walked into the kitchen.

Sam was speechless as both girls looked at her in expectation. "I'll get you some blankets," she mumbled and quickly walked away from them. Sam brought out a pillow and blanket for Bridget and then looked for Trina.

"She's taking a shower," Bridget said as she watched Sam. "Thanks for letting me stay here."

Sam forced herself to smile. *If only she knew*, she thought. Sam noticed that Kyle was not in the kitchen and she got a sickening feeling wondering if he was in the shower with the other young girl. She turned and went back to her own room and laid the extra blanket and pillow on the floor. She wasn't sure what Kyle would expect of her this time so she left all of her clothes on and climbed into her bed. She could hear the shower turn off and she waited to see what was going to happen.

Kyle opened her door and escorted Trina into Sam's room. Sam could see that Trina was only wearing a towel and she giggled as Kyle laid the blanket out for her. Sam saw him lean down on the floor with her and she could hear them whispering and laughing. Sam thought she was going to be sick as she realized what Kyle was doing. Suddenly he stood up and he looked at Sam with an evil grin. He was naked and her heart starting beating harder in fear. He smiled again and he yanked the blanket off of Sam.

"You really didn't need this, did you?" He laughed and leaned back down on the floor with the young girl. Sam covered her ears and tried to stop the sounds of their lovemaking on the floor below her. She was relieved that he hadn't forced her to have sex with him. *At least he is not hurting her like he does me*, she thought. It finally got quiet and Sam carefully looked over the side of the bed. Trina was lying in Kyle's arms and they were both asleep. Sam tried not to gag as she realized that they were lying on Sam's blanket. Sam curled herself up on her bed and shivered slightly. There was nowhere she could go and she hugged her knees as she laid awake the rest of the night.

Sam sat up quickly. She realized that she must have fallen asleep and she tried to wake herself up as she looked around the room. She slowly glanced over the side of the bed and saw that Kyle and Trina were gone. She did not hear any voices so she slowly got out of bed and walked out into the hallway. The blanket Bridget had used was still on the couch and neither of the girls seemed to be there. Sam looked up at the clock on the wall and was shocked to see that it was almost ten o'clock in the morning. Kyle would have been at work for an hour already. She had been so tired from trying to stay awake all night that when she did fall asleep, she must have slept really hard. She looked down at her wrinkled clothes and shook her head again.

"I don't even want to know what else is going to happen around here," she mumbled as she made her way to the shower.

That night the girls came back again. Kyle had taken Trina in his room this time and Sam was relieved. In fact, Kyle did not talk to Sam at all and Sam was just fine with that. The next morning the girls were gone again and Sam did not see them or hear about them again.

A couple of nights later Kyle came home later than usual. He was whistling when he walked in the front door and he barely even noticed Sam watching him. *I wonder where he has been that would make him so happy,* she thought to herself. Sam walked over to the living room window and looked out. She could still hear Kyle singing to himself and she realized he was coming in the living room. She did not turn around but just listened to where he was.

"I had such a great time tonight," he said as he watched Sam. "I had such a great time that even you couldn't ruin it for me." She was still quiet and he continued talking. "Well, aren't you going to ask me what I did? I went out and had a nice dinner and went dancing... I don't even know how long it has been since I had such a good time. Aren't you going to ask me who I was out with, Sam?"

Sam knew what he was trying to do but she refused to fall into his trap. Instead she surprised him.

"I'm glad you had such a great time tonight, Kyle," she said as she turned around to look at him. "I was just thinking that I might like to go out to dinner. You have been telling me how good I have been lately, so why not let me go out and have some fun for a change."

Kyle's eyes turned cold and he started screaming at Sam. "How dare you criticize my decisions, Samantha!"

"No Kyle, I didn't mean..."

"No, Samantha, I guess I was wrong about you after all. I thought you had changed. I thought that you had finally understood what I wanted. Man, you just know how to ruin a nice evening, don't you?"

Kyle started coming toward Sam and Sam was walking backwards, bumping into furniture.

"Just forget it, Kyle, it's no big deal, really," Sam said as she inched her way towards the hallway.

"I guess it is over, isn't it? I guess I will never be able to trust you." Kyle's eyes glazed over and it looked as if he was looking right through her. "I'm really sorry we had to end it this way, Samantha."

Kyle started coming after her and Sam screamed and ran down the hallway towards her room. She jumped into her room, slammed her door hard, and screamed as loud as she possibly could.

"Dear Jesus, please help me! Help me, God! Please hear me and rescue me! Please God! Pleeeasse God!" Sam cried as she pleaded for help, hoping that someone would hear her.

Suddenly it got completely quiet. Sam could feel her heart pounding hard in her chest and she held her breath, not sure what to expect. Suddenly, her door opened and Kyle stood in the doorway with a blank look on his face. Without saying a word, he dropped to the floor. Sam sat dumbfounded. She was not sure if this was an act or if he was suddenly ill, or what exactly happened. She waited for a few minutes and when he did not move, she cautiously leaned slightly over the edge of the bed. She looked down at him and he actually appeared to be unconscious. She backed herself up on the bed until she fell off the opposite side and she grabbed part of the blanket that was now hanging off of the bed. She pulled the edge of the blanket over her knees.

"I don't get it," she cried as her trembling hands kept pulling the blanket closer to her chin. She sat there for a moment and when Kyle still had not moved, a strange calmness came over her. "He can't hurt me anymore," she said quietly as her eyes got bigger. *Maybe physically, but he can't touch my mind, my spirit or my soul. Not anymore,* she thought to herself reassuringly. "God," she whispered as she looked around the room as if someone was really there, listening to her. "I don't know if you really are listening to me and if you had anything to do with this, but if you are – please help me to get away from him. I know now that he can't hurt me anymore." Sam let go of the blanket and cautiously crawled around the back of the bed and looked at Kyle. He was still lying motionless on the floor. She took a deep breath.

"You will never hurt me again," she said softly.

CHAPTER 22

Sam sat on the edge of her bed, watching Kyle. He eventually woke up from his trance and, without saying a word, he left the house. Sam knew that the door had been opened for her to finally leave and she spent the next several hours planning her escape. All of the time she had spent in her closet planning had finally helped her.

Sam had a feeling that Kyle would be coming home that night, and as she had anticipated, he did.

Sam waited for about an hour after she heard Kyle close his bedroom door, and then she quietly sneaked into the hallway. She stopped in front of Kyle's door and listened. She could hear him softly snoring and she knew that he was asleep.

"Please God, don't leave me now." Sam whispered as she went back into her room and grabbed her purse. She dumped out everything in her purse until she found what she had been looking for – the spare key to her car. "I can't believe I did not think of this before," she whispered. "I mean, what woman does not carry a spare key in case she locks herself out of her car?" Luckily Kyle had not thought about that himself. Sam knew why she had not tried to leave before, but as she looked at the key, she shook her head and saw how close freedom could have been.

Sam quietly made her way to the front door and stopped. She took a deep breath and slowly opened the front door. The sound the door made when it opened seemed horribly loud to Sam, but she knew that Kyle would not have heard it. She closed her eyes and felt the cool evening air tickle her face and slide down her arms. She opened her eyes and ran her hand along the goose bumps on her arm. She took another deep breath and stepped outside. She quietly closed the door and then quickly ran down to her truck. It felt strange to be driving again, not to mention to be out of the apartment at all. She wondered if any of the neighbors had ever heard her cries and wished that someone had and would have called for help. "I can't do anything about that now, she mumbled and then she drove to the nearest gas station. Her plan was going to be easier than she thought – the truck was already almost out of gas. Sam went into the gas station and explained to the clerk that someone had threatened to steal her truck. Her plan was to take the gas out of her truck just for one night until she could buy some sort of security device the next day. Sam thought the story she had come up with sounded crazy, but luckily the clerk was more than happy to help Sam, as her own car had recently been stolen. She gave her a long tube and a gas can and explained to her what she needed to do. Sam thanked her for her help and promised to return the can the next day.

Sam drove back to the apartment and parked the car. She immediately siphoned the remaining gas into the can and hid the can in a bush and ran back into the apartment. She tried to be as quiet as she could, but she could hear her own heart pounding vigorously. She stopped in front of Kyle's door again, and he was still snoring softly. Relieved, Sam slipped quietly back in her room and undressed. As she lay in bed, she tried to calm her pounding heart and she thanked God again for his guidance and protection.

She looked up at the ceiling and shook her head. "I don't know why you are helping me now, God, but just please don't stop."

Sam went over her plan again in her mind. She could not believe how easy it had been to sneak out of the house.

"Why couldn't I have done this before? Why did I have to go through so much abuse before I got away?" she whispered to herself. She realized that she had to stop thinking about all of the what ifs. What if she had not called Greg; what if she had not accepted the ride from Kyle in the first place; what if she had not moved in with him; what if she had not moved out of her mother's house in the first place; and of course, what if Kyle really did find her.

Sam shook her head. "Stop it, Sam. The first part of your escape has been taken care of. Now you have to just concentrate on getting out of here," she mumbled as she leaned back into her pillow and closed her eyes. That night Sam woke up several times thinking that Kyle was in her room, standing over her with a pillow above her face. Each time she would calm herself down and then remind herself that soon she would be free.

CHAPTER 23

The next morning Sam awoke to hear Kyle getting ready for work. She decided to stay in bed until seven o'clock, which was the usual time that she got out of bed. *Nothing must happen any different than usual*, she thought to herself. She waited until seven and then rose out of bed. She casually strolled into the kitchen to get a cup of coffee and smoke a cigarette. She lit her cigarette and glanced at Kyle who was reading the morning paper while eating a bowl of cereal. Sam kept her back to him and listened to his movements as he put the bowl by the sink, grabbed his coat and went outside. He was only gone for a few minutes when he came stomping back into the apartment, and Sam could tell that he was furious.

"Stupid kids, always stealing gas out of the cars. Now I am going to be late for work. Where is the damn phone?" He grabbed the phone and dialed his work.

"Hey, Rex, yeah it's Kyle. Some stupid kid stole the gas out of my car." He stopped and listened as apparently Rex was saying something on the other end. "Yeah, I know. Hey, I'd appreciate it. You know where I live, right? I'll just go and wait outside in about ten minutes. Thanks buddy!"

Kyle hung up the phone and looked over at Sam. Sam looked back at him with a look of concern, but did not say anything. She wanted him to think that she was sincerely worried, but nothing more.

Kyle looked away, apparently satisfied that Sam did not have anything to do with the missing gas. He grabbed his newspaper and headed back outside. Sam went to the living room window and watched as Kyle sat down on the sidewalk and opened his paper. From time to time he would glance at his watch, until finally his ride arrived and he left.

Sam waited for about an hour and then went up to the phone. She started to pick it up, but she stopped and nervously rubbed her hands together. She took a deep breath and then picked up the phone and hit redial.

"Auto shop, this is Rex speaking."

"Kyle please," she said as she bit her nail nervously.

"I'm sorry ma'am, but he is working on a car right now. Can I take a message and have him call you back?"

SHERRY MOORE

"No, I will try again later. Thank you."

Satisfied that Kyle was safely at work, Sam quickly gathered her clothes and, after about three trips back and forth, and with her adrenaline pumping, she got her things thrown into the back of the truck. She kept trying to push aside the thoughts that Kyle would always find her, no matter where she went. She quickly grabbed the gas can from behind the bushes and replaced the gas. She opened the driver's side door and stopped to look back at the apartment that had been her jail cell for so long. After nearly two years of being abused, Sam was finally free. She got back in the truck and started on her way to freedom.

CHAPTER 24

Sam went back to the gas station, returned the gas can, and put a couple of dollars worth of gas back into her truck. She had found some change scattered around the house – just enough to get her where she needed to go and to make a few phone calls.

Sam drove for about ten miles in the opposite direction of where Kyle worked. She did not want to take the chance of him seeing her driving around. She pulled into a twenty-four hour truck stop called Sam's. The name alone appealed to her.

She walked up to a pay phone and pulled some change out of her pocket. She knew who she had to call first, but she was not quite sure what she was going to say. Sam put the money in the pay phone and as soon as her mother answered the phone, Sam started to cry.

"Mom," was all she could say.

It was silent on the other end for a moment. "Samantha?" Her mother finally asked.

Sam took a deep breath. "I know you are mad and I can only imagine what you might be thinking. A lot has happened and I, well, look, I'm at a truck stop that is about forty-five minutes from where you are. Would you mind coming here? I'll try to explain everything when you get here."

"Oh sure, no problem," her mom said sarcastically. "I haven't heard from you in, oh, how long has it been? Maybe a year? Of course I'll drop everything and come running to see my darling daughter."

Sam looked down at her feet and tried not to cry again. "I don't need the sarcasm, Mom. I've been through a lot in the last year." She paused for a moment and then, with true sincerity, she spoke calmly into the phone. "Mom, please, I need you."

Caught off guard by her daughter's honest plea, her mother was silent for a moment, but then she laughed. "I don't know if I really want to know what you have been up to this last year or so. I told you that you wouldn't be able to make it on your own. You are just not responsible enough to handle what the real world has to offer." Her mom sighed. There was something different about her daughter's voice. Reluctantly, she gave in. "Well, where are you?"

Sam told her where the truck stop was and when she hung up she had to take a deep breath. Facing her mother was not going to be easy.

While she waited for her to arrive, Sam made a mental list of what she would need to ask of her mother. She picked the phone back up and, using the phone book as a guide, made some calls to apartment communities that she hoped would have a small, inexpensive one-bedroom apartment. After several tries, she was relieved to find an available unit and she wrote down how much she would need for the deposit and first month's rent. When she got off of the phone, she also tried to figure out what she would need to hold her over until she could find a job. She knew that she did not have any time to waste and this time, she was not going to live out of her truck. She was glancing through the want ads in the newspaper when her mother arrived. As soon as her mother sat down, Sam lit up a cigarette.

"When did you start smoking?" Her mother immediately asked with a surprised and yet disapproving look on her face.

"I don't know. What's the big deal? You smoked for years." Sam looked annoyed but went ahead and put the cigarette out. She sighed loudly. She was tired but grateful that her mother had come. She may have been mad, but Sam knew that she would still be there for her. "Thanks for coming, Mom."

"Yeah, sure. So what troubles have you gotten yourself into this time?"

"Well, I don't know quite how to tell you." Sam looked down and tried to hold back her tears. She always wanted to cry when she was around her mother. "Basically you were right. Kyle turned out to be a real creep, to say the least. Let's just say things have not been too great and I had to get away from him. He doesn't even know that I'm gone."

Sam's mom laughed sarcastically. "I knew I was right about that guy, but then again, how many times did I tell you that you would get yourself in trouble? You just had to beat the world, didn't you? Well, I told you that you would fall on your face and here you are. Whatever has happened, I'm sure that you brought it upon yourself. Don't think that you are going to come running home either. You seem to think that you can do things on your own; you made your bed and now you have to sleep in it."

Sam did not say anything but just looked at the floor.

"So, Samantha, what do you plan to do now?"

Sam could not look up at her mom. "I made some calls and found a couple of apartments that I could move into for pretty cheap. I honestly don't know exactly what I am going to do, but I have been looking through the paper to see what jobs are out there." Sam ran her fingers over the newspaper sitting in front of her. She had circled a few prospects and she saw that, from the look in her mother's eyes, she had noticed. "Can you please, I mean, is there any way that I could possibly borrow some money? I'm already trying to find a job, but I just need enough to hold me over."

Her mother sat across from her for a moment without speaking. "I can't believe that you are even asking me this, but I suppose it had to take a lot of courage to even call me. God, Sam, I hope this isn't some new ploy you have kicked up." She sighed loudly and looked pensively at Sam. "I suppose I could loan you some money, but remember that it is just a loan. You have to pay it back." She watched Sam's reaction and was surprised by how grateful she actually seemed. "How much do you think you will need?"

Sam told her what she had come up with and her mother wrote her a check.

"You know Sam," her mother said as she was signing the check, "I don't exactly know where this is heading, but I want you to know that, just because I am helping you now, it doesn't mean I trust you. You have to earn trust and that takes time. A long time." She tore the check out of the checkbook and handed it to Sam. "If you ever really want to regain my trust, you will have to work hard at it. Like I said, it won't happen overnight." She stared hard at Sam for a moment and then stood up. "I am glad that you are ok, Sam," she said quietly.

"I will pay this back to you, Mom," Sam said as she looked at her mom gratefully. Her mom looked at her for a moment and the left without saying another word.

Sam slowly stood up and went into the bathroom. She looked at the worn look on her face and then looked down at the check in her hand. Suddenly the tears came and she could not stop them. She cried for everything that had happened; the abuse, her mother, and just everything that had built up inside of her.

Once Sam had regained her composure, she set out to cash the check her mother had given her. She also had called the apartment complex and they said that they could meet with her the following morning.

She returned to the truck stop and as she sat back against the chair that she would be staying in for the night. She vowed to herself that eventually she would repay her mother. Somehow she would show her that she had changed.

That night she watched all of the people that came and went and it gave her a feeling of security. She knew that Kyle would not find her there.

After Rex had dropped him off he quickly walked up to the apartment door. The night before had shaken him up pretty badly and he realized that it was time to regain control over the situation.

He walked in and immediately felt an odd silence. He ran down the hall to Sam's bedroom and threw open the door. The room was empty. The closet was open and all that hung inside were a few empty hangers.

Furious, Kyle ran back outside to the parking lot and saw that the truck was gone. He stood there for a long time, alone and disbelieving, and with eyes filled with fury.

CHAPTER 25

On the first new morning of her newfound freedom, Sam was exhausted but anxious to get her life going again. Her heart raced nervously as she left the safety of the truck stop and drove to what would hopefully be her new home. She did not have a job yet, so, with a little deception, a lot of promises, and a phone call to her mother, she finally won the heart of the manager. She signed all of the paperwork and when the manager handed her the keys, she couldn't help but smile.

Sam grabbed a handful of her things and then stepped inside her new home. She stopped and looked around. The apartment was completely empty but to Sam it looked like a castle. She turned towards the front door and sighed.

"Ah, to be free!" she said and went back out to her truck.

Sam's mom had given her more than she had asked for so she decided to get a few things for her apartment. She drove to a nearby indoor flea market and was able to get an old phone, a cot to sleep on, an old dresser, and a beanbag chair. She wanted to keep things very simple so that she would have a little extra money left over in case she might need it. There was an older man that worked there who was nice enough to load all of her things in his own truck and bring it to her home. She tried to give him ten dollars, but he refused. Instead, he took her hand and said, "Just take good care of yourself, young lady. God bless you." Sam smiled and thanked him for his generosity.

That night Sam went to a pay phone and called her sister collect. Although Jessica was just as surprised as their mom to hear from her, her sister's comforting and supportive voice was like music to Sam's ears.

"Where have you been hiding out, little sister?"

Sam smiled. "It is so great to hear your voice, Jess. How's Missouri treating you?"

"Forget about Missouri, are you ok? Where are you?"

Sam looked around her and laughed. "Well, believe it or not, I have left Kyle and I am at a pay phone near my new apartment."

"Is this really my sister calling me? Did I hear you right? You actually have your own apartment?"

Sam laughed. "Oh shut up, you crazy fool! Of course I have my own apartment. What, did you think I would live off of other people my whole life? Wait, don't answer that."

Jessica laughed. "Hey, seriously though, where have you been? Mom and I have been worried sick."

Sam looked down at the ground and thought about how her mother had reacted to her just the day before. "Well, Jess, I hope your feelings are more sincere than Mom's were. I saw her yesterday and she wasn't all that happy to see me."

"Well, after everything that has happened between you two, I guess I'm not all that surprised. You still haven't answered my question, though; where have you been?"

"It's a long story, Jess. I really don't want to get into it right now. All I know is that I don't think I have ever been as scared as I have been for the last year."

"I don't know that happened Sami, but whatever it was, don't blame yourself. It is over now and you are safe. We all make mistakes in our life, but just remember that it only means something if we learn from those mistakes."

Sam appreciated her sister's wisdom. That was something she had never done before. "Thanks, Jess. I'd better get off of this pay phone, but I promise as soon as I get my phone hooked up that I will call you."

When she hung up the phone, she felt comforted knowing that her sister cared so much for her. She smiled as she walked back to her new apartment. No matter how bad she messed up in life, her sister seemed to always be there for her. That made the mistakes a little easier to deal with.

Several days later Sam found a job in a small office that was close to her apartment. The pay was not the best, but it paid her bills. She made sure that she could put a little aside to start paying her mother and hopefully she would be able to open a checking account soon.

After three months, Sam finally was able to have her phone hooked up. Her landlord was even nice enough to give her an old answering machine that she no longer used. Her life was starting to finally settle down and she decided it was time to call Laura and tell her what had happened. It was hard to talk about it, but Laura was Sam's closest friend and she deserved to know.

Sam sat down on her beanbag chair one evening and dialed Laura's number.

"Hello?"

"Laura, this is Sam." She waited for a response.

"Sami? Oh my gosh, girl, where are you? I saw Kyle the other day and he said you had moved out. What happened?"

That's an understatement, she thought. "Laura, I need to see you, can I come over?"

"Of course, come right over!"

Sam drove to Laura's house and when she answered the door, she immediately hugged her. Laura saw the strain on Sam's face and knew that something horrible had happened.

They sat down on the couch and Sam started telling Laura as much as she could about what Kyle had done to her.

"You mean to tell me that this has been going on for over a year?" Laura sounded astonished.

"Yes. And I was too stupid to try to get away from him. I should have left him a long time ago."

Laura looked very somber as she held Sam and listened to her say over and over again how grateful she was for her friend's support. When Sam finally had to leave, she made sure to give Laura her new phone number.

CHAPTER 26

"Samantha, it's Kyle. Why did you leave me? Please forgive me. I love you. Please come back to me – let's work this all out."

Sam listened in shock at the message on her answering machine. It had been two days since she had seen Laura, and when she had seen that there were messages on her answering machine, she never imagined it would have been from Kyle.

She slammed her finger on the delete button and just stared at the machine as the next message came on.

"Samantha, you can't get away with this. I WILL find you! You are going to regret ever leaving me."

Sam could not believe what she was hearing. "How in the world did he find me?" she shouted. "How could he have gotten my phone number?"

Sam listened in disbelief as two more messages played. This time Kyle sounded warm and loving.

Sam shook her head and then chills ran down her entire body as the final message played.

"DIE, BITCH, DIE."

Sam leaned against the wall and looked down at her hands which were shaking. *How did he get my phone number?* She thought again. Nobody except her mother and Laura had it. Suddenly Sam looked up. Laura? No, it couldn't be. Not Laura. Why would Laura give Kyle her number? Especially after Sam had spilled her heart to her just two days before.

She immediately went to the phone and dialed her phone number. When Laura answered Sam immediately started to question her.

"Laura, Kyle called me today. How did he get the number? Did you give him the number, Laura?"

There was silence on the other end. Sam could hear her friend breathing hard.

"Laura, you have to answer me. Please, did you give Kyle my number?"

"Yes," she said softly.

"How could you? After I sat there and told you about all of the awful things that he had done to me, how could you give him my phone number?"

90

"You don't understand, Sami. All of those things you said, those accusations, they were just so hard for me to believe. So I called Kyle and asked him about it. He said that you made it all up to make him look bad. He said you two had a fight and you stormed out and now you are trying to turn me against him, too."

Sam sat there astonished. How could she believe what he was saying?

"Laura, why would you listen to that creep over me? I thought you were my best friend."

Laura took a deep breath. When she started to talk again, it was evident that she was very upset.

"Sami, I am in love with him."

"What?" Sam could not believe what she was hearing.

"We have been seeing each other for almost a year now. He said you two were only roommates and that you wouldn't mind. Sam, I thought you knew."

Sam was speechless. What could she say? Her best friend was in love with the man who had made her life hell for the last year.

Laura continued to talk about how Sam should try to resolve her problems with Kyle, but Sam had stopped listening to her. She didn't know what to do or what to say. Her friend was obviously so lost in her feelings for Kyle that she would never believe anything that Sam had to say.

Sam closed her eyes and hung up the phone. She leaned forward and put her face in her hands as she took a deep breath. She really was going to have to start over.

Sam picked the phone back up and dialed Jessica. When she answered, Sam asked her if she could come out there to see her. She still had not told her sister or her mother about what had happened, but she felt confident that Jessica would help her. As she predicted, Jess told her to take the next flight out and gave her one of her credit card numbers.

Sam made the arrangements and that night she was on a plane headed for Missouri. Sam only took her clothes with her and figured she would worry about everything else later. Her job, her apartment, her truck – it would all have to be dealt with at some point. Right now, she just wanted to get as far away from Kyle as she could.

As the plane descended into some clouds, Sam leaned back into her seat and sighed. She wondered if her past would finally stay in the past, or if it would follow her forever.

PART 11
Starting Over

CHAPTER 27

Sam's mind had been filled with so many thoughts during the flight that she had been surprised when the stewardess announced that they would be landing shortly. It was late when Sam's plane arrived at the airport, and she was exhausted. As the passengers started to stand up and walk out into the aisle, Sam stood up and stretched. She waited for most of the passengers to leave before she started down the aisle. As soon as she entered the waiting area, she saw Jessica looking frantically for her. Sam smiled and shook her head. Just then Jessica spotted her and ran like a maniac towards her. The two girls hugged and laughed. They had not seen each other since that last Christmas.

"It is so wonderful finally seeing you again. Mom and I have been so worried about you, Sami. Are you ok?" Jessica looked at her younger sister with a look of concern on her face. "You sure have lost a lot of weight."

"I'm ok, Jess. Just really worn out, you know? I have so much to tell you and I really don't even know where to start." Sam looked down at her hands and then when she looked back up she had tears streaming down her cheeks. "God saved me, Jess. I don't know why, but He saved me."

Jessica looked gently at her sister and took her in her arms.

"You're with me now, sis. Everything is going to be ok."

"But Jess, He did. He saved me."

"Come on, let's go home. I know that we are going to have a lot to talk about, but first I am going to stuff you with my horrible cooking and then I am going to put you to bed."

Sam nodded appreciatively and then followed her sister down to the baggage department. Once she got her bags, Jessica led Sam into the parking garage. Sam immediately noticed the humidity and had to almost gasp for air. Jessica laughed and then she started to ramble on about her last semester of school and some teacher who was so difficult that "not even the smartest person in the world could have passed his class," she was explaining. Suddenly Sam stopped and her face turned pale white.

"Sami, what's wrong?" Her sister searched her face.

There in front of Sam was a large pickup truck just like the one Kyle owned. *Could he be here? Could he have followed me again?* she thought in a panic. Then she remembered the pole he had hit, him attacking her, and her trip to the hospital. He had totaled out the truck to protect himself. *Besides,* she realized as she shook her head in embarrassment, *how could he possibly drive fast enough to beat an airplane?* Feeling humiliated and overwhelmed, Sam dropped to her knees and started crying hysterically. Jessica dropped down next to her and pulled her sister close to her.

"Shhh. Everything is going to be ok. Come on, let's go home." She helped her sister up and guided her to her own car which was parked only a couple of spaces away. Jessica had an uneasy feeling about what Sam had gone through and knew that no matter what had happened, she would be there for her.

Jessica drove back to her home. From time to time she would glance over at Sam, who was being very quiet and looked really pale. Jess watched the dazed looked on her sister's face and wondered what she was thinking about. Once they got to Jess's house, she was unsuccessful at getting her sister to eat and she finally ended up leading Sam to the spare bedroom. Jess tucked her sister in and Sam looked up at her and smiled weakly.

"This reminds me of when we were little kids. Do you remember, Jess, when you used to imitate Mom as she tucked me in for the night?" Sam smiled as she pictured it in her mind. "Do you ever wish that you could go back in time? Maybe be a child again? If I was able to go back in time, I would change a lot of things, you know?"

"You just get some sleep. Ok, Sami? I have a feeling tomorrow is going to be a very difficult day for you. I just hope you know that I was totally offended that you didn't like my cooking tonight." She tried to sound humorous and Sam laughed lightly.

"I'm sorry. I promise I will eat something tomorrow." Sam's eyes started to close so Jessica got up, closed the door and went back into the kitchen.

Sam could hear her sister walking around the house. She had acted like she was falling asleep so that Jess would let her be. She just really needed to be alone.

She could faintly hear her sister talking to someone and she figured that she was probably talking to their mom.

"I wonder what they are talking about. Probably me," she mumbled. She tried to listen to what her sister was saying but Jessica was talking too quietly for Sam to hear her. She got out of bed and quietly opened her bedroom door just enough so that she could listen to her sister.

"I don't know what happened, either, but I do know that whatever it was, it left her pretty shaken up," Jessica was saying. "Yeah, me too. Well, I think that I am going to try to convince her to stay here for a while. It would be good for her to get away from Denver, you know? Yeah, I agree. Ok, Mom, I'll let her know that you send your love. I'll talk to you soon."

Sam quickly closed the door so that her sister would not know that she had been eavesdropping. She felt guilty, but she had to know what was being said about her. She sat back down on the bed and thought about her mother.

"Yeah, I just bet that you send your love to me. You are probably laughing so hard about how right you were, that you probably don't have time to love me," she mumbled.

Suddenly there was a light knock at the door, startling Sam. Her sister opened the door slightly and peeked in.

"Sam? I thought I heard you talking in here. I also thought that you had gone to sleep. Is everything ok?"

"Yeah, Jess. You go on to bed, I'll be fine." Her sister started to close the door again. "Oh, Jess," Sam called out quickly, stopping her sister. "Would you mind leaving the door open a little bit?"

Jessica smiled and said goodnight.

Later on that night Sam screamed in her sleep as once again the lights flickered around her and the shadows came at her so fast that she could not get away.

"Sam? Sam?" Sam heard the voice but it seemed so far away. Someone was shaking her and she screamed again. "Sami, it's ok. It's Jessica, wake up." Sam jerked awake and saw her sister standing right above her.

"Jessica, how did you get here?" She asked, dazed. As she tried to wake up completely she remembered that she was not at Kyle's apartment but at her sister's home.

"Sami, you were screaming in your sleep. You were tossing and turning and I couldn't get you to wake up."

Sam remembered the dream. "I was having a nightmare. I'll be alright."

Jessica sat down on the edge of the bed and took Sam's hand. "Remember what Mom used to tell us when we were little? Whenever we had a nightmare Mom would tell us to think about good things like ice cream and birthday parties and ponies. I know you are a little older now, but it still might help."

Sam smiled and hugged her sister.

"Good night, little sister," Jessica whispered. "Sweet dreams."

As Sam drifted off to sleep again, she tried to think of only good things. "Ice cream and birthday parties," she said with a smile. She softly laughed and then drifted into a deep slumber.

CHAPTER 28

The next morning Sam woke up dazed but rested. It took her a moment, once again, to remember where she was. *It is Saturday and I am at my sister's house*, she thought to herself. She sat up in her bed and looked at the blanket covering her. It had a southwest style design with beautiful earthtone colors on it. Everything in the room was done in the same style; it was the most amazing bedroom Sam had ever seen. Sam stretched and then stood up. She opened up one of her suitcases and then put on her robe and slippers. The bedroom alone gave her a cozy feeling and she could only imagine what the rest of the house must be like. The night before she had not been in any condition to notice her sister's home, but this morning she felt pretty good.

As Sam walked down the hall towards the kitchen, she was greeted with the scent of breakfast cooking.

"I thought you said your cooking was horrible. Something sure smells good," Sam said, startling her sister.

"Well, if it isn't sleeping beauty. I started to wonder if you were ever going to wake up." Her sister smiled and gave her a big hug. "Good morning! And don't judge my cooking by the way it smells. Wait until you try to eat it first."

Sam laughed. "What a beautiful house you have, Jess. I never knew that you could decorate so well." Sam was looking around the kitchen. Her kitchen looked like something straight out of a country magazine. It was a nice size kitchen, with an island in the middle. Sam sat down on a stool that was set along a long counter that bordered one side of the kitchen. There was a good sized window over the sink where curtains were tied open to bring in lots of sunshine. Sam noticed that there was only open farmland outside.

"Let me just cover this pan, and I'll show you around." Jessica checked all of the food that she was cooking, and then she walked towards Sam. "Let's go!"

Jessica's house had two stories with a small basement. It was amazing to Sam that her sister could actually own a house and be out in the middle of nowhere by herself.

"It is a lot less expensive to live here than back home," she explained as if she had read her sister's thoughts. "I know I could not have gotten this place if it hadn't been for Mr. Steward."

George Steward was an eighty-year-old man who had lived by himself in a small home in Denver. He had advertised that he needed someone to come in every day to clean his house and take care of him. Jess had been seventeen and had jumped at the job. He apparently had a lot of money and he paid her very well. During the year that she worked for him they both had grown very close. He was like the father she had needed, and when he died it had been devastating to her. A week after he had died, an attorney had contacted Jessica to inform her that he had no living relatives and he had left a great deal of money to her, which would be held in a trust fund until her twenty-first birthday.

As soon as she turned twenty-one, she received a substantial check. Jessica now explained that she had put some of the money towards purchasing the house, and the rest she put away in case of an emergency and to help with her schooling. Because it was the middle of summer, she was also working full-time so that she could save as much money as possible to help to pay for her bills later, when she would be going back to school. She really wanted to invest the money that was left over from her trust fund.

Sam listened in amazement as her sister explained everything. "I never knew that he had left you so much money. Good things always seem to find you, Jess." Sam looked down and sighed to herself.

"Oh, don't you start pouting, little sister. Good things come when you least expect it. That money won't go as far as you seem to think, that's why I have to be smart about it."

Sam nodded. *I wonder if I will ever have anything good happen to me,* she thought to herself. *I sure didn't start off right.*

It was as if her sister had read her thoughts again as she smiled. "Sam, you have to realize that life is not about what party you can go to. It's about surviving, and in order to survive you have to learn to make good decisions, and utilize what resources you do have."

Sam thought about what she had just said. "Jess, I am really starting to realize that. It is kind of like when you are a child and you don't have to worry about surviving because your parents take care of that for you. But suddenly you find yourself having to take care of yourself." Sam stopped and shook her head. She looked up at her sister. "You may wake up one morning and see the sun shining and the birds singing, but you still have to be prepared in case a storm comes through."

Jessica smiled. Her sister was growing up. "Well, enough serious talk for right now, let me show you the rest of the house. Then I want you to eat, take a shower, and get ready so I can show you around town." The rest of the house was just as nice as what Sam had already seen. The upper level was the main living area with a living room, kitchen, small dining area, and two bedrooms. Sam laughed when she saw Jessica's bedroom. There must have been twenty teddy bears of all different sizes all over the room. The wallpaper and even the drapes had teddy bears on them. Sam loved to tease Jessica about her fascination with teddy bears. No matter where she was or what she was doing, if she saw anything that had to do with teddy bears, she had to have it.

Sam shook her head and laughed as she looked around the bedroom. "Gee, sis, what is this? The Teddy Bear Fan Club?"

Jess put her hands on her hips and smiled. "You better be nice or I will make you sleep in here with them," she said as she pointed around the room.

Sam laughed. "Ooooh, is that a threat?"

"That's a promise," Jess said as both girls laughed and then they walked back into the hallway.

Sam walked down some stairs and saw that there was another bedroom and a family room that had a sliding glass door that went out to the back of the house. The small basement had a laundry room, water heater and furnace. They walked into the family room and Jessica opened the sliding glass door.

As soon as Sam stepped outside she noticed the humidity again. She gasped for air and Jessica laughed.

"It takes some time to get used to the air around here."

As soon as she had caught her breath, she looked around in every direction. "This is incredible, Jess. All you can see is farmland, and I can't believe how quiet it is out here. There isn't any smog, or traffic, or anything." Suddenly Sam looked seriously at her sister. "How can you stand it?"

Jessica laughed and the girls walked around the house to where she had parked her car. She explained to Sam that she never locked her doors. Maybe she was too trusting, but she just never felt she needed to worry about it.

As the girls walked around the house, Jessica explained that her home was just north of Main Street. She explained that the farmland that was around her house actually belonged to a middle-aged couple with four children. This couple had owned several acres and had built themselves a home set far back into the property. At first they had built Jessica's house as a guest-house, but then they had realized that with the small college nearby, they could rent it out to several students and make a little extra money. The last group of students had been so wild that they nearly destroyed the house, and that was when the owners decided to sell it. They were thrilled that Jessica turned out to be the buyer.

The owners maintained all of the land, except for about one-third of an acre that surrounded Jessica's home. Jess had loved having a small lot to take care of and had even planted a small strawberry patch in front of the house.

The girls got in Jessica's car and when they drove over to Main Street, Sam laughed when she saw how small the town was.

"I don't think many people have even heard of this town," Jessica was telling her. The town's main street was maybe eight blocks long and it consisted of a hardware store, a small food store, an ice cream parlor, and some other small shops. There were also two diners and one bar. On the east side of the town was the Mississippi River, and farmland surrounded the town in all of the other directions. It was small and quiet and Sam loved it.

"This place is incredible! Other than the fact you can't breathe here, it is just so peaceful. I could stay here forever." Sam turned around, taking in the trees and the buildings and even the blue sky. Jessica had told her it rained a lot, but today it was clear and beautiful.

"I was hoping you would like it here, Sam. I wanted to see if you would like to stay with me for a while."

Sam thought about the night before, when she had overheard Jessica telling their mother that she was going to ask Sam to stay. She smiled now as she looked at her sister. "You know what, Jess, I would really love it. This might just be the kind of medicine I need right now."

Jessica smiled and then treated her sister to an ice cream cone at the small parlor. She watched Sam closely. Although she was smiling and seemed to be enjoying herself, there were clouds in her eyes that never seemed to go away.

CHAPTER 29

After Jessica had given Sam the tour of the town, she brought her down the hill to see the Mississippi River. Sam's eyes opened wide as she watched a barge go by. Not far behind it was a steamboat with a large wooden paddle wheel. It was moving fairly slowly and Sam could see people standing on the different levels looking out. When the boat was across from where the girls were standing, some of the people started to wave. Sam waved back and then sat down in the grass smiling.

"This is great, Jess. I keep waiting for Tom Sawyer to come walking by."

"Sorry, that's another town." Both girls laughed.

"Sorry to burst your bubble, Sami, but there are some clouds coming in and it looks like it might rain. Why don't we head back to the car and then I'll drive you to where I go to school. It's closed for the summer, but I can show you what it looks like."

Sam stood up and followed her sister. When they got back to the car, Jessica drove Sam to the college where she was taking her classes. Once again Sam was astonished as she saw how small the campus was and how old the buildings appeared to be.

"Boy, you really feel like you are going back in time here. Are these buildings even safe?" Sam looked amazed as Jessica drove her around the campus.

"Of course, silly. They have been maintained really well. You are going to love this, come on." She stopped the car and motioned for Sam to follow her. Once again they were overlooking the river. "From the back classrooms you can look out the window and see the river. Same with this side of the library. Neat, eh?"

"If I were to go to college, this would be the way that I would want to do it," Sam said.

All of a sudden it started pouring and the girls had to run back to the car.

"I told you it would rain," Jessica said laughing. "Why don't we go back to the house now?"

Sam agreed.

When they got back to the house, they both headed for the living room and sank down onto the couch. Sam got quiet as she realized that maybe it was time to tell her sister what had happened to her. She knew it would have to come out sooner or later, and she had been thinking on and off all day about what she was going to say. It was not very easy to talk about, but Sam knew that it would help to talk about it. She took a deep breath and looked at her sister.

"Jess, we need to talk. I don't even know where to start."

Jessica gave her sister a reassuring look. She had been able to tell all day that Sam had a lot on her mind. One minute she would seem to be ok, and then suddenly the next minute she was lost in her own thoughts, oblivious to everything around her. She watched her sister's face now as she patiently waited for her to begin her story.

Sam looked down at her hands. "When I left home two years ago I thought I could beat the world." She laughed sarcastically. "You hit the target when you said earlier that life was not a party. I was so worried about what parties there were to go to that I ended up being homeless, and I was too proud to go back home.

"I lived in my truck for about two months and then I met Kyle. Do you remember meeting him on New Year's that year I had first left home?" Sam waited for Jessica to acknowledge that she remembered him, and then she continued. "He had seemed so nice at first and he was always concerned about what I was up to. Well, one day he told me that he had been worried about me living in my truck and that he wanted me to move into an apartment with him. 'We will just be roommates,' he had said.

"I was so stupid, Jess..." Sam started crying and had to stop talking for a moment.

Jessica got up and went to get a box of tissues. She did not say anything, but just squeezed her sister's hand and then sat back down next to her. Sam looked up towards her sister and Jessica saw the pain in her eyes.

"At first things were fine, and I thought that we had become good friends. But slowly I started to see strange things about him, like that he had a really bad temper, and then he started to hit me." Sam stopped to blow her nose, and then continued. "He put me in the hospital once." Sam saw the look of shock on her sister's face. "Would you believe that he staged a car accident to hide the abuse?" Sam shook her head. When she looked back up Jessica saw so much pain in her sister's eyes that she almost started to cry herself. She was not expecting what Sam said next.

Tears started coming down Sam's cheeks as she spoke. "He raped me, Jess," she said as she brought her hands up to her face and cried.

Jessica leaned towards her and held her as she held back her own tears.

She knew that, right now, she needed to be strong for her sister.

"It's ok, Sami, I'm here for you. Let it all out." She held her for a moment and then looked into her eyes. "Sami, I don't understand something. Why didn't you ever call me or Mom, or the police for that matter – or just leave?"

"I couldn't. He said that if I ever told anyone or tried to leave him that he would kill me and you guys. He had also told me about some other girl from his past. He said that she had tried to get away and that he found her and caused her to have a fatal car accident. That thought stayed with me the rest of the time I was there. I was so scared. All I could think about was that if I ever left, he would find me."

Jessica looked pensively at Sam. "You know, Sam, that girl could have been drinking and driving, for all you know, and could have run off the road. He might not have had anything to do with her accident or death, but in his infinite insanity he wanted to take claim for it. And who knows; there may have not even been another girl at all. I think he was just trying to scare you and intimidate you into staying."

That had never even crossed Sam's mind. Nonetheless, his plan had worked; she had always been too scared to leave. She looked at Jess and shrugged. "There were so many times I could have left and just didn't. Of course at one point he had gone as far as disconnecting the phone for a while. Not that it mattered, I mean, who would I have called? At the time I didn't think that Mom would care. I knew that you would, but what could you do from here? You were in school and couldn't just take the first flight out. You know, I think when it comes right down to it, I was so ashamed that I had gotten myself into that mess in the first place, that I couldn't get myself to call anyone for help."

"Sam, I had no idea."

"Oh wait, it gets even better. The night that he raped me I found out that he had been part of some kind of satanic cult. Then, after I got away from Kyle, I called my best friend Laura and told her everything that had happened just to find out that she had been sleeping with him for who knows how long. She said that she had fallen in love with him. Can you believe it? As it turned out she was the one who told Kyle where I was living, and that's why I had to leave."

Jessica looked stunned. "You aren't talking about your old high school friend Laura, are you?" Sam nodded. "Oh, Sami." Jessica held her sister and let her cry. Suddenly Sam pulled away from her sister with a determined look on her face.

"God saved me, Jess. Kyle was coming after me and he was going to kill me. I screamed out for God to save me and Kyle dropped to the floor. It was the weirdest thing I have ever seen. I don't even think you would believe it unless you had seen it for yourself. Somehow, though, that gave me the strength I needed and I ran away the next day."

Jessica looked at her sister and shook her head. "Wow. I can't even imagine what that must have been like. All I know is that you are ok now and that you are here with me. I'm really glad that you decided to stay here, too."

Sam looked at her sister with a serious look on her face. "Jess, I have to go back. My truck and all my belongings are still at my apartment. Plus, I just started a new job."

Jessica took her sister's hand. "I'll call Mom and see if she can take care of your things. Right now you need time to heal and going back home is not going to help you. You know, Mom does care and she really was worried about you. Maybe you can't see it right now, but it is the truth."

Sam nodded her head and thanked her for listening to her. When Jessica got up to call their mother, Sam went out onto the patio and watched the rain. *I wonder if Jess had ever had a really bad experience,* she thought. *I guess it really doesn't matter. She is doing enough just trying to help me right now.* Sam turned and looked towards the house. "I know Mom loves me. It will all work out," she said as she looked back out at the rain.

Sam sat down on a lawn chair and continued to watch the rain for a while until she finally went back inside to be with her sister.

CHAPTER 30

Sam had been staying with her sister for a couple of weeks and she had finally started to relax. Telling her sister about what had happened to her had released a huge burden in Sam's mind.

One afternoon she decided to go for a walk down to the river. She grabbed a notebook and headed outside. It was a gorgeous day and Sam smiled as she listened to the birds singing and the leaves that were softly moving from the small breeze that was tickling Sam's face. She had known from the moment that she had woken up that morning that it was going to be a fantastic day.

She sat down in the grass and looked out towards the river. It was a quiet day and Sam closed her eyes and enjoyed the sun on her face for a moment. She could not remember the last time that she had felt this much peace.

She opened her eyes and watched the water again for a moment and then she opened her notebook. The breeze lifted the edge of the paper as she wrote.

"Dear Mom," she wrote. She took a deep breath before she continued. "I don't know if you are still upset with me about everything that had happened, but I feel that it is time to put the past in the past and to get on with our lives. Life is too short and too precious to be upset with each other.

"I love living here with Jess. It is so beautiful and so peaceful that I can't imagine ever leaving. As you know, she offered to let me stay for a while and I happily accepted. If I can actually find a job out here I will start sending you money again. One way or another I will pay back the money you loaned me.

"I hope all is going well your way. Please write back or call soon so that I know where you stand with our relationship. I do love you Mom, and I am sorry for all of the pain and worry that I have caused. Love always, Sam."

Sam read over the letter and was satisfied with what she had written. She closed her notebook and leaned back into the grass. She felt like she was opening the door for a new beginning in her life.

One Saturday afternoon in July, Sam was trying to help Jessica decide which classes she should register for. That fall would be the start of Jess's junior year in college, and classes were starting in September.

"You know, Jess, there are some really neat management classes here. Have you taken Management 305 yet?" Sam asked her with a look of interest.

"No, but I do need that one this year. I hate trying to figure out these schedules."

"Oh, it's not that bad. Hey, here is another one that looks really interesting. This class goes through how to deal with people you work with, whether it is your boss or co-workers, or even your customers."

Jessica gave her sister a questioning look. "Sami, have you thought about going to college? Your grades in high school were not that bad."

Sam looked up surprised. "How on earth could I possibly afford to go to college?"

"Well, they have all kinds of loans and grants. You already said that you wanted to live here with me, and that alone would save you a lot of money. You have to at least check into it. What do you say?"

Sam looked down at the descriptions of classes she had been reading. "There sure are a lot of good courses. How would I apply, though?"

Jessica smiled. "Come down to the school with me on Monday and the admissions office can help you. There is an application you will need to fill out and then, if they accept you, you take a couple of placement exams and you are off. You should probably see the financial aid office too so you can hurry and apply."

Sam looked interested. "Isn't it a little late to be doing all of this?"

"Not at all. The way this college really works with people is just incredible. It's a small private college and they really take the time to help the students. You'll see!"

Sam was excited. Who would have ever thought that the girl who used to live to party would actually be going to college. She helped her sister with the rest of her schedule and then she looked at some possibilities for herself. They talked for hours about the school and what kinds of jobs they would someday get. It was seven o'clock in the evening and Sam stood up to stretch.

"Where does the time go?" she asked. "Why don't we stop and eat something and then go and take a stroll by the river."

Jessica glanced up briefly from the mess of papers lying on the floor before her. "You go ahead, I need to get some more of these papers put together. Don't be gone too long though, because we need to get up early tomorrow morning for church."

Sam ate a sandwich and then left the house and started to walk towards the water. She loved these evening strolls even more than her day walks. When she reached her usual spot, she sat back into the grass and glanced up at the stars. It was so quiet and peaceful here. She looked back towards the river and started throwing small pebbles into the water.

Out of the corner of her eye, Sam thought she saw some sort of movement. She quickly glanced to her right and saw a dark figure standing next to a tree at the edge of the river, a small distance from where she was sitting. She could tell by the height and build that it was a man. At first she just ignored the figure standing in the shadow, but then it started to make her a little nervous. She sat still for several minutes and the man never moved. Suddenly Sam felt her pulse quicken. *What if it was Kyle? What if he has found me again and he is going to try to kill me here, where no one will find me?* she thought frantically to herself. She started to get up. She was going to try to make a run for the main road. As she stood, she noticed the figure also move. Sam was so scared that she felt like she was moving in slow motion. Suddenly, out from behind some other trees, a smaller figure emerged. Sam heard a girl laughing and the two figures walked off in the opposite direction.

Sam started to shake and she put her hands up to her face as she started to cry uncontrollably. She suddenly felt the heat of the night overwhelm her and she started running toward the road that led back to the house. By the time she reached her front door she was crying hysterically. She flew into the house and ran past Jessica, who was caught by surprise.

"Sam, what's wrong..." Jessica put her hand out towards Sam but her sister just brushed by her and ran straight to her room. Jessica stood up and went to her door. She knocked softly and then opened the door, but Sam was not there. Jessica started to leave her sister's room but stopped when she heard something coming from the closet. Jessica opened the closet door and was shocked to see Sam sitting on the floor of her closet, hugging her knees and sobbing uncontrollably. She was rocking back and forth mumbling to herself.

"Oh God, please help me," she was saying over and over again.

"Sami, what are you doing in here?" She bent down and stroked her sister's hair, but her sister only pulled her legs closer to her chest. "Please tell me what happened. Are you alright?"

Sam looked up at her older sister. "Jess, will I ever be able to live without fear?" she said in between breaths. "Will the shadows of the past ever leave me?"

Jessica sat next to her sister and held her as she cried. She tried to comfort her until Sam finally let her lead her out of the closet and into her bed. She stayed with her until she finally fell asleep. Jessica said a quiet prayer and then went back into the living room to finish her paperwork.

CHAPTER 31

Jessica did not ask Sam what had happened the night she had gone for a walk, and Sam had never told her what had gotten her so upset. It had really bothered Jess to see her sister so upset and especially to find her hiding in her closet. All she could hope for was that somehow Sam would work through her problems. Sam had not taken any more evening walks by the river and she seemed to be always looking over her shoulder. Jessica was getting very worried about the sudden changes in her sister's behavior; it was as if suddenly she was paranoid about everyone and everything. Jess tried to get her to agree to get help, but Sam always refused.

Jessica finally took Sam to the college to apply. It did not take long for Sam to find out that she had been approved and she was thrilled. She would not be able to get the financial aid until after the semester had already started, but Jessica had agreed to help her until then.

Jessica mentioned again that maybe she should look into getting some help to deal with what had happened to her.

"Now that I am going to be starting school soon, that will keep my mind busy," Sam had told her.

"Sami, you have to deal with what has happened to you. You just can't keep hiding away in a closet somewhere waiting for the bad memories to go away by themselves."

Sam glared at her sister. "Just mind your own business, ok?"

Jessica shook her head and walked away.

When September came and it was time to start classes, both girls were ready. Sam had even found a part-time job working in the campus library.

Sam fell into her new schedule easily, and loved all of her classes. The way her schedule was set up, she had most of her classes on Monday, Wednesday, and Friday. She only worked for two hours in the library during those days. On Tuesday and Thursday she only had one class, so she spent most of those days in the library, whether it was to work or to study.

One afternoon in October, Sam was sitting in the library looking out the window. The sky was gray and overcast, and it looked like it was going to rain. She noticed how the trees were all starting to change colors. There were reds, oranges, purples and browns. It was incredibly beautiful.

"It is beautiful here, isn't it?" Sam jumped. She turned to see a young man standing next to her.

"I'm sorry, I didn't mean to scare you."

Sam brushed a strand of her hair away from her face and she looked back up at the man and smiled politely.

"I noticed that you were looking out the window. I think that fall is my favorite season here, and I don't even mind that it rains a lot. Are you from this area, Missouri, I mean?"

Sam looked back out the window for a minute. Why was this man so eager to talk to her? Unsure of his motive, she decided to try to be polite.

"No, I'm from Colorado. Obviously you are not from around here."

The man laughed. "No, I'm from California. Big difference, eh? From the big city to this. I may never go back! By the way, my name is Austin Sinclair." He reached out his hand to her and she hesitated. "We are in the same psychology class," he added.

Sam accepted his hand briefly. "Samantha Higgins."

"May I join you for a moment, Samantha?" He looked down at her with a hopeful look on his face.

Sam sighed and signaled for him to join her. *Can't he see that I want to be alone?* she thought to herself.

"So, is this your first year of school?" Sam nodded. "This is my second. This is a great place to start out, don't you think?" Austin started fidgeting in his chair. He was starting to realize that she was not very interested in holding a conversation.

"Look, Samantha..." he started saying.

"Please, call me Sam," she said quickly.

"Sam," he smiled at her, "I just thought it would be nice to know someone from class that I could study with. If you have a boyfriend or if you are just not interested..."

"No, I'm sorry if I am being rude. I pretty much keep to myself around here. You are right, though. It would be nice to have someone to study with. Mr. Johnston seems like he is not going to make psychology all that easy."

Austin leaned back in his chair and relaxed again. He had been immediately attracted to Sam the first day school had started. He had broken up with his girlfriend back in California so that he could start fresh here, as he was not one for long-distance relationships. His luck with the girls last year had not been very good and he wondered if there was any chance that he and Sam might eventually get together. Although he did see something strange in her eyes now, he could only be hopeful that she might eventually lighten up.

They talked for a while and then Sam looked at her watch.

"I'm sorry, Austin, but I really need to get going. It was nice meeting you." She stood up.

Austin immediately stood up as well. "Please, let me walk you to the main door."

Sam allowed him to walk with her just outside the main library door. The wind was blowing and her hair had blown into her face. He reached his hand out to move her hair and she jumped back away from him. She had a look of pure panic on her face.

"Sam, I didn't mean... I was just going to move your hair out of your face." He looked concerned for her. *Why was she so scared?* he thought to himself.

Sam was still backing away from him. "I really have to go now. Bye." She turned and started running for her car.

Austin did not follow her, but just watched her run frantically away from him. He shook his head and walked back in to the library.

CHAPTER 32

December came, and with it also came finals and very cold weather. The girls did not know which they hated more.

Sam had received a letter from her mom and they had continued to write back and forth. Although she could still sense some tension from her mother, Sam knew that everything was going to be alright. Her mother had taken care of Sam's apartment, her job, her truck and the rest of her things for her. Sam was surprised by how much it meant to have her mom helping her, but even more so when the last letter she received ended in "I love you."

Sam was overwhelmed with all of the studying that she had to do and she finally decided to get together with Austin to study for the psychology final. As it turned out, they had other classes in common, although they did not have any of them together. Sam liked Austin, but she had also liked Kyle when she had first met him. She would not let down the barrier that she had built up in her mind. She could not take that chance.

Sam had called Austin one cold and icy evening to see if he would meet her at the library to study for their final. He had agreed to meet with her and had even offered to come and pick her up so that she would not have to drive, but she quickly declined. She did not want him to know where she lived, although she didn't want to be rude and tell him that. She just explained that it was not that far and that she could drive herself.

The roads were so bad that it took Sam twice as long as usual to get to the campus. She parked her sister's car and wrapped her scarf tightly around her face. She was really glad that Jessica did not mind sharing her car because it made it a lot easier for Sam to get around.

Sam headed out into the brisk wind and hurried to the library. She had several layers of clothes on and yet the cold seemed to bite right through all of them. She pulled open the door to the library and stepped inside. Despite the weather, there were several other students there as well, as was always the case during finals week. Sam had anticipated this and was relieved to see all of the people that were walking around. She pulled off her scarf, hat and coat and looked around for Austin. She noticed him sitting at a table hunched over some books. She smiled to herself. She had to admit that he really was handsome. He stood just under six feet tall and had a large, muscular build. He had blond hair and blue-green eyes. Although he took his studies very seriously, he could also have a great sense of humor. No matter how locked-up inside herself Sam tended to get, he could always seem to make her laugh. Sam reminded herself that she had to stay in control and that she could not let herself get too close to any man again. She just couldn't.

Austin looked up and saw Sam watching him. He smiled and waved her over to join him.

"Hey, girl, I'm really glad you made it. I was starting to get worried," he said as she approached him.

Sam draped her coat on the back of the chair and sat down across the table from Austin. "I'm from Colorado, remember? I am used to bad weather in the wintertime, although the roads seem to get a lot more icy here."

"I wouldn't know. I went to Colorado a couple of times to ski, but I am mainly used to the smoggy, but clear streets of L.A. This weather is still pretty new to me. I just can't seem to get used to it."

Sam glanced back towards the door and watched as some snow blew around some students as they entered the library. "Yeah, well, I know firsthand that you have to be really careful when you are driving around in this stuff," she said, remembering what she had done to her mother's car. It felt like ages since the accident. So much had happened since then and Sam was a very different person now because of it.

"Earth to Sam," Austin said as he watched the faraway look on her face.

"Sorry," she said as she tried to shake off the thoughts that had drifted in her mind.

They talked for a few more minutes about the weather and then got into their books. They read together and then quizzed each other on what they had read. They studied for several hours until someone announced that the library was closing for the night.

Austin insisted on helping Sam back to her car. When they got to her car she motioned for him to get in on the passenger side. He jumped in and shivered.

"Man, that cold bites right through you, doesn't it?"

"Yeah, that is why I told you to jump in here. Why don't you sit in here while the car warms up and then I will take you to your car. There is no reason for you to freeze when I have a heater that works." It was so dark and cold that Sam actually felt better having him there with her. The darkness of the night always made her nervous because she could never see what was out around her.

Austin could sense her uneasiness, but he was grateful for the warmth of the car. "I really appreciate you letting me stay warm. I, of course, parked in the lot on the other side of the building. So," he said as he rubbed his gloves together. "What are you going to do during Christmas break?" He was trying to make light conversation while they waited for the heater to warm up.

Sam shrugged. "I really don't know. My sister, Jess and I will probably try to get home for Christmas and New Years." Sam looked down at her hands.

"You really don't want to go back to Denver, do you?" Austin said softly.

"No, I don't. But I do want to see my mom. So what are you going to do, go back to California?"

"No, my folks travel a lot and they are not planning to be around for the holidays this year. I just decided to stay here and watch football, if I can get it in on the TV. Have you noticed that this town doesn't have any good channels?"

Sam laughed. "Yeah, the only two stations here show sports or soap operas and that is about it. You should be able to keep entertained."

"Wow, I can choose between football players killing each other and housewives that are having affairs with each other's husbands. Sounds like a great combination."

Sam laughed again. The car had warmed up so she decided she better get him to his car and try to make her way back home.

"Hey, would you like to come over to my place for a little while? You know, so we can finish studying," he asked with a hopeful look in his eyes.

"I don't think so, Austin. I just want to get you to your car and go home," she said somewhat annoyed.

"Well, do you at least want me to follow you home to make sure you make it ok?" Austin asked, before he got out of the car.

"No, but thank you. You go on home and I will see you tomorrow in class."

Austin waved goodbye and got into his own car. Sam made sure his car started, and when it did, she proceeded to head home. There was a fear in the back of her mind that he might try to follow her despite her telling him not to. She watched her rearview mirror closely the entire way home, but she saw only darkness and the snow that was continuing to fall.

CHAPTER 33

Sam quietly turned nineteen that December. She had made Jessica promise that she would not do anything special for her this year. They still had a lot of finals to study for and Sam really was not in the mood to party. Jessica laughed when she told her that.

"What? The party girl not wanting to party?" Despite the teasing, Jessica knew that her sister had not been in the best of moods lately. Nonetheless, she had a surprise for her sister that she hoped would cheer her up.

"Sam, take a break from studying for a moment, I want to talk to you."

Sam marked her page in her book and looked up at her sister.

"What's up, sis?"

"Well, as you know Christmas is coming up. You missed last Christmas and we both know that you really don't want to go home right now, so Mom and I decided to bring Christmas here, to you. Mom is even going to try to remember to bring some of our old Christmas decorations with her. What do you think?"

"Mom is coming here? Oh, Jess," Sam jumped up and hugged her sister. "Now that Mom and I are getting along, I am really starting to miss her a lot. This is perfect! Besides, you are right. I wasn't looking forward to going back to Denver just yet, you know?"

Jessica nodded. "We kind of figured it would be hard for you."

"I can't believe she is bringing some of the decorations, too. Do you even have any here?"

"I bought a tree last year to make it festive around here, but since I went home for Christmas, I really didn't bother to get much in the way of decorations."

"Oh Jess, we have to go get some things to put up! We can get some decorations, and some lights. This is going to be great! So where in the world are we going to find this stuff around here anyway?"

Jessica laughed. She was thrilled to see Sam so alive again.

"So when will Mom be here, anyway?" Sam was excited as well as nervous to see her mother. After all, their last meeting did not exactly go all that well.

"She should be here on the twentieth. Right around the corner! That way all of our finals will be over, too."

The girls sat down together and tried to write down everything that they would need to do to prepare for their mother's visit. The more they talked about it, the more excited they got about the upcoming holidays.

Suddenly Jessica jumped up. "I almost forgot, I also have another surprise for you; wait here." She ran out of the living room and then came back with her hands behind her back. "Ta daa! Happy birthday, little sister," she said as she handed her a small box.

"What did you do, you brat?" As Sam spoke, she was thrilled that her sister had not listened to her and had still bought her something.

"Well, open it up. It is from both Mom and me. We hope you like it."

Sam opened the small package and inside was the most beautiful necklace she had ever seen. It was a gold chain with a small angel hanging down.

"Mom actually found it. She thought that you might like having an angel watching over you," Jessica said as she watched her sister.

"It's beautiful, thank you!" She reached over and gave her sister a tight hug and then put the necklace on. "Will you please hand me the phone—I want to call Mom and thank her, too."

Sam dialed their mother's number and when she answered she immediately thanked her mom.

"It's so beautiful, Mom!"

"So are you, Samantha. You have changed so much that it is hard to believe that you were once the crazy teenager that I called my daughter. Now look at you. You are in college and you have blossomed into a beautiful young woman. We are both very proud of you, honey. I hope you know that."

Sam had tears slowly sliding down her cheek. "Thanks, Mom, I needed to hear that."

"By the way, before I forget, an old high school friend of yours named Sarah called for you yesterday. She said she had not seen you in a long time and wondered where you were. I told her you were living with your sister, but I did not give her the number. I was going to get hers for you, but I had a call coming in on my second line, and when I got back to her, she had hung up."

Sam searched her mind. "Mom, I never knew anyone named Sarah, are you sure that is what she said her name was?"

"Positive. I even wrote it down. Let's see," she said as she grabbed a piece of paper. "Here it is; Sarah Brown. That's the name she had given me."

"Mom, I know for a fact that I have never known anyone by that name. How weird. Well, if she ever calls back, try to get a phone number from her.

And Mom, do me a favor. Please do not tell anyone I am out here, ok? Oh, and before I forget, did you get my last payment that I sent to you?"

"Yes I did, but I also had told you that while you were in school that you didn't need to send me any money."

"I know, but as long as I have it, I want to get it to you."

"Thank you, Samantha. Well anyway, happy birthday. You better let me say hello to your sister. I'll see you soon and I love you."

"I love you too, Mom." Sam handed the phone to her sister and then she sat back down on the floor again. She looked down at the angel pendant and touched it gently with her finger. She smiled and then glanced down at all of her school books. She sighed and crossed her legs. As she reached for a book she thought about the strange person calling for her. *I have never known anyone by the name of Sarah, especially not in high school.* She straightened herself up and bit her lip. *I hope it's not Kyle trying to find me again,* she thought to herself.

She decided not to think about the strange caller, and instead tried to put her mind back on her studies. She found that she could no longer concentrate and decided to go to bed and get some rest instead. That night, she prayed that God would protect her and keep her safe.

CHAPTER 34

December twentieth, Sam's mother left her house to head for the airport. She was so preoccupied with making sure that she had not forgotten anything, that she did not notice the car that had followed her from her house to the airport. She parked her car in the security parking lot and headed for the terminal. As always she was running late and almost missed the flight. She quickly dropped off her bags and ran to board the plane.

He watched as Mrs. Higgins ran to catch her plane. He glanced down at his watch and sighed in frustration. Which plane are you heading for? Luckily for him she had been so caught up in catching her flight that she had not even noticed him behind her. He followed her though the airport and watched as she ran to a particular boarding gate. He smiled triumphantly and quickly went back to that flight's ticket counter.

"May I help you, sir?" the lady behind the desk asked.

Kyle looked at her name tag. "Yes, Linda, I would like a ticket for flight 303, heading to Missouri, please."

"I'm sorry, sir, that flight is completely booked. In fact, I believe that flight has just left the terminal as well. Can I get you a ticket for a different flight?"

"No, thanks anyway." He turned away, frustrated that he could not completely go through with his plan. He walked over to a window that overlooked the planes and sighed. There will be other times. Oh yes, there will be other times. He wondered what Samantha was doing in Missouri, but that didn't matter right now. He would have all the answers he needed soon enough. He turned away and went back to where he had left his car.

CHAPTER 35

Sam and Jessica sat impatiently in the waiting area where their mother's plane would be coming in. They were so excited that they had gotten to the airport forty-five minutes early, just in case the plane might arrive early.

"Knowing Mom, her plane will probably be late," Jessica said laughing.

"Knowing Mom, she probably was running so late that she missed the plane and she is trying frantically to reach us right now," Sam added.

Both girls laughed and then they saw the plane taxi in. When the passengers started coming off of the plane, the girls could not hold back their excitement.

"Can you see her yet, Jess?" Sam cried out.

"No, yell if you see her, Sami."

Suddenly, they saw their mother and they both ran to her and attacked her with hugs. They laughed and hugged for several minutes.

"Hey girls, I better go get my luggage," she said as they started walking. "You would not believe it. I was running so late earlier that I thought I would miss my plane. Wouldn't that have been fun?"

Both girls started laughing and their mother looked at them strangely.

"What's so funny?" she asked.

"Don't ask, Mom," Sam said as the two girls continued to laugh.

They went down to the baggage area and when they saw the huge box come down the chute, they knew that the box most likely contained all of their Christmas presents and decorations for the tree. The girls were thrilled; it was going to be a great Christmas!

When they brought their mother back to the house they gave her a quick tour. They had worked for hours to get the house cleaned. Somehow knowing that their mother was coming made them clean in corners that they normally ignored. Their mother always gave them a hard time about that.

"Oh darn, I left my white gloves back in Colorado." They all laughed and were pleased that she liked the house as much as she did. Her reaction was the same as Sam's had been when she first arrived.

"It is so quiet here! Cold, but quiet," she had said.

They helped their mother put her things away and then Jessica pulled her tree out of her storage room. Their mother was exhausted, but she also knew that there was no way that the girls would possibly wait until morning to put up the Christmas tree. Just like they had done every year when they were children, Sam and Jessica starting laughing and throwing tinsel at each other. Sam was just so happy to be with her family for the holidays again, that she felt like a child.

Sam was putting up candy canes on the tree when she picked up an ornament she had never seen before. It was a bulb that had Santa Claus and last year's date on it.

"I got that one from someone at work last year," Sam's mom commented when she saw Sam looking at it.

Sam's eyes clouded over as she stared at the ornament. Last year at this time she was lying across a bed, alone and scared. Her Christmas had been spent thinking about her family and trying to hold onto her sanity.

Jessica noticed the look that came across her sister's face, and she went over to her. She put her arm around her shoulder.

"Sami, you are with us now, not locked away with Kyle. Let's enjoy this wonderful, precious time tighter." Suddenly the serious look left Jessica's face as she stuffed an old Santa's hat over Sam's head. "Now, let's HO HO HO and do the Jingle Bell Rock!"

Sam shook her head and smiled as she tried to push all of the bad memories aside. She was with her family now and she was not about to ruin anyone else's Christmas. The rest of the night they sang and danced to Christmas songs until they all dropped from exhaustion. It was late and their mom finally had to go to bed. Jessica and Sam decided to stay up and watch *It's a Wonderful Life* which was playing on TV. They sat together on the couch, eating popcorn and crying while they watched the movie. Sam was happier than she had been in a long time.

CHAPTER 36

The morning after their mother had arrived, Sam and Jessica helped her bake some bread and cookies, although they seemed to have more flour and sugar on themselves then in the mixing bowls. As Sam was working, she started to think about Austin, and how he would be spending Christmas alone.

"You sure must be thinking about something important, Sam, because you just put about four cups of sugar in that mixing bowl," Sam's mom said as she took the bowl away from her.

Sam looked up and blinked. "What? Oh, I'm sorry, Mom." She laughed at herself. "We could always make that batch into sugar cookies."

"Ha ha, very funny. What was so serious that you lost track of what you were doing?" Her mom hoped she had not been thinking about the past again.

"Actually I was thinking about a friend of mine from school." She turned to look at her sister. "Jess, you remember Austin, the guy I have been studying with?" Jessica nodded. "He's from California. His family is going to be away for the holidays and he is spending Christmas here by himself. I was just thinking about how sad it will be for him to not be with his family for the holidays."

Both Jessica and their mother knew that she referring more to herself than she was to Austin.

"Sami, why don't you invite him to come over here for Christmas?" Jessica said, not sure what her sister's response would be.

"I don't know." Sam looked worried.

"He's not Kyle, Sam. Give it up! Austin is a nice guy and there is not reason for him to be alone for the holidays. Besides," Jessica started laughing, "I don't think Kyle would have stepped foot on a college campus; he wouldn't have know what to do with himself."

Sam glared at her sister annoyingly. "I know he's not Kyle, Jess. You don't have to remind me."

"Girls, settle down. Samantha, if you want to invite your friend, go ahead. If not, let's all drop it now, ok?" Their mother was always good at ending arguments quickly.

Sam sent a nasty look towards her sister, but Jess had already turned around. Sam knew that there was no reason to be mad at her, but she did not want to have to face the decision of whether or not to invite Austin over. On the one hand, she remembered what it was like being alone for Christmas, even if it was under horrid circumstances. On the other hand, she was not sure if she trusted Austin enough to tell him where she lived. If there was one lesson that she had learned, it was not to trust anyone too soon.

Sam walked out of the kitchen and went back to Jessica's bedroom. She sat on her bed and grabbed one of the teddy bears that was lying next to her. She held it up and looked at it. "What do you think?" she asked the bear and then she laughed. She tossed the bear back behind her and then grabbed the phone. She held the receiver for a moment and the dialed his number.

"Austin?" she asked when he answered the phone. "How are you? Keeping warm, or what?"

Austin stretched. "Well, this is a surprise, Sam. Isn't your mother there? Did her flight make it in ok?"

Sam smiled. "Yes, she made it just fine. In fact we stayed up late putting up Christmas decorations. Jess and I watched *It's a Wonderful Life*. I couldn't believe we got it in on the TV last night." Sam knew she was stalling, but she wasn't sure just how to ask him to come over. She finally decided that he would probably decline anyway, so she just decided to hurry up and ask him. "Hey, Austin, my sister wanted to know if you would like to come over here on Christmas day." Sam put her hand on her face. *Could you be any ruder about it, Sam?* she thought to herself.

"Sure, I'd love to. What time do you want me over?"

Sam looked up in shock. He accepted. She was not expecting him to accept.

"Uh, I'll call you later and let you know."

"And give me directions?" he quickly added.

Sam smiled and shook her head. "And give you directions. I'll talk to you later. Bye." Sam hung up the phone and looked around in disbelief.

She slowly got up and walked back into the kitchen. "Well, Austin is coming for Christmas," she said as her mother and sister looked up at her. "Oh, no. That means I will have to get him a gift." Sam quickly ran to get her purse. "I'm going to run down to Main Street and see if I can find him something really quickly."

Jessica and their mother looked at each other and laughed.

"Honey, you don't have to buy him a gift just to be nice. I'm sure he will just appreciate having someone to spend the holidays with," her mother said.

Sam smiled. "I know, Mom, but I was going to get him something anyway. Besides, I really don't want him to just be sitting here watching all of us opening our gifts. That seems so rude. I was going to wait until after Christmas to pick him up something, but I'll just go grab him something now instead. I'll be back in just a few minutes."

She drove to the town's only clothing store and ended up buying him a warm sweater. It was the only thing she could think of that he might like. She had the store wrap it for her and she was quickly back on her way home. She was surprised how fast she had found one she liked. She just hoped he did too. As soon as she got home she put it under the tree.

When Austin arrived on Christmas morning, he also had a gift for Sam. She blushed as she accepted it and she put the box under the tree with the other gifts.

Austin said hello to Jessica and then Sam introduced him to her mother. Her mother smiled approvingly and Sam shook her head and laughed.

They all had a wonderful time and it turned out that Austin loved the sweater. He tried it on and it fit him perfectly. When Sam opened her gift from him, she gasped with delight. He had gotten her a beautiful pen and pencil set.

The morning wore on as the rest of the gifts were opened. The group laughed and sang and ate all day. There were so many delicious things to eat, as they had baked fudge, breads, cookies and pies. Sam and Jessica even attempted a ham dinner, which surprisingly came out really well.

"Do you guys always have this much fun and eat this much food at Christmas time?" Austin asked as he stuck a large amount of food into his mouth.

"Well, I always tried to give the girls a nice Christmas," Sam's mother said. "I love to bake and this has always seemed the only time of year I have the time to do it. I think we have always had fun, except for last year of course. But I think this year has more than made up for it!"

Sam panicked and shot a cold look at her mother as if to try to say, "Please don't say another word."

Her mother ignored the look. "I'm just glad that we could have this Christmas together. Oh well, you know teenagers."

Sam jumped up from the table as everyone looked at her in surprise. She looked at her mom in frustration and then quickly went into the kitchen. *How could she do this to me?* she thought as she paced back and forth, fighting back tears.

Jessica came into the kitchen and looked at Sam in annoyance.

"Sami, everything has been so wonderful, don't ruin it now."

"Me? Mom is the one that was saying all of those rude comments. If

124

anyone is going to ruin the holidays, it will be her."

"Mom is just being honest. She was hurt that she had not heard from you in so long and especially at Christmas time. You might as well come back out here and stop acting so crazy. She can't help how she feels."

"How she feels? What about my feelings? How do you think I felt knowing that while you guys were eating cookies and opening presents, that I was locked away."

"Don't you dare get mad at Mom right now, Sam. You chose not to tell us what was happening. At least I know now, but she still doesn't. Either tell her what happened or let it go." Jessica said and she turned and left the kitchen.

Sam waited for a moment and then she slowly followed after her sister. Jessica was right, but Sam still did not want Austin knowing what had happened. She was quiet for most of the rest of the evening and just forced a smile when she needed to. She was relieved when Austin left and she immediately went to her room and turned off her light. After a few minutes she heard her door being opened and she acted as if she were asleep and then the door closed again. She wondered if it had been her mother or her sister, but at that moment it really did not matter. No one could possibly replace the time that she had lost, and only time could heal the pain that she was constantly reminded of.

Kyle paced in front of the bedroom window as the snow fell lightly outside. He shook his head and sighed loudly as he thought about how close he had come to knowing exactly where Sam was hiding. Missouri. Oh, if only he had paid attention to where her sister had said she was going to school. He was convinced now, more than ever, that Sam was hiding out there. His anger rose as he thought about how she had gotten away. "It should never have happened," he mumbled angrily. Suddenly a hand gently touched his arm.

"What should not have happened," he heard the female voice ask.

He turned to look at Laura, who was holding out his wineglass, and he just smiled.

CHAPTER 37

The semester of school that followed Christmas went by fast. Both Sam and Jessica had been maintaining high grade point averages, and Sam had also been spending a lot of time with Austin. She was feeling a lot more comfortable with him, especially after having spent so much time with him over the holidays. She finally had admitted that it was nice having a friend, although her actions made it clear to him that she was not willing to be anything more.

Austin, on the other hand, was starting to have very strong feelings towards her and refused to give up on the possibility that they might have a future together.

One afternoon in early June, Sam was sitting outside with Jessica. She was playing with a blade of grass and watching her sister work on her strawberry patch. Sam was frustrated because she had been trying unsuccessfully to decide what job she should get for the summer.

"There are not a lot of choices for jobs around here, Jess," she was telling her sister, "unless, of course, you want to shovel manure on someone's farm. How did you manage to get that office job, anyway?"

Jessica looked over at her sister and noticed how tan and lazy she had become. She basically fit right in with everyone else around town. "I don't know, Sami, I guess it was mostly luck. The secretary that had been there before me had gotten pregnant and was having twins. Her pregnancy was taking its toll on her and she decided to quit. In fact, she had just left when I came along looking for a job."

"Must be nice. I will probably be stuck shoveling manure." Sam leaned back into the grass and looked up at the sky. "It is hard to believe that I have already been here for almost a year."

"I can't believe that this is my last year of college," Jessica said looking worried. "Pretty soon I am going to have to decide where I am going to go to get a good job, and what I am going to do about this house."

Sam rolled onto her side and watched her sister. "Why not just let me stay here, Jess? After I graduate then sell it or rent it out."

"Let me think about it, Sami, ok?" Jessica jumped up to her feet and wiped her hands on her shorts. "I think I hear the phone ringing, I'll be right back."

When Jessica went into the house, Sam though about what they had just discussed. *I sure hope I can convince her to let me stay here,* she thought to herself. Jessica had only been gone for a couple of minutes before she came back outside.

"Sami, Austin in on his way over here, and he sounds kind of upset."

When Austin pulled up to the house, Sam could see that indeed he was upset about something.

"Hi, Sam, are you busy right now? I really need to talk to you."

"Let me just run in and get my keys." When she came back out she yelled over to Jessica that she was leaving. Jessica, who was once again busy working on her strawberry patch, waved back to her sister.

Austin took Sam to the ice cream parlor. They each got a cone and then went outside. There was a bench right outside that was not being occupied so they sat down. Austin was looking down at his cone and was not saying anything. Finally Sam could not take it any longer.

"Austin, there is obviously something bothering you, what is going on?"

Austin looked up into Sam's eyes. "I just got some bad news from back home."

Sam put her hand on his leg. "Is it your parents?"

"No, they are fine," he paused for a moment. "I just found out that a good friend of mine, a female friend, has been killed. She was raped and then the bastard killed her." Austin's eyes were watering and Sam just sat there staring at him in shock. She did not know what to say or do. She moved her hand and put it on his arm and he reached over to her and put his arms around her. Her entire body immediately tensed up and she sat there without responding to him. Austin felt her resistance and he pulled away from her. "I'm sorry, Sam, I just really need you right now." He seemed disappointed.

Sam cleared her throat. She could not look at him when she finally did speak. "What happened?"

"I really do not know all the details yet. All I know is that she had a lot of bruises and that she had been raped. Apparently it looked as though he had been trying to keep her quiet and ended up choking her to death. I can't even imagine what she must have gone through."

Warning bells went off in Sam's head. *This is a trick,* she thought. Somehow he had found out about what had happened to Sam and he was trying to get her to talk. He probably hated her now.

Sam jumped up off of the bench and threw what was left of her ice cream cone to the ground. "Why did you have to make up such an awful story? If you want to know what happened, than just come right out and ask me, ok. How could you do this to me?" Sam turned and started running. She could hear Austin screaming out her name, but he did not come after her, and she did not stop or look back.

CHAPTER 38

Sam ran for what felt like miles. Before she knew it, she ended up by the river. She sat down on a rock and looked out at the water. She was furious. How could he do this to her? Why would he make up such a horrible story? If he wanted to find out what had happened to her, why didn't he just ask?

Sam brought her hands up to her face and tried to understand what was going on. She stayed there for a couple of hours and then realized that it was getting late. She never stayed out late when she was by herself because she hated to be out alone when it got dark. Sam stood up and looked back out at the water. She took a deep breath and started walking back home.

When Sam got home, Jessica was waiting for her.

"How could you do that to Austin?" she shouted as soon as Sam walked through the front door. "How could you be so selfish as to call him a liar and run off when he has just found out that a good friend has been killed? How could you, Sam?"

Sam stared at Jessica with a blank look on her face.

"Yes, I know all about what happened. After you ran off, he came here. You should have seen him, Sami, he was so upset. What possessed you to be so cruel?"

Sam walked over to the couch and sat down. Could it be possible that he had been telling her the truth?

"Oh, what have I done," she mumbled to herself.

"I'll tell you what you have done, Sam. You have instigated a lot of curiosity as well as a lot of pain in a man who is in love with you."

Sam looked up at Jessica in surprise.

"That's right. While you were so busy treating him like he was some sort of maniac getting ready to harm you at any time, he fell in love with you. Imagine that."

Sam straightened up. "Should I call him?" she asked softly.

"If you have any shred of decency in those bones, I would skip the phone call and go to him." Jessica walked over to her sister and put her hand on her shoulder. "He needs you right now, Sami. Go to him."

Sam grabbed her keys and with tears running down her cheeks she ran out to her sister's car. She drove to his house and then sat in the car for a moment, staring at the house he was renting.

"I don't even know what to say or do," she mumbled. She finally gathered up her strength and walked up to the front door. When he opened the door Sam did not say anything but just took him in her arms. Together they cried; he for his friend, and she for the cruelty that she had inflicted upon him. They held each other for a long time and then they slowly pulled apart.

"I am so sorry, Austin. Please forgive me."

Austin gave her a small smile and touched a strand of her. She did not flinch this time.

"Sam, I know that something horrible has happened to you. I don't know what, but I hope that someday you will trust me enough to tell me. I suppose that Jessica probably told you that I have feelings for you." He stopped talking long enough to see the confirmation in her eyes. "Please don't hate me for caring about you. You may never feel the same way about me, but I can't help my feelings."

"Austin, I hope that someday I can confide in you about my past. But for right now please just be patient with me, ok? I do care a lot about you, but I just can't give you what you want right now."

He nodded his head. They were still standing on his front porch and he motioned for her to come inside his house. As they walked into the living room, Sam felt the secure feeling that she always felt when she came to his house. You could tell that a man lived there. Almost everything was decorated in a country western style. There were small cowboy statues and paintings of Indians and horses. There was even a cowboy hat hanging on a lamp. It was almost like entering a different world for Sam and she always laughed when she pictured this California man turned cowboy. Even so, his place gave an air of strength and security that Sam could not help but enfold.

They walked into the living room and sat down. Austin leaned back against the couch and started telling Sam about his friend who had been killed. Her name was Suzanne and they had known each other since elementary school. They grew up together and once, they had even tried to date one another.

"We knew that we had a very special relationship and we were afraid that we would lose it by dating, so we stopped. Our friendship just seemed to keep growing stronger after that," Austin explained.

Sam did not say a word but just listened. Austin continued to tell her about all of the crazy things that he and his friend Suzanne had done. He told her about a lot of things that they had shared as they were growing up.

"When I left California, she was so upset. She was afraid I would never keep in touch with her. She knew that I was not much for long distance relationships and that I had even broken up with my girlfriend before I left. Although there were more reasons behind the breakup, she had convinced herself that I would probably forget about her, too." Austin smiled to himself. "I proved her wrong, though. As much as I hate writing letters, I wrote her twice a month and called her once a month. You just can't let a lifetime friendship like we had slip away." He stopped talking for a moment and a sad look came across his face. "You know, she will always be my greatest friend," he said and Sam was touched. Not many men would ever let down their guard and show their sensitive side.

Austin talked about his friend for a long time and then around midnight he stretched his arms and looked at his watch.

"I'm sorry, Sam, I have been talking for hours."

Sam smiled and touched his arm. "Don't be sorry, Austin, sometimes it helps to talk about the things that are bothering you." Austin noticed her eyes cloud over as she spoke.

"Sam, you don't have to explain anything to me until you are ready, that is, if you ever get to a point where you feel you can talk to me. Just remember, I am here for you, just as you were here for me tonight." He laughed softly. "And I promise I won't even run away from you."

Sam smiled, although she felt horribly guilty for having run from him when he had first told her about his friend. She knew that Austin was being more goodhearted about it than most people would have been.

She stood up to leave and Austin walked her out to her car.

"Thank you again for being there for me," he said as he looked down into her eyes. He leaned forward to kiss her goodbye and she quickly pulled back away from him.

Austin looked at her, annoyed. "You know, Sam, you confuse me. When you came back here I thought that it would mean a possible turn in our relationship. I shared a lot of personal things with you tonight, and yet this is the treatment I still get. I don't understand you."

"I came back here because I care about you, Austin. I acted like a jerk when you were hurting, and I felt horrible. Is it so bad that I wanted to be here for you?"

"If you want to be here for me," Austin said as he stepped closer to her, "then why don't you show me and really be here for me."

Sam stepped back again and shook her head. "For someone who claims to have feelings for me, I'd say it's definitely not your heart that wants the attention. You know, for a moment there I actually thought you were different. But now I see that you men are all the same."

Sam jumped into her car and quickly pulled away from Austin's house. She looked in her rearview mirror and saw that he was still standing there and he was shaking his head as he watched her drive away.

CHAPTER 39

Sam did not call Austin before he left for California to attend his friend's funeral. She was frustrated with the way he felt towards her and she did not know how to handle it. She did not understand why he could not just be her friend and nothing more. It was true that she had some feelings toward him, but it was definitely not the same as the feelings he had towards her. She had no intention of having any kind of physical relationship with him. She knew well enough just how men did things; first it would start with a kiss and then he would force her to have sex with him. She would not put herself in that position again.

Until Austin left, however, Sam did not realize just how much time she had been spending with him. Suddenly she had no idea how she was going to pass the time. She had never realized before just how boring the town she lived in could be.

Thinking about how Austin was going home suddenly made Sam homesick and she really wanted to see her mother again. She had not seen her since Christmas and she missed talking to her as well. They wrote letters from time to time, but Sam was not the best about writing. She would set the letter down and suddenly, two or three weeks later she would realize that she had not written her mother back.

She grabbed the phone and decided she would call her.

"What the heck," she mumbled as she dialed her mother's number.

"Hello," her mother said as she answered the phone.

"Hi, Mom."

"Samantha, is that you? Is something wrong?"

Sam shook her head. Her mother could always tell when if something was bothering her, even over the phone. "No, Mom, I was just thinking about you, that's all. I was also thinking about coming home for a visit. Would you mind?"

"Of course I wouldn't mind, but I really think you should wait until the holidays again. Flying can be very expensive and you said yourself in your last letter that you had not been able to find a job. Why don't you girls wait and come out for Thanksgiving?"

"I don't know, Mom," Sam sighed. "I wanted to come home now. It is so boring here and I miss you. Thanksgiving is still practically five months away. What am I supposed to do to keep busy around here?"

Sam heard her mother laugh on the other end of the phone. "Sam, I'm sure you will find something to do, but for right now we better get off the phone before you rack up a huge phone bill. Tell your sister that I love her, and let me know about Thanksgiving. Good bye, honey."

Sam hung up the phone. She picked up a pen and threw it across the table. She wished that she had told her mother about Austin, but for some reason she hadn't. She knew that her mother would have reacted the same way as Jessica had and she wasn't in the mood to get lectured again. She stood up and walked over to the window. *I am so bored,* she thought. *There has to be something around here to do during the summer.*

Sam grabbed her keys and headed out the front door. She walked over to the river and sat down. She may be too scared to be out there at night, but she still loved to go there during the day. Today, however, it was too quiet and Sam needed some excitement. She started to get back up when she noticed something blue in the river and it was heading towards her. As it got closer, she saw that it was a small boat that looked like a fishing boat and there were three people in it. They looked like they were having a great time and Sam wished that she could join them. When the boat was across from where she was standing, Sam saw that the three people happened to be all women around her own age. They were laughing and then they noticed Sam and started waving happily at her. She waved back and then one of them shouted something at her. She put her hand up to her ear to show that she could not hear her and then the girl shouted towards her again.

"Would you like to join us?"

Sam was thrilled. She screamed, "Yes!" back to them and then they motioned for her to follow the boat until they could get it over to the shore. The water was very calm that day and they were able to bring it over to the side fairly quickly.

She laughed as she stepped into the cold water and then the girls helped her into the boat. It was crowded in the small boat, but the girls had a blast as they floated down the river, waving at people, laughing and splashing water at each other. When some gray and nasty looking clouds started to pull in overhead, they immediately made their way over to the shore.

"Where is your car?" Sam asked, concerned that they would have to carry the small boat in the rain.

"Don't worry," one of the girls said to her, "I parked my truck right up the road. "I'll go get it and be right back." She ran up the road as the rest of them pulled the boat out of the water.

"Wow, this thing is really easy to lift," Sam said amazed.

Once the girl with the pick up truck arrived, they all helped to set the small boat onto the trailer that was hooked up to the back of the truck. When they were done, one of the girls, a short redhead, asked Sam if she wanted to join them for lunch and she happily accepted. Sam realized as she jumped into the back of the truck that this was the first time since she had left Kyle that she had actually associated with anyone besides her family or Austin.

They drove to where another of the girls' vehicles was parked and then they went to a place called *Jan's Diner*, which was a popular hangout for college students. As it turned out, this is where the other two girls had left their cars. It was just starting to rain when they arrived and the girls quickly went into the restaurant and found a large table. As they were sitting down, Sam smiled at her new companions.

"It never ceases to amaze me how nice people are out here. You guys are going to have to tell me your names again, though, because I am just horrible about remembering names."

The little redhead popped her head up. "I'm Georgie. Actually it's George Ann, but, man, do I hate that name. Would you believe that my mom named me after one of her old boyfriends whose name was George? I mean, who would name their girl George?"

Sam raised her eyebrow and looked questionably at George Ann as the other girls laughed.

"Just ignore her, she is always mumbling about something. I'm Gina, by the way." The girl who now spoke was tall, thin and had short blonde hair. "What was your name again?"

"Sam." She looked over to Georgie who was humming to some song and bobbing in her seat. "Really it is Samantha, but I prefer to be called Sam."

The girls laughed again as they watched Sam's reaction to Georgie's behavior and then the third girl spoke. She was medium height and had jet-black hair. When she spoke, she had a very soft voice.

"I'm Emy. It is really nice to meet you, Sam."

Sam smiled. "It is really nice to meet you, too."

They all ordered hamburgers and then they talked about school. As it turned out, they were all getting ready to start their second year as well and Sam was thrilled. They discussed the different classes that they might take and then Gina asked if Sam was dating anyone from campus.

"Well, I have a good friend, but I would not say I am dating him. I am really not interested in dating anyone right now." She tried to sound casual, but she saw the questioning look that the other girls gave one another. Sam was not quite sure how to respond. "What about you guys? Are you dating anyone special?" she asked as she looked around the table.

Gina was dating a guy from campus whom she had met the first day of school. Emy had a boyfriend back home in Michigan, and little Georgie just could not seem to understand why men never asked her out.

Sam did not want them to think she was strange, so she made up a story about a guy in one of her classes the last semester who was "just so good looking and had a body that you just would not believe," she explained. "But he didn't even notice me."

"How sad," the redhead said. "And you are so pretty you could be a model or something."

Sam shook her head and laughed. "Eat your hamburger, Georgie," she said back to the girl, relieved that they had believed her story.

As the girls talked, Emy excused herself from the table. When she came back she looked over at Sam with a worried look on her face.

"Sam, it is raining really hard outside, would you like a ride home?" She spoke so softly that Sam had to strain to hear her over all of the other noises in the restaurant. She looked down at her watch.

"Yeah, I had better get going. Is anyone heading towards Lily Lane?"

Emy nodded, "I can take you home."

Sam wrote her sister's phone number down on different parts of her napkin and gave it to each of the girls.

"Call me, ok? Who knows, maybe we will have some classes together next semester and we can study together."

The other two girls waived goodbye to Sam, and then Emy led her out to her car. It was raining so hard that the streets were already starting to flood over with water. Emy drove the short distance to Sam's home and Sam asked her if she would like to come in.

"I better not, I really need to get going home. My boyfriend is supposed to be calling."

Sam said goodbye and ran into her home. She could not wait to tell Jessica about her new friends.

CHAPTER 40

When Austin returned from California, he was very quiet and hardly spoke to Sam. She was not sure if it was because of what had happened to his friend or if it was because of their fight before he had left. Sam had finally taken it upon herself to call him.

"Look," she had told him, "we can't let what happened end our friendship. You know how I feel now, so why can't we just start over?"

Austin had not seemed thrilled, but he did like the idea of spending time with Sam during what was left of their vacation. He still had hopes that things might change between them. He had thought a lot about her during the time he was home. He finally decided that, unless something better came along, he would wait it out and see what happened.

The summer went by fast and Sam had spent most of the time with either Austin or her new friends. She really enjoyed having people to do things with, although she was worried about Emy. Every time they got together, Emy would always be very quiet and withdrawn. Finally, one warm afternoon in late August, Sam invited Emy over to her house. When she arrived, she just sat on the porch, looking down at her hands. Sam could not take it anymore.

"Emy, I know I have not known you very long, but has there been something bothering you?"

Emy looked up at Sam with a look of panic on her face. "Why would you ask that, Sam?"

It was as if Sam was looking in a mirror as she watched the look on the girl's face and the way her hands started to shake. She looked warmly at Emy and put her hand on her shoulder. "I have been though enough in my own life to know when someone else is going through a hard time. You know that I am your friend and you can trust me if you need to talk about anything."

Suddenly Emy leaned forward, covered her face with her hands and started to cry. Sam moved closer to the girl and put her arm around her shoulder.

"Shhh. It's ok, Emy."

When Emy looked up, she had a very serious look on her face. "If I tell you what happened, do you promise not to tell the others? They just wouldn't understand," she said as her eyes pleaded with Sam.

"Whatever you tell me will always stay here with us. I will never say a word to anyone, I promise."

She looked back down at her hands. "I don't know why I am telling you this now. I guess I just need to get it out, and for some reason I trust you." She smiled at her and she continued. "Just before I met you something happened to me." Emy looked out at the land around them and sighed. Tears were slowly coming down her cheeks and she had a look in her eyes that seemed as if she were miles away. She did not look at Sam while she spoke.

"Everyone thinks that I have been dating a guy that is back in Michigan, but I'm not. I have been lying to everyone because I was afraid that someone might find out the truth." Emy took a deep breath and let it out slowly. "Sam, I was raped back in Michigan. I moved out here because I had to get away, you know?"

Sam was shocked. She leaned her head back and closed her eyes for a moment. When she opened her eyes she saw that Emy was watching her, and she looked scared. Sam knew from her own experience that Emy was probably waiting for Sam to tell her that it was her own fault. Sam smiled at the frightened girl. She had a pain of her own in her own eyes.

"Emy, I know what you are feeling. I know how scared you are, and how invaded you still feel." Emy looked at Sam with a questioning look on her face and Sam continued. "I was badly abused, to say the least, for over a year just before I came out here, too." She saw the look of surprise on her face. "It's a long story, but the main point is that we have to get on with our lives. We can't let this haunt us forever. What was done was horrible and vicious, but we can't let it ruin our lives. I know that it is easier said than done, but somehow we have to get past it."

Emy was shaking her head. "I just can't get it out of my head. I wake up frightened in the middle of the night, and I am always looking over my shoulder during the day. I just don't know how to go on."

"I know, I have been living my life the same way. Did you press charges on the guy when it happened?"

"No, I was too scared to. Plus I didn't want my family or friends to find out about it. How about you? Did you press charges?"

Sam shook her head. "No, I was too scared also. Now I look back and wish I had."

"Yeah, me too."

Sam looked at Emy and took her hand. "I'm glad you told me about what had happened. It helps to have someone to talk to, especially when we have both been through it. Please try to work through it though, ok? And never forget that, no matter what anyone ever says to you, it was not your fault."

Emy smiled. "I will. You have really helped me, Sam, thank you."

"You're welcome, Emy."

Emy stood up and stretched. "I really should get back. I feel like a thousand pounds have just been lifted off of my shoulders. I have never told anyone about what happened, not even my family."

"I told my sister. I was lucky she was really supportive. She has put up with a lot from me this last year, and she has been really great," Sam explained as she walked Emy to her car. She thought about how she had told Laura, too, and what had happened. She knew that Emy had enough to deal with than to be bothered with the details of Sam's ordeal, though.

Sam smiled and waved as she watched Emy drive away. Talking about what had happened had helped her as well, although she wondered if she would ever be able to take her own advice.

CHAPTER 41

When the new semester started that fall, it turned out that Sam had Emy in one of her classes, although she very rarely ran into any of the other girls that she had met over the summer. As the semester went on, Sam started to spend a lot of time with Emy, and less time with the other girls.

As Thanksgiving was getting closer, however, Sam started acting quiet and somewhat withdrawn again. Everyone was worried about the sudden change in her personality, but they were afraid to ask her what was going on. Finally Austin decided he had better talk to her.

He found her one afternoon sitting in the library, staring out the window. He smiled as he approached her; it was just like the day when he had first met her.

"It is beautiful here, isn't it?"

Sam jumped and turned around. She laughed when she saw it was Austin. "You nearly scared me to death, Austin."

"Do you realize that this is exactly how we first met? You were staring outside at the trees with a far away look in your eyes, just like you were just now." He hoped that she would catch on to what he was implying, but she just looked down at her hands. Austin shook his head and sat down across the table from her.

"Ok, beating around the bush isn't getting us anywhere so I'll be blunt. What's going on with you, Sam?"

"Don't worry about me, Austin," she told him as she looked back out the window.

"Sam, please. Everyone is worried about you. What is going on?"

She looked over to him and then looked back out the window again. "There are a lot of bad memories waiting at home for me and I just don't know if I am ready to face them yet."

Suddenly Austin understood what had been bothering Sam. The closer it got to her having to go home, the more distraught she had become. "Sam, whatever had happened to you is in the past and you need to leave it there. You can't keep digging it up and torturing yourself like this, not to mention what you are doing to your friends."

"I don't mean to be taking out my problems on my friends, but it is just not that easy, Austin. Why do you think I have been trying to stay away from everyone?"

"Well, I'd say that you are having just the opposite effect."

"Look, I have been having nightmares again, ok? I really had thought that I had moved on, you know? I was even looking forward to going home again. But now that it is getting closer, it is really bothering me." She took a deep breath. "You just don't know how horrible it had been."

"I have my suspicions, Sami."

Sam looked back over at Austin. "What are you talking about?"

"Sam, I'm not stupid. When certain things set you off the way they do, well, it kind of makes you think. Take my friend Suzanne, for instance. You remember, the one that was raped and then killed."

A look of panic came across Sam's face.

"Don't look so frightened Sam. We have been friends for a while now, and I think it is time that you open up to me. I can't be there for you if you keep hiding things from me."

"Look, I don't need this kind of pressure right now."

"What pressure? I'm just trying to be a friend. It seems like I can't even do that anymore without getting my head chewed off. Just forget it. I'll se ya later, ok?" Austin started to turn away but Sam stood up and stopped him.

Sam sighed. "Hold on, Austin. Let me go home for Thanksgiving first and I will tell you everything when I get back, ok? I just need to deal with this myself right now."

"Ok, but I promise that when you get back, I will not stop bothering you until you talk to me."

After that conversation with Austin, Sam had tried desperately to find Emy. When she finally did find her, she was about to tell her about her feelings, but Emy started to talk first. She was very excited about something.

"Sam, you won't believe what I am about to tell you. I took your advice and I have been really dealing with what had happened to me. I told my parents last night and they want me to come home. Sam, I am going to do it! I am going back home after this semester. Isn't that great? I think I am finally ready to let the past be in the past and go on with my life."

"Emy, that is really wonderful."

"I have never been happier. So, what was it that you wanted to tell me?"

Sam tried to smile. "Oh, it wasn't that important."

From that day on, Sam avoided everyone. Everyone was starting to get used to it and most people avoided Sam as much as she avoided them. She was hiding from everyone's questions, and her friends knew it. Whatever her problem was, they figured it just wasn't worth the hassle anymore and they all got tired of all of her excuses and how she would "tell them everything after Thanksgiving."

Two days before Thanksgiving, Sam and Jessica were on a plane headed for Denver. Sam was sitting at the window and when Denver came into sight, she started shaking. *I sure hope I can handle this,* she said to herself.

Their mother was waiting for them when they got off of the plane. She was so happy to see her that Sam temporarily forgot about everything else. They walked out to the car and then headed for home.

Sam watched out her window as they passed all of the familiar sights. Despite her fears, it felt good to be home again. When they pulled up to the house, Sam tried to convince herself that everything was going to be ok. Seeing her childhood home brought back the memories of how she had left home and how all of her problems seem to really start from that point on. As she walked into the house, she hoped that when she left this time, that it would be on good terms with a fresh start on life.

Thanksgiving Day Sam was helping her mother in the kitchen when the phone rang.

"I'll get it, Mom," Sam said. She brushed back her hair and then answered the phone. "Hello?"

"Hello, Samantha. Welcome home." It was Kyle. The voice she had feared for so long now echoed in her ear and then he laughed.

Sam's eyes widened as she stood frozen in fear.

"Samantha darling, you should never have run away from me. You will not have anything to be thankful for when I get done with you. Happy Thanksgiving and give my love to your family." He laughed and it sent shivers down her back.

Sam slammed down the phone then fell down to her knees. Her mother and sister ran over to her. Sam was shaking violently and they did not know what was wrong with her.

"No, no, no…" were the only words that she spoke.

CHAPTER 42

Jessica tried desperately to calm Sam down while their mother stood by them confused and worried.

"Sami, talk to us, what is wrong? Who was on the phone?" Jessica asked softly.

Sam did not respond; it was as if she had gone into shock.

Jessica put her hand on her sister's arm. "It was Kyle, wasn't it?"

Sam nodded her head and looked away.

"Will someone please tell me what is going on? And why does Kyle's name keep coming up," their mother cried out.

"Not now, Mom," Jessica quietly told her.

Jessica sat and comforted her sister until Sam finally took a deep breath and said "I'll be ok." She looked at her sister and then her mom. "I'm sorry, Mom. When I left Kyle, I left behind his back. He seems to be determined to find out where I am living and I don't think he will give up until he does."

"Maybe he is just all talk. I mean, he probably knows that he is getting to you and that is all he wants to do. You need to not let him know that he is scaring you and then maybe he will leave you alone."

"It's not quite that easy, Mom. It is hard to explain, but he has to get his way and he is not used to someone defying him. I am the fish that got away, so to speak, and he is furious."

Her mother leaned down and touched her daughter's hair. "Well, honey, then I think it is time you called the police."

Sam looked at Jessica and she nodded in agreement. "She's right, Sam. If he is still trying to find you after a year, then when does it stop?"

"I don't know. If I go, will you guys come with me?"

Jessica stood up. "Why don't I take her, Mom? We'll call you as soon as we know something."

Sam hugged her mom tightly and then Jessica drove Sam to the police station. As they got out of the car, Jessica looked over at Sam. "I figured it might be easier if Mom didn't come. She doesn't know everything that happened and knowing you, you would probably be more emotional if she was with us."

Sam laughed and rubbed her palms together nervously.

"Are you ok, sis?"

"Yeah, let's just get this over with, ok? They probably won't be able to help me anyway."

They approached the main desk where a large woman was standing. She noticed the girls walk up to her and looked at them in annoyance. "May I help you girls?"

Jessica stepped aside to let Sam come forward.

"I was wondering if I can talk to someone about a man that is stalking me."

"One moment," the woman said as she turned to say something to another officer. She turned back to Sam again. "Follow me, please."

The girls followed her as she led them to another waiting area. "Sign your name on this list and you will be called shortly," she said and briskly walked away.

Sam signed her name and then sat down. Then minutes later she heard her name being called. She approached the window nervously.

"What can I help you with, ma'am?" the officer behind the window asked as he was tapping a pencil on his desk.

Sam took a deep breath. "Ok, so how do I start?" She took another deep breath. "Last year I was abused by a man I had been living with. I ran away from him and now he is following me and he won't leave me alone. I am scared and I don't know what to do. I am just tired of being paranoid and, well, I know that it has been a year, but I was hoping that I can talk to someone about putting an end to this." Sam knew she was rambling but she was nervous, and she was also relieved to finally be telling someone what happened.

The officer showed no emotions as he watched her. He made sure she was done talking and then addressed her as if he was reading off of a cue card.

"Have you had any reports written up on him in the past?"

"No, sir."

"Have you ever placed a restraining order on him in the past?"

"No, sir."

The man looked annoyed. "Why not?"

Sam fidgeted for a moment and then started to twirl her hair with her fingers. "I was too scared of him. He had me convinced that he would hurt me and my family if I ever tried to get away from him. I was afraid of what he would do once I did get away."

The officer watcher her for a moment. "If you would like to place a restraining order against this man you can go around the corner..."

"Excuse me, officer, but this man has threatened my life before. In fact, he has beaten me beyond belief. What good is a restraining order going to do? A piece of paper won't stop him." She was starting to shout and Jessica was trying to get her to calm down. "Don't you see, this man is crazy. Why can't you arrest him or something? Please…"

A man in a suit came up behind the officer. "It's ok, Lou, I'll take care of this one." He looked over towards Sam and motioned for her to follow him to the back.

"I'll wait here for you, Sami. Good luck." Jessica squeezed her sister's hand and went to sit down.

Sam followed the man back to a small office. He went behind a large desk and motioned for her to sit down. Before he sat down, he leaned towards her and introduced himself.

"I am Sergeant Joe D'Vincio. And you are?"

"Samantha Higgins." They shook hands and he sat down.

Sergeant D'Vincio looked at Sam seriously for a moment. "You were causing quiet the commotion out there."

"Yes, sir, I'm sorry."

"Well, why don't you start from the beginning and tell me everything you can about this man that is bothering you and what led up to this point. Take your time, Ms. Higgins." He picked up a pen and wrote her name at the top of his paper.

"Yes, sir." She took a deep breath and then explained to him how she had moved in with Kyle. She told him about the abuse that had started, how he had held her against her will, constantly threatening herself and her family. She told him that he had raped her as well and how he had been involved in satanic activities.

"He found me almost immediately when I had first left him because someone who I thought was my friend told him where I was. After that I left the state and went to Missouri. There has also been some mysterious woman calling my mom's house asking where I am. She claims that she is an old high school buddy of mine, but I have never heard of her. Personally, I think that it is another one of Kyle's tricks to try to find out where I am living." Sam took a deep breath. "Earlier today he called me at my mother's house. He said that he knew that I would come home for the holidays."

The sergeant looked down at his pad and then tapped his pen on the desk. "Let me back up for a moment. This girl that has been calling your mother, what has she been saying to her?"

"She said that she was an old high school friend of mine and that she wanted to know where I was living now. She apparently won't ever leave a

145

return number. I know for a fact that I have never known or even heard of anyone by that name before."

"Ok. When did you say that Kyle called you and what did he say?"

"He just called today and he said I should never have left him and that I would not have anything to be thankful for when he got done with me. Then he told me to give his 'love' to my family and laughed this horrible laugh. That is when I hung up on him."

"I see." He was writing something down again and did not say anything for a moment.

Sam looked over at him. "I know you are probably wondering why I didn't deal with this when it happened, but I was scared. I still am scared. I was just so glad to have gotten away from him finally, that I didn't think about what I should have done. I am still scared, Sergeant. I am always looking over my shoulder, always wondering if he will be there. Is there anything that can be done to stop him?"

"Well, you are right, I do wish that you had called the police back when he was abusing you, Ms. Higgins..."

"He had the phone disconnected, too," Sam said, interrupting him. She felt like she was defending herself and she knew that that was not going to help her.

He waived a hand in front of her. "I understand that you went through a terrible ordeal, ma'am. I can only imagine how scared you were. The problem we have here is that we are going merely on your word. There are no bruises or marks to prove there has been abuse, and he has only called your mother's house once. If you file a complaint, we would have to question him and I guarantee that he would deny everything that you have told me. Now don't misunderstand me, I do believe what you are saying, but there is no way to prove that he is harassing you. I understand that you are scared and understandably so. I really hope for your sake that he is only talk."

He stopped and tapped his pen on the desk. "I know that this seems cruel, but until we have some kind of proof, all you can do is issue a restraining order against him." He reached into his inside pocket and pulled out his card. "Make sure to call me if he does or says anything else, ok?"

Sam took his card and looked down at it. She was numb with disbelief. "So basically you are saying that until he actually kills me or someone in my family, there is nothing that the police can do for me."

"I strongly urge you to obtain a restraining order, Ms. Higgins," he said as he stood up. "I'm sorry that I could not be of more help."

Sam stood up and shook his hand. "Thanks for your time," she said coldly and then she walked back to where her sister was waiting. Jessica stood up when she saw her sister approaching her. She could tell by the look on her face that it had not gone well.

"What did he say?" she asked her.

Sam wiped away tears of frustration. "They can't do anything without proof," she said.

Jessica put her arm around Sam's shoulders and they quietly walked back to the car.

CHAPTER 43

Sam and Jessica rushed around the house making sure that they had not forgotten any of their things.

"I can't believe that you were up so early this morning, Samantha," her mother said as she grabbed her purse.

"I couldn't really sleep, so I figured I might as well do something useful and get our things put in the car."

"Hey, I don't mind," Jessica screamed from the bedroom. "It sure as heck made it easier for me to get ready this morning."

"I just can't believe how fast time went. It seems so silly to fly back for such a short time just to fly right back out here again for Christmas," Sam yelled back.

Jessica came around the corner of the hallway and lightly hit her sister's shoulder. "You just don't want to deal with finals again. Admit it!"

Sam laughed. "You know me just too well!"

They looked around one last time and then they headed out to the car to head for the airport.

He watched as the car slowly pulled out of the driveway. He could see Sam sitting in the back seat. She was leaning slightly forward while talking to her mother and sister who were in the front. For a moment, her face seemed so close that he wanted to reach out and touch her.

He quickly stepped back into the safety of some shadows as they drove by him and he smiled as he watched the car disappear around the corner. This time he had not followed them; they were probably just going shopping and he was not in the mood to chase them around some crowded mall. He had decided not to call her again during her visit home. There was no need as he had made his point. Once he had known that she was here, he had enjoyed just sitting across the street; watching the lights and shadowy movements within the house. Often he would close his eyes and try to picture what Sam would be doing. He had already forgotten how bad she had looked while she had been with him. Instead, he remembered what she looked like when he had first met her. Seeing her now, looking as good as she had then, just made

148

him want her that much more. Next time he would make sure that she looked that good for him at all times.

Suddenly he was brought back to the present when he noticed the car pulling back into the driveway. He looked at his watch. They had only been gone for an hour. He watched as Sam's mom got out of the car and walked up to the house, but there was no sign of Sam or her sister. He waited there until late that night before he finally acknowledged that Sam was not coming back.

"Damn, how could I have been so stupid." He took a step forward from where he had been hiding and, as he looked over at the house, he had a look of pure hatred on his face.

When their plane arrived back in Missouri, Austin was waiting for them, and Sam was actually relieved to see him. He could see the worn look on her face and guessed that her trip home had not gone as well as she would have liked it to.

Sam surprised him by asking if she could come over to his house after they dropped Jessica off. She had decided on the plane that she would tell him everything, but she knew that if she did not tell him immediately, she might change her mind.

They dropped Jessica and all of the luggage off and Austin took Sam to his house. They went into the living room and sat down. For the next two hours, Sam proceeded to tell him everything, including the last phone call and her visit with the police. When she had finished talking, Austin was shaking his head.

"No wonder you have been so upset. You poor thing." He put his arms around her and held her close. She had bared her soul to him and she was relieved to see that he still wanted to be there for her.

She pulled away from him and looked at him very seriously. "Austin, I didn't tell you about what had happened so that you would feel sorry for me. I wanted you to know because, well, I just figured it was probably the right thing to do. To be perfectly honest, I thought that you would pull away form me if you knew the truth."

Austin looked shocked. "You *thought* that I would pull away or you *hoped* that I would?"

Sam looked down at her lap. "I'm sorry. It's just that I have a hard time trusting men right now. I know that I should be able to trust you, but sometimes these little warning bells go off in my head. Besides that, I'm well, you know. Damaged merchandise."

Austin smiled. "I don't think you are damaged merchandise. You look

SHERRY MOORE

perfectly fine to me!" He leaned towards Sam and touched a strand of her hair. "Sam, how do you expect to find out who you can trust, if you don't give someone a chance?" He shook his head. "So anyway, do you think that wacko is going to bother you again?"

Sam looked serious for a moment. "Something inside of me tells me that something bad is going to happen. It may just be that I am being paranoid again, but I don't think so."

"If that creep ever comes around here, you just let me know. I'll take care of him for you."

Sam laughed and then she told him about the rest of her visit with her family.

Austin drove Sam home and that night, she dreamt that Kyle was coming after her again.

CHAPTER 44

Winter came once again and brought with it its dreadfully cold winds and icy rains. Everyone finished taking their finals and prepared for Christmas. Sam tried to see as much of Emy as she could, but they both did not have a lot of free time. When her friend left to go back home, Sam was sad to see her go.

Sam's mom had decided to come out to see them again for Christmas, rather than have the girls fly home. As their mother had pointed out, they were college students and had already spent enough money over Thanksgiving. Between that and what had happened with Kyle, Sam and Jessica were both thrilled and relieved.

Just as it had happened the year before, a few days before Christmas their mother frantically rushed to her car with her bags. She did not want to be late for her flight.

Just as he had waited and watched the year before, he was again watching her. He knew that either Sam would come home to her, or she would go to Sam for Christmas. When he saw her dragging her suitcases out to her car, he smiled.

"It looks like I'll get to see where Samantha is living this year."

He once again followed her to the airport. This time; however, he was prepared. As he was heading towards the airport, he picked up his newly purchased car phone and dialed the airport.

"When is your next flight to Missouri?" He waited and was happy to hear that the next flight was leaving within the hour and that there had been a cancellation. He smiled to himself.

"Yes ma'am, I would like to take that seat. Can I also schedule a return ticket back to Denver? Great, let me give you my credit card number." Kyle drove around Mrs. Higgins and went on to the airport. There was no need to follow her anymore as he knew where she was heading and this time, he would be there too.

When the plane arrived, Kyle quickly left the plane. He saw Sam and Jessica and waited until they had looked the other direction and then he ran behind the ticket counter. His heart was pounding as he watched Sam laugh

151

and hug her mother. He made sure that he had not been seen and then quickly ran out to get a cab. He had not bothered to bring any luggage as he was not planning to stay for very long. All he wanted to know right now was which town Sam lived in and the rest would come later.

He hailed a cab and then sat and waited for Sam and her family to go to their car. He then had the cab follow them until they reached the outskirts of the town where they lived.

He smiled victoriously. "Merry Christmas, Samantha," he said as he laughed and then he told the driver to turn the cab around and head back to the airport. The driver shrugged and turned the car around.

Kyle sat back in the seat and put his hand under his chin. He had to get back to Colorado quickly as he had a lot of planning to do.

CHAPTER 45

Christmas was better than the year before and Sam had been relieved that she had not had to go back to Denver again. Although time went by fast, Sam and her mother spent the short time trying to build a new bond between them. When it was time for their mother to leave, both Jessica and Sam were sad to see her go.

Sam spent a quiet New Year's with Austin and then, before they knew it, their vacation was over and everyone was back to studying again.

One Saturday afternoon in early February Sam and Jessica were at home studying. There was a cold wind blowing outside and there was a chill in the air. Sam was lying on the couch with a blanket wrapped around her, studying for a test, while Jessica was staring blankly at the wall next to her. She blinked and then dropped her book on the floor. The loud *thump* startled Sam.

"Alright, Jess, what's wrong now?"

"I can't do it, Sami." Jessica shook her head in frustration. "It is my last semester and I can't seem to keep anything in my head. The way I am heading, I will probably never graduate because I am going to flunk all of my classes. My last semester and my brain freezes."

Sam laughed. "Oh, you silly girl. Just take a deep breath and try to forget that it is your last semester. You are just letting yourself get overwhelmed."

"Yeah sure, easy for you to say. You still have a couple of years to go."

"Believe me, I would rather be in your shoes right now. Just think," Sam tilted her head back. "By June you won't have to study anymore whatsoever. You will actually be able to turn on the television, or read a good novel. Suddenly I don't like you anymore."

Jessica laughed and threw a pencil at Sam. "Oh, leave me alone!"

The girls studied for a while and then Jessica jumped up to get a drink of water.

"Would you like anything while I am up, Sami?"

"No thanks." Sam set her book aside and stretched.

Jessica came back into the living room and sat down. "So what are you and Austin planning to do for Valentine's Day?"

"What makes you think I am planning to spend Valentine's Day with Austin?"

"Who else would you be spending it with?"

"Well, gee, I was kind of hoping to spend the day with you. Of course, if you are going to be busy…"

Jessica looked surprised. "You really want to spend Valentine's Day with me? How sweet. Hey, we could go out for breakfast and then go ice skating."

"Actually, I was thinking that I would try to cook you breakfast for a change. Then, if you are still alive from my cooking, we can go ice skating."

Jessica laughed for a moment. "You know, we are both pretty pathetic. Neither one of us is spending Valentine's Day with anyone special."

"Hey," Sam said as she put her hands on her hips. "I resent that! Actually I am spending the day with the person I think is the most special around here. So there."

Jessica smiled warmly at her. "Thanks, sis." Sam smiled back at her and then they both got back to their studies.

Sam called Austin later that week and, when he asked her about Valentine's Day, she explained that she wanted to spend it with her sister.

"I think that is really great, Sam. Do you think, however, that I might be able to at least sneak in dinner with you that night?"

"We'll see, Austin."

The next couple of weeks were very cold and the weather forecaster was calling for a nasty storm to blow through town.

At two o'clock in the morning on Valentine's Day, as Sam and Jessica slept, a dark gray van pulled into town. The van stopped and parked along the side of the road just on the edge of Main Street. The tinted window on the driver's side started to slide down and he looked out at the heavy falling snow.

"Looks like that storm has arrived," the radio announcer said over the radio.

He smiled and rolled the window back up.

CHAPTER 46

Sam woke up at seven o'clock in the morning on Valentine's Day and cursed to herself. She could hear the wind blowing hard outside her window. She got up and looked out to see a horrible snowstorm.

"Figures, brrrr," she mumbled to herself and then she quickly grabbed her robe and slippers. She walked out into the kitchen and saw Jessica holding a cup of steaming coffee and looking out the kitchen window. Jessica turned when she heard her sister coming into the room.

"Good morning," her cheerful voice rang out, "sleep well?"

Sam gave her a nasty look and grumbled to herself.

"What is wrong with you this morning, you little grumpy head? Did you wake up on the wrong side of the bed?" She laughed and poured Sam a cup of coffee. Sam took the cup and held it in both of her hands.

"In case you haven't noticed, there is a horrible snow storm outside. Besides that, I didn't sleep very well and I have a horrendous headache. Do you have any aspirin or something?"

Jessica looked in the drawer where she kept her vitamins. "Nope, sorry. I guess you'll have to run to the store if you want some." Jessica chuckled to herself.

"I'm glad you are finding this so amusing. The way my head feels right now, I am going to have to get something. I guess I'll go throw on some sweats and drive down to Harvey's store really quick. I sure hope he is open."

Sam got up from the barstool she had been sitting on and went back to her room. She quickly dressed and grabbed the broom to brush the snow off of the car. She went outside and took a deep breath. *Man it is cold out here*, she thought to herself. She started the car and then hurried to brush the snow off. She let the car run for a few minutes and then proceeded to make her way to Main Street. There was a lot of snow on the road and Sam could barely see in front of the car. She passed a dark gray van that was on the side of the road. The windows were tinted so she could not tell if anyone was inside.

"I wouldn't want to be the owner of that vehicle," she said to herself as she continued to drive the short distance to the drugstore. She parked the car and, while leaving the car engine running to keep it warm, she ran into the store.

He sat back in the van and watched as the car drove by him. He had been barely awake when he saw the car go by.

"Who is crazy enough to be out driving around in this weather," he mumbled as he pulled the blanket tighter around his body. A couple of hours ago he had turned the engine off to save gas and he had hoped that he would not look too suspicious. He had thought that, with the weather being as bad as it was, no one would be out driving around the small town. He had stayed warm for a while, but then it had started to get pretty cold.

He watched in fascination as the car stopped and the driver's side door opened. He had to blink a couple of times when he realized that it was Samantha getting out of the car. He straightened up in his seat and grabbed the wheel.

"Well, I'll be. This is going to be easier than I thought." He started the van back up and as soon as she had disappeared into the store, he drove over to where Sam had parked. He smiled as he realized that she had driven right by him and that she had no idea that he was even in town.

He grabbed the rose that he had been saving for Sam. He wished that it could have been a real one, but it would have wilted in the cold. He smiled at the thought of giving her a wilted rose.

He got out of the van and quickly opened her car door. He guessed that she would not be very long so he placed the rose on her seat and quickly got back into his own vehicle. He carefully drove back to where he had originally parked and waited.

Sam walked out of the drugstore and rushed back to her car. It was extremely cold, and she hoped that the car had finally warmed up. She opened the car door and saw the rose sitting on her seat. She picked up it and quickly looked around but there was no one in any direction. The streets were just as quiet and bare as they had been when she had first arrived. She noticed the tire tracks next to her car and smiled. It must have been Austin. She jumped into her car and carefully drove back home. She was concentrating so hard on her driving, that she did not even notice the van that she had passed earlier was now following behind her. She pulled into the driveway, quickly got out of the car, and then ran up to the front door.

Kyle stopped the van long enough to watch Sam run to her door and he smiled. "Soon you will belong to me again, Samantha." He laughed and then decided to try to search the area to see what was available for him. The weather was getting nastier by the second and he was going to need a warm place to sleep. The heavy snow was going to make it hard for him to watch her, but it did not even bother him. As he slowly pulled back onto the road, he smiled at how incredibly well things were going. "Luck may have been on your side once, but this time, Sami," he said with a smile, "luck is on my side." He slowly drove away and only glanced back once in his mirror as Sam's house quickly disappeared within the fog and blowing snow.

CHAPTER 47

Sam ran into the house and went into the living room where her sister was sitting. Jessica had just started a fire in the fireplace.

"Hey, sis!" Sam said cheerfully as she plopped herself down on the couch.

Jessica looked at her surprised. "Is this the same girl that just left here with a bad attitude? What was in that aspirin? Whatever it was, I want one!"

Sam laughed. "Nah, there was a rose sitting in my car when came out of the drugstore." She held the rose out for her sister to see. "That was so sweet of Austin." Sam smiled and got back to her feet. "I need to call him and thank him. Besides, I want to know why he just dropped it off and disappeared."

Jessica shrugged. "Maybe he was trying to be mysterious and romantic."

Sam laughed and then went into the kitchen. She picked up the phone and dialed Austin's number.

"Hello," he answered, sounding groggy and tired.

"Don't try to fake your voice to sound like you just woke up, you bum! I know you were out running around just a little while ago." Sam twirled the phone cord and smiled.

"What are you talking about, Sam? What time is it?" He moaned. "Sam, I thought you said you were going to be spending the day with your sister. I was up really late last night studying." He yawned. "I hope you know that you woke me up."

Sam tensed up. "Why are you playing these games, Austin? I found the rose that you put on the driver's seat of my sister's car while I was inside Harvey's Drugstore. I was just calling to say thanks."

Austin cleared his throat. "Sam, honey, I wish I could have put a rose in your sister's car for you, but I was sound asleep while you were out running around. Sorry, it must have been someone else."

"But who else would be crazy enough to be out driving around in this weather? And why would that person follow me to give me a rose?"

Suddenly Sam's eyes opened wide. *No, it couldn't be,* she thought. *He couldn't have found me here.*

"Sami, why are you so quiet all of a sudden? What are you thinking about?"

"Oh, it's probably nothing. Let me call you back later, ok, Austin?"

Austin heard the shakiness in her voice. "You don't think that crazy guy Kyle left you that rose, do you?" Sam did not respond. "Oh come on, Sami. There is no way that he could have found you in this hole-in-the-wall town."

"But what if he did? What if he did somehow find me?" Her voice was so low that Austin could barely hear her. Sam suddenly remembered the van that she had passed. "There was a strange van parked on the side of the road just on the edge of Main Street. I thought it was deserted, but what if Kyle was in it, watching me?" The thought gave Sam chills all over her body.

"Sam, why don't I get dressed and drive over there and see if the van is still there? Ok? It looks like it is snowing pretty hard out right now so if someone was following you, there should be tire tracks in the snow."

"Ok," Sam took a deep breath. "Why don't you stop off here after you look around."

"Everything will be ok, Sami; just relax and I will be over there soon."

They hung up the phone and Sam walked back in the living room. Jessica looked up at Sam then stood up.

"Sam, what is wrong? Your face is so white that you look like you have seen a ghost."

Sam did not say anything but just walked to the window and looked out at the blowing snow. She glanced down at her watch and nervously waited for Austin to arrive, although she knew that it would take him a little while. She shivered as she looked out into the white fog and realized that if Kyle was out there, she could not even see him and she wondered if he would be able to see her. She pulled herself away from the window and sat down. All she could do now was wait and pray.

CHAPTER 48

Austin drove slowly over to where Main Street began. It was snowing so hard that he doubted that he would be able to see anything, and the roads were becoming a solid sheet of ice.

He stopped the car along the side of the road and pulled up on the emergency brake. As cold as it was outside, he knew that as soon as he stepped out of the car it would only be a matter of minutes and he would be jumping back into the car to warm up again. He wrapped his jacket tightly around him and went out into the icy wind and blowing snow. He walked along the side of the road and was about to turn back when something caught his attention. He walked a little farther up and saw that there was a large area that had less snow than anywhere else. He realized that, from the way it looked and as hard as it was snowing, a vehicle would have had to have been parked there for several hours. He could barely see slight tire tracks leading up Main Street. It was too cold to follow them on foot and the visibility was too poor to follow them by car.

Austin got back in his warm car and rubbed his hands together. He saw something out of the corner of his eye and turned to see the town's only sand truck putting sand out on the roads.

"Oh great, there goes what little I could see," he said as she watched the truck make new tracks up Main Street. He sighed, released the emergency brake, and then slowly made his way to Sam's house.

When Austin arrived, Sam was anxiously waiting to hear what he had found.

"I'm sorry, Sam, but between the blowing snow and the sand truck, all I could tell was that there had been something parked on the side of the road for quite a while. Whoever it was is gone now. Other than that, I could not tell anything else."

Sam slapped her hand against her leg and walked over to the couch. "Thanks for trying."

"I really wish someone would tell me what is going on around here," Jessica said, looking very annoyed.

"Nothing is going on, sis. I was probably just being paranoid again, although we will probably never find out who gave me this rose. Look, would you mind giving me some time along with Austin?"

Jessica smiled. "Sure, but don't forget you promised me breakfast!" When she left the room, Sam looked over at Austin, who had moved in front of the fireplace.

"I just can't shake the feeling that he is here."

"Yeah, but, Sami, how would he have found you?" Austin sat down in the recliner that was across from her.

"I don't know, but who else could it have been?"

Austin smiled. "Maybe you have a secret admirer."

"Yeah, right." Sam picked up a pen off of the coffee table and started tapping it against her leg.

"Sami, I don't want to sound rude, but you really need to forget about this guy." Sam looked up at him angrily and Austin put his hand up before she could speak. "Don't look at me like that, Sam. You really do need to get on with your life. It's like you are still obsessed with what has happened."

Sam jumped up to her feet and started pacing. "How can I possibly get on with my life when he is following me everywhere I go? I can't go anywhere without looking over my shoulder. You have never had anyone throw you into a wall or follow you around. You don't know what it's like to have to keep moving because you fear for your life. Don't you even dare tell me to get on with my life."

"Hey look, you don't know that he has followed you here, and to me it seems pretty inconceivable the he could have found you here, anyway." Austin stood up. "Why don't you call me later when you have settled down, ok? Happy Valentine's Day," he said sarcastically as he bolted out the door.

He watched as the young man quickly got in to his car and drove away. Who is he? The anger rose within him as he wondered if Sam had a boyfriend.

Whoever he was, he was not there for very long, and he seemed upset when he left. Could Sam have figured out who had left her the rose?

He smiled confidently. In a way he hoped she did know, because that would make the game that much more interesting.

His stomach growled and he suddenly realized how hungry he was. He smiled victoriously as he left to find a place to eat.

After Austin had left, Jessica came back into the living room.

"Are you alright, Sami? I heard all of the commotion from the kitchen. Do you want to talk about it?"

"Oh, Jess." Sam threw herself back onto the couch. "Nobody understands why I am so scared. I had thought that I could forget about what had happened, but things keep happening to bring it all back again. It was easy for me to tell Emy that she needed to get on with her life and leave the past in the past, but I can't seem to take my own advice. I had started to make some new friends and even they have stayed away from me lately. Austin even acts like he is ready to just say forget it, too. Sometimes it just seems easier to avoid everyone than to keep hearing the lectures, you know?"

"Ok, Sam, so what exactly happened that set this all off?"

Sam sighed. "Well, you remember that rose that I found on the front seat of the car after I left the drugstore?" Jessica nodded. "Well, Austin didn't put it there. In fact, he was still in bed when I called to thank him for it."

"Who do you think left it there for you?"

"That's just it, I don't know. There was a strange gray van parked on the side of Main Street this morning and, to be honest, I thought it might be Kyle." She saw that her sister was about to protest the idea and she waved her hand in the air. "Please, don't start lecturing me, too. Jess, I feel it deep down inside my stomach. He is here; he has found me."

Jessica looked at her sister, but did not say a word. What could she possibly say? She shook her head and left the room, leaving Sam wide eyed and frightened.

He returned from the small market and quickly ate the sandwiches that he had bought. He watched the house and smiled. He had a feeling that Sam knew that he was there. Maybe it was just hopeful thinking, but he thrived on the hope that she was worried and scared. He sat back and smiled again as he sang to himself.

Hush, little baby, don't say a word,
Mama's going to buy you a mocking bird,
If that mocking bird don't sing...

He laughed.

Then Kyle's going to take care of everything!

CHAPTER 49

A couple of weeks had passed since Valentine's Day and Sam had started to relax. Much to her relief, there had been no other strange events. She was starting to believe that everyone was right and that she was just being paranoid.

It was a Saturday night and Sam and Jessica had gone over to Austin's house to play cards. It was starting to get late and they decided to head back home.

"Just wait, I'll beat you next time," Jessica had said to Austin as he walked them to their car. They all laughed and he waved goodbye to them as they got into the car.

As they headed down the road, Sam stretched. "That was fun, Jess. It felt good to get out of the house for a while. I have been so burnt out on school that I needed to do something fun for a change."

"I know what you mean." Jessica yawned. "I am so tired that I don't know if I can keep my eyes open."

Sam laughed. "You better, because otherwise we won't have to worry about studying; we will be in a ditch somewhere between here and home."

Jessica laughed. "Oh shut up, you backseat driver!"

They were both still laughing when Jessica pulled the car up onto the driveway. Both girls got wearily out of the car and stretched.

"I'm sure glad you remembered to turn on the outside light, Sam."

"I thought you turned it on." Sam said as she looked over at her sister.

"Oh, maybe I did. I'm so tired that I can't remember."

They walked up to the front door and about half way up the walkway, Sam stopped, looking down at the ground.

"I wonder if a package came for us. Look, someone has been here." She pointed down and Jessica saw that there were large muddy footprints going to and coming from the front door.

Jessica shrugged and reached out to open the front door. She stopped and just stood staring at the front door; it was already slightly open.

"Sami, someone's been in the house."

Sam stood frozen, afraid that whoever it was would still be in the house.

"Maybe we should call the police before going in, Jess."

"I don't even want to go in to get the phone. Let's just go back to Main Street and go directly to the police station. I don't even want to take the chance."

"Oh, Jess, what if it is Kyle?" Sam's heart started to pound and she could not move.

"I am so sick of you thinking that everything that happens must have something to do with Kyle. I mean, come on, Sami, you don't even know that he is here in town. If anyone has even been here, it was probably one of the college guys playing a prank. You know, one of those fraternity things."

Suddenly they heard a loud crash and both girls jumped. They turned and saw that a dog had just knocked down their trashcans that were sitting out in front of their house. Jessica put her hand to her chest and took a deep breath.

"Come on, sis, let's get over to the police station."

They quickly got back in the car and drove the short distance to the sheriff's department. The girls walked into a small office where two officers were. One was sitting on a chair with his feet set up on the desk and a newspaper across his lap, and the other was leaning against the wall smoking a pipe. They both stopped what they had been doing and looked over at Sam and Jessica when they walked in.

"Can we help you girls?" the one standing asked.

Jessica cleared her throat. "Yes sir, we think that someone has been in our house and we were wondering if someone could please come and check it out for us."

"What makes you think that someone has been in your house?" the one sitting down asked.

"There were large footprints outside the front door and the door was open," Jessica said.

"And someone has been bothering me a lot lately," Sam added.

Jessica shot Sam a nasty look and then looked back at the officers. "I'm sure that it was just a fraternity prank or something, but we would feel a lot better if you could just please check it out for us," she explained.

The officer that had been leaning against the wall looked over to the one sitting down and spoke with a humorous tone and an obnoxious look in his eyes.

"Gee, Bob, you better rush on down there and make sure that there is no one in their house. I'll keep watch around here." He laughed as he grabbed the newspaper and the other man grumbled.

"Thanks a lot, you owe me one." He stood up and grabbed his coat. He was a short but large man with a belly that hung over his pants. "Let's go,

164

girls. I'll follow you back to your house."

When they arrived back at the house, the officer walked in and checked it for them. He went through the entire house and then came back to the living room where the girls were nervously waiting.

"I have checked everywhere for you and no one has been in here that I can see. If you find anything missing or disturbed, give us a call in the morning. 'Night, ladies." He tipped his hat and, without waiting for a response, he walked out the front door.

Jessica and Sam looked at each other and laughed.

"Well, I guess he was amused," Sam said.

"I guess. Well, since everything is ok, let's just go to bed and get some rest. I do think that Austin is right though, maybe you do need to settle down. Now you're even starting to get me paranoid."

"I don't know. Do you really think that I am just being paranoid, Jess?"

Her sister shrugged. "I don't know. You have been through a lot and I'm sure that it is normal to be a little nervous, but you do seem to overreact to everything."

"Yeah, I guess. Well, good night, sis."

"Good night."

The next morning Sam woke up fairly early and decided to get a little studying done before they went to church. She strolled into the living room and sat down on the couch. She stretched her arms back and then picked up her notebook that had been lying on the floor. She opened it up and then screamed. Inside the notebook was a note from Kyle.

CHAPTER 50

Jessica heard her sister scream and she quickly ran into the living room. Sam was sitting on the couch, and her face had gone completely white.

"Sam, what's wrong? What happened now?"

Sam could barely speak. "He *was* here last night," was all she could say as she handed the note to Jessica. "I haven't read it yet."

Jessica looked over the note for a moment and then started to read it aloud. "Hello Samantha," she read, "I bet you are surprised to hear from me again. I have been in town for a while keeping an eye on you. You and your sister have a really nice place, it is just so cozy, and I really love how small-town people live so trustingly. You know, how no one ever bothers to lock all their doors."

Sam and Jessica looked at each other. "Oh Sam, I'm sorry. I never thought that I'd have any problems out here." Sam nodded and then her sister continued to read the letter.

"You know, Samantha, I have really been missing you lately. It has just been too long since we have been together, but don't worry, that will change soon enough.

"I hope you enjoyed the rose I gave you for Valentine's Day. Do you still have it, Samantha? I would have liked to have given you a real one, for real ones have thorns. Yes, real ones have thorns and as you well know, they eventually will also wither and die, won't they? I will see you soon, my love. Forever, Kyle."

Jessica put the letter down and went to sit next to her sister. "What a creep," she said. "I'm so sorry for doubting you, Sam. Please forgive me. I just didn't think that he would really be here."

Sam was silent for a moment and then looked up at Jessica. "That rose he left for me wasn't even real. I wonder what he meant by…" Sam stopped and put her hand up to her head. "Valentine's Day last year. How could I have forgotten? He got me a rose and had written me this bizarre letter about how our friendship was like a rose and he hoped that it would never wither and die. I guess this is just his sick way of trying to remind me of how much he had control over me. Well, not this time. First thing tomorrow morning I am going to call Sergeant Joe D'Vincio from Denver. Maybe he can somehow help me now."

The next morning Sam called Sergeant D'Vincio. Luckily he happened to be available to talk on the phone and Sam updated him on what had been going on. When she read him the note, he sighed.

"I'm really sorry, Ms. Higgins. I know you must be scared, but we cannot arrest a man for writing a letter to you. Although you know that he was in your house, there is nothing that we could use in court to really prove it. He could merely say that he had put the letter in your book at school. There is also nothing in the letter that directly threatens you. I'm sure that he knew what he was doing when he wrote that note to you, and it sounds to me like his is just trying to scare you. I'm sorry; I wish I could be more help. Just be careful and make sure you lock all of your doors and windows from now on."

"But, Sergeant," Sam pleaded, "The man followed me to another state. He watches my house. Doesn't that classify as stalking?"

"Once again, there is no law that says that he can or cannot go to another state. It may feel like stalking, but I'm sure he'll get over it and go home. He has not harmed you or threatened you in any way. You don't have any recorded messages from him showing that he is calling your home. You haven't seen him following you around. You just can't have a person arrested because he is annoying you. If you are that worried about him, why don't you notify your local police and they can keep an eye out for you."

"Oh, yeah," Sam mumbled, "they will just be thrilled to help."

"I'm sorry?"

"Oh, nothing. Thank you for your time, Sergeant. Sorry to have bothered you." She hung up the phone, looked at Jessica, and shook her head.

"Let me guess, the note is still not enough to do anything with."

"You got it, Jess. He suggested that I notify the local police." Sam stood up and looked around for her textbooks. "Would you mind if I took the car for a while? I'd just like to go to the library and bury myself in some books. I don't feel like going to classes today."

"Go ahead, but please be careful. Oh, and also be back by one so I can use the car to go to the office. My only class was canceled for today and I told my boss I would come in for a while this afternoon."

"Thanks, I'll be back around noon." Sam put on her coat and headed out to the car. She pulled out of the driveway and started to make her way up the road. Back at the house, Jessica started putting the dishes in the sink and came across Sam's wallet.

"Oh shoot, she is going to need this." Jessica wrapped her robe tightly around her and ran out the front door. She ran out into the road to try to wave at Sam before she got too far when she heard a horn behind her. She started to turn away but it was too late.

CHAPTER 51

Sam was in the library studying when she heard the school's church bells ringing twelve o'clock noon.

"Jessica is going to kill me for running late," she mumbled to herself. She gathered her books and ran quickly down to her car. She turned on the radio and, as she drove, she listened to the country music and thought about how lucky Jessica was to be graduating soon. When she got to her house and walked in, she immediately noticed how quiet it was.

"Jessica," she shouted out, "Where are you?" She did not hear a response so she shrugged and then walked into the kitchen to see if she had left her a note. *She could not have gone too far without the car,* Sam thought.

The red light was flashing on the answering machine so she hit the play button to see who had called.

The tape started to rewind and Sam poured herself a glass of water. The tape stopped and she looked over at it expectantly.

"Ms. Higgins? This is Jane Waters from the community hospital. Your sister has been in a terrible accident, please come immediately." Sam dropped the glass of water on the floor, shattering it. She left the shards of glass on the floor and ran back out to the car. She could hear the sand and snow spitting out from under her tires as she slammed on the gas and took off towards the community hospital. It did not take her long to get there and the nurse who had left her the message immediately greeted her.

"Are you Samantha Higgins?" the nurse asked her.

"Yes, where is my sister? What happened?"

"Ms. Higgins, you sister has been injured pretty badly. We are going to be airlifting her to the hospital in Quincy because they are better equipped to take care of her injuries."

"What happened to her? When I left her she was at home and she was just fine."

"Well, for some reason your sister ran out into the road and someone pulled out from around a curve and could not stop in time to avoid hitting her. He did not even check to see if you sister was ok, but just kept on driving. George Watkins, who lives in a farm not too far from you girls, saw the whole thing. He tried to chase the guy down and, although he lost him, he did get the license plate number. It was a dark gray van and the plates were from Colorado."

Sam shook her head in disbelief and tried to clear her head.

"I can't believe this is happening. You said that someone got the plate number of the van. If you have that number here, I would like to get a copy of it." She stopped and took a deep breath. "How long will it be before I will be able to see my sister?"

The nurse put her hand on Sam's arm. "She is being prepared to be moved right now. I'm sure that once the hospital evaluates and stabilizes her condition, they will let you see her then."

Sam was desperately trying to hold back her tears. "Can I at least go with her?"

The nurse smiled kindly at Sam. "No, I'm afraid they won't have enough room in the helicopter, but there is a ferry you can take to cross the river. We can give you directions and it won't take you very long to get there. Oh, and before I forget. The police will want to talk to you as well. I have already given them the information we got from Mr. Watkins and they were going to go talk to him first."

Sam thanked the nurse for her help and then followed her to get the directions to the hospital and the license plate number of the van. She opened her purse and pulled out Sergeant D'Vincio's card. For some reason she felt the need to keep talking to him. There was something almost fatherly about him and she was convinced that sooner or later he would help her. *I'll call him once I get to the hospital in Quincy. Surely he will listen to me now,* she thought to herself as she put the card back in her purse.

As Sam walked back out to the car, the realization of what had just happened to her sister really hit her and she started to cry. She got behind the wheel and put her hands up to her face.

"Jessica did not do anything to you, Kyle. How could you do this to her," she screamed. If Kyle had been there, Sam knew that she would have attacked him with all of her strength. She knew, of course, that he was a lot bigger and stronger than she was, but she did not care. She hated him with everything that she had inside of her. Kyle had not just seriously injured Jessica, but he had also taken away her future. Jessica had been only two months away from graduating and had a wonderful job lined up. Now she would have to wait until she was out of the hospital and fully recovered, and who only knew how long that would take. The realization of all that hit Sam hard as she thought about everything that was happening.

"God, how am I going to tell Mom," she thought as she hit her head back against the seat.

Sam wasn't sure how long she would be at the hospital so she decided to run back to her house to get a few things before heading over to Quincy. Once back at the house, she started to head quickly towards the front door but suddenly stopped. She turned and looked towards the road she had just pulled off of. As if being pulled by string she found herself walking down the driveway back towards the road. Shortly past the driveway she could see her sister's blood, lying there, standing out in contrast against the light, dusty color of the road. She felt nauseous as she knelt down by where her sister had lain helplessly. She closed her eyes and could almost feel her sister's presence. When she opened her eyes, she stood up and glanced around. The sun reflected off something lying just off of the road and she walked towards it to see what it was. She was surprised to see her wallet laying there, partially covered in dirt from the road.

"What the... why would my wallet be here?" Suddenly she realized why her sister had come running out into the road. "Oh no," she mumbled. She rubbed her hand on her temple, picked up her wallet and tried to hold back tears as she headed back to the house.

She felt strange being back in the house after everything that had happened. She quickly went into the kitchen and saw the broken glass that was all over the floor. She was feeling weak and wanted to grab something to eat while she was driving. As she reached for the refrigerator door, she saw a paper that Jessica had placed on the door with a magnet. There was a phone number and the name Tom Jones written in big, bold letters and a happy face written next to it. This was the man that was going to be hiring Jessica when she graduated. Suddenly Sam had an idea. She looked at her watch and saw that still had some time before the hospital would be moving her sister.

"I'm responsible for her getting hurt, but maybe there is something that I can do to help her." She quickly picked up the phone and dialed the number to Denver.

When the receptionist answered, Sam asked for Mr. Jones. Sam was only on hold for a minute.

"This is Tom Jones, may I help you?"

"Yes, sir. My name is Samantha Higgins. You recently hired my sister Jessica to start working for you in June. I wanted to let you know that she has been in a very serious car accident and might be in the hospital for some time. I know that there has been some correspondence back and forth between my sister and you, and I did not want her to lose this opportunity."

"Yes, I do remember your sister. Is she going to be alright?"

"I don't know yet. She is being airlifted to a hospital in Quincy and I am on my way there now. Mr. Jones, I just want to make sure that this won't affect her new job. Will she still have a job waiting for her once she has recovered from this?" Sam bit her nail, waiting for his response. He was silent for a moment and Sam heard some paper being shuffled in the background.

"Well, Ms. Higgins, we do appreciate your calling to inform us of this unfortunate incident. We have waited a long time to find just the right person for this position and we strongly believe that your sister fits that bill. Please give our best wishes to her when you are able to and rest assured that the job will be hers once she is ready. We will be anxiously awaiting her recovery."

Sam sighed in relief. "Thank you, sir. I will let you know as soon as I can what is happening and what the time frame we will be looking at will be. Thank you so very much."

"Thank you for your call, Ms. Higgins."

Sam hung up the phone and took in a deep breath. She released it slowly and then went to her sister's bedroom. She grabbed an overnight bag and filled it with some of Jessica's clothing and makeup. She started to leave her room but stopped and ran back to her bed where she grabbed a teddy bear lying by her pillow. She then went to her own room and filled another bag with a few of her own things. She took one last look around the house and then went back out to the car. She put the bags in the trunk and headed to the hospital.

CHAPTER 52

When Sam reached the hospital, she checked to make sure her sister had arrived and checked on her condition. As she drove to the hospital, Sam tried to figure out how she was going to tell their mother. She finally decided she would wait until someone told her exactly what was going on. She didn't want to worry her mother any more than she needed to and at the moment, Sam still did not know just how badly Jessica was hurt.

Sam went to a pay phone and pulled out her calling card. She looked at the sergeant's business card and said a quick prayer. As she dialed his number she could feel her heart racing.

"This is Sergeant D'Vincio, how may I help you?"

"Sergeant, this is Samantha Higgins again."

"Hello, Ms. Higgins, what can I do for you?"

"I'm sorry to bother you, but I thought you might want to know that my sister is in the hospital. She was hit by a car." Sam started to cry again and had to stop for a moment to regain control of her emotions.

"I am really sorry to hear that, Samantha."

"Sergeant, the reason that I am calling is that a witness who saw the accident said that a van with Colorado license plates had hit my sister and then left the scene. I'm positive that it was Kyle."

"Why don't you give me the license plate number and I will check into it for you. How do you know it was Kyle?"

"I saw the van before, back when he was first following me. It was last Valentine's Day in fact, when he left me the rose that I told you about. If you remember the letter he had written me, he referred back to the rose again. Anyway, besides the fact that no one had ever seen the van before, it also had Colorado plates."

"Well, go ahead and give me the license plate number and the phone number where I can reach you. I also want to see if we have anything on file on Kyle."

Sam read him the license plate number and told him to have her paged at the emergency room lobby. After she hung up with him, she dialed Austin's number.

"Hello," he answered.

"Austin, it's Sam."

"Hey there. I must have left a million messages on your answering machine. Where have you been?"

"Austin, I'm at the hospital in Quincy. Jessica was hit by a car."

He sounded shocked. "What happened?"

"She had just run outside for some reason when it happened. There was a witness who described that same van that I had seen on Valentine's Day. And the plates were from Colorado. Austin, it was Kyle."

She heard Austin take a deep breath. "I'm on my way, you hang in there." He hung up and Sam leaned back, relieved. It would be a lot easier to handle everything with Austin by her side.

Sam sat in the waiting area, flipping through magazines for over an hour before a doctor finally came out to see her. When she saw him approaching, she stood up.

"Samantha Higgins? I'm Dr. Martin."

"Doctor, is my sister going to be alright?"

Dr. Martin looked very seriously at Sam. "Your sister has a fractured femur," he explained, "which is basically the thigh bone. We will need to do surgery to place pins in the damaged area."

Sam looked worriedly at the doctor. "How long will she be in surgery?"

"This type of surgery typically lasts about an hour and a half, if there are no complications. She has also sustained a concussion and we were worried at first about possible head injuries."

Sam took a deep breath. "Do you know how long she will have to be in the hospital?"

"I'm sorry, but it is too soon to say. I'm sure that she will be here for at least two weeks."

Sam looked surprised. "Two weeks?"

"There are a couple of things that we will need to watch for, Ms. Higgins. One, of course, is the possibility of infection after the surgery. We could also see a problem with an embolism."

"What's that?" Sam asked.

"You have what are called fat embolisms inside your bone marrow, and when you break a bone, these embolisms can travel through the blood and get into your lungs."

"What would happen to her if that happens?" Sam was trying to keep her composure while she listened to the doctor.

"Don't worry about that, Ms. Higgins; she will be here where we will be able to watch her closely. If either problem exists, we will be able to take

174

care of her. There is something else about your sister that I need to discuss with you, though." Sam looked up at him with a panic look in her eyes. "Don't worry, it is nothing life threatening. Your sister has some facial lacerations. This is not physically serious now, but she will need some plastic surgery later on in the future. I can tell you that the plastic surgery will happen in stages and your sister may have a hard time dealing with it psychologically. This kind of situation can be very traumatic, especially in younger women. I wanted to mention this to you ahead of time so that your family can start to prepare for it now."

"Thank you, doctor. When can I see her?"

"Well, we are prepping her for surgery now. You can see her about an hour after her surgery."

"Thank you again, doctor."

Just as the doctor was walking away, Austin appeared. Sam fell into his arms, relieved that he was there. Up until now she had managed to hold up her strength, but now she needed someone to hold her up. Austin waited for a moment and then he pulled away from Sam and asked her about Jessica.

"Well," she took a deep breath. "The doctor told me so much, I am not totally sure of everything that has happened to her. From what he told me, it sounds like she has a fractured thigh bone and a pretty messed up face. They are getting ready to put her into surgery for her fracture. She is going to be here for about two weeks, Austin."

Austin took her hand and led her to a seat that was in the waiting area. "I said a prayer for her on the way over here. I know she will be just fine. Let's just hope for a quick recovery. Have you called your mom yet?"

Sam shook her head. "I didn't want to call her until I could find something out about Jess's condition. It is going to be traumatic enough for her to find out that Jess was in an accident, but at least I can let her know that she will be ok. I better go call her now, though."

Austin touched her arm reassuringly and then watched as Sam walked up to the pay phone. Her face stayed serious and she fought back her own tears as she listened to her mother get hysterical on the other end. When she hung up the phone she walked back over to Austin.

"She's going to get the first flight out she can," she said as he approached her.

Sam sighed and as soon as they sat down she rested her head against his shoulder. They sat there for about three hours and then the doctor finally came out to say that she could see her sister.

"Only one visitor at a time though, please," the doctor said, "and only direct family members for right now."

Austin squeezed her hand for encouragement and then she followed the doctor to the recovery room.

"She is still out from the surgery, but you can see her for a few minutes. We will let you know what room we will be moving her to," Dr. Martin explained to her as he led her to the room where Jessica was recovering.

Sam smiled weakly at the doctor and then entered the room. If he had not pointed to where Jessica was, Sam would have never recognized her. She had tubes everywhere and her face was worse than Sam could have ever possibly imagined. Her face was several different colors and it was completely swollen. There were also several slashes across her cheeks and chin. Her sister looked like something out of a horror movie.

Sam dropped down in the chair that was next to her sister's bed and she put her hand on Jessica's arm.

"I am so sorry, sis. Please forgive me." She brought her hands up to her face and silently watched her sister until the nurse tapped on her shoulder and asked her to go back out to the lobby. Sam stood up and wiped a tear from her cheek.

"Please, God, let her be ok," she whispered and then she walked back out into the lobby.

CHAPTER 53

Sam was sitting with Austin, feeling helpless, when she heard her name being called out. "Samantha Higgins, please pick up the courtesy phone. Samantha Higgins, you have a call on the courtesy phone."

Sam went over to the phone and picked it up.

"Ms. Higgins, this is Sergeant D'Vincio."

"Hello, Sergeant. I hope you have some good news for me."

"I don't think you are going to like what I have to say." Sam sighed and he continued. "First of all, the plates on that van were reported stolen about a week before Valentine's Day. Our only hope there is that, if we can find that van, Kyle will have left his fingerprints somewhere inside of it. That will, of course, help towards the evidence we will need to connect him to your sister's accident. We are just lucky that there was a witness.

"I also found out some other information that I think you should know about. Apparently Kyle has been in jail before on assault and battery charges."

"What happened?" Sam's heart was racing as she listened.

"I don't know all of the details, but apparently police were called out to a home where Kyle ended up being detained due to violent behavior. He spent the night in jail but then there were never any formal charges. The female who had been abused never pressed charges."

Sam shook her head. "I know how that girl must have felt. You are too scared to do what you know is right. When you are being abused, you just don't think rationally."

"That isn't all I found. Kyle is also wanted for questioning in the death of his mother. About three years ago around Christmas time, his mother was found murdered. She was living in a secluded area back east and apparently the police had not found her body for practically two months after she died. Although Kyle was never officially named as a suspect, police have wanted to question him. Unfortunately they have never been able to locate him."

Sam stood there listening to the sergeant and felt overwhelmed and almost sick to her stomach. She had to sit down as she felt she might otherwise fall to the floor. She could not believe she had gotten herself into this situation.

As she thought about what he had just said, something came to her mind.

"Sergeant, when I had first moved in with Kyle around three years ago, I remember that he had gone to visit his mother, but had come back early saying that he had gotten in an argument with her. Although he had never spoken about it again, you could tell that something had been bothering him for quite some time after that."

Sergeant D'Vincio cleared his throat. "Samantha, I am not going to beat around the bush. I wish that I had checked into this situation when you first came to me, because this man could be very dangerous. Is there any possible way that after your sister gets released from the hospital, that both of you could come back to Denver for a while? I'm sure that you probably won't want to leave there, but I think that at this point, the safest thing for you to do is come here where I can watch over you and try to help you. We are still faced with the problem of finding enough proof to nail this guy."

Sam turned around and looked back at Austin. He was flipping through a magazine and looking at his watch. He glanced up and smiled at Sam.

"Samantha, are you still there?" the sergeant asked.

"I'm sorry. It's just that we both have a lot here that is definitely worth staying for, Sergeant, but with Kyle wandering around, what's the point." Sam sighed. "I will figure out a way to get my sister and myself back to Denver as soon as possible. If anything, I would feel better having her closer to home."

"Good. Now I have made some calls and I am sending someone out there to stay with you. I strongly recommend that you do not go back to your sister's house for any reason. We will worry about your things later. Do you have any questions?"

Sam was surprised that suddenly he was going to so much trouble for her. "You are sending someone out here from Denver?"

"Well, not exactly. I have a friend that lives not too far from there. Let's just say he owes me."

Sam laughed and rubbed her neck. "I really appreciate all that you are doing for me. Will you please call me if you hear anything else?"

"Of course, and you let me know if anything else happens out there."

They said goodbye and she hung up. She walked back over to Austin and then sat down. Austin watched her face closely.

"Don't tell me that they are still not going to do anything about this guy."

"No, Austin, this time they are going to do something. Apparently Kyle has been in some trouble before and the police have been looking for him. I could have told them myself that he was dangerous; I have learned that firsthand."

178

Austin was relieved. "So what do they want you to do?"

Sam looked at Austin, dreading what she was about to say. "He wants us to go back to Denver. He thinks he can help us more there and that we might even be safer."

Austin sat back in his chair and looked away, shocked at what she had just told him. What could he possibly say to her? He had not anticipated that she would have to leave.

"Austin, I know how you feel about long distance relationships, but I hope you will still at least write to me. I'm sure that once this is all over with we can see each other again."

Austin did not say anything for a while. Sam kept looking at him, hoping and almost willing him to try to be optimistic, but instead he only looked away from her. He finally stood up and when he spoke, he avoided looking directly at her. "Look, I'm going to go and see if I can catch your mother at the airport. Her plane should be arriving soon and she'll need a ride to the hospital." He turned and, without waiting for her to respond, he quickly rushed off.

Sam sat back against her seat and the tears once again started to flow down her cheeks. Austin had not even asked which flight her mother would be arriving on.

Kyle was once again ruining her life.

CHAPTER 54

Austin found Sam's mother and dropped her off at the hospital and then left, saying that he had some things to take care of. As happy as Sam was to see her mother, she was also quite upset that Austin had not stayed.

Once Jessica's condition had stabilized, she was moved into a private room and Sam and her mother were both relieved to finally be able to sit with her.

It was not until the day after her surgery that Jessica fully woke up. Sam had been standing next to Jess's bed talking with their mother, when they both noticed Jessica stir. She looked from her mother to her sister and then smiled.

"Hi, guys; what's up," Jessica said weakly.

Sam and her mother smiled and for a short while, Jessica talked to them like she was at home. Suddenly her face changed and she looked around the room.

"I'm sure that this is going to sound really strange, but where am I?"
Sam took her sister's hand and smiled at her. "Don't worry, Jess. You are in a hospital, but you are going to be just fine."

"A hospital? What am I doing in a hospital? The last thing I remember was that I was trying to get you to stop the car because you had forgotten your wallet."

Sam flinched and then looked helplessly at her mother. Their mother stood up, walked around to the other side of the bed, and sat down next to Jessica.

"Honey, when you ran out to get your sister, you were hit by a van."

Jessica looked from her mother to her sister, hoping that one of them would tell her that this was all a joke. Instead, they both just looked at her sympathetically.

Jessica sighed. She was still pretty groggy and she was not sure how to respond. "So, what's the damage?"

Sam told her what Dr. Martin had said, although she left out the part about the plastic surgery. The doctor would be telling her that himself when he felt she was ready to hear it.

Jessica cried for a while and then she finally calmed down and relaxed.

"I just wish I could remember something. Did they catch the guy who did this to me?"

Sam panicked as she did not know quite what to tell her. She was about to say something when the doctor came into the room, sending Sam and her mother back out to the waiting area for a while. Sam sighed with relief that she did not have to tell her anything quite yet. Sam looked at her mom and was amazed how calm and in control she seemed.

"I'm so glad you are here, Mom!"

Her mom took her hand and they walked down the hallway together.

"I don't know how I would have gotten through all of this without you," she said as they walked. "I can't believe everything that has happened. When does it all stop?"

Her mom put her arm around her daughter's shoulders and they stopped walking. She touched a strand of Sam's hair and smiled. "We have been through hard times before, Sam, and we will get through this, too. You know, it is said that love and faith can carry us through the hardest of times. When we are on our knees because the weight on our shoulders is too heavy a hand reaches out and takes our hand and lifts us to our feet. Then hugs from miles away keep us standing. It has been hard being so far away physically from you girls, but I have been at your side in spirit and my love will always surround you and try to bring you strength."

Sam was speechless. She had never heard her mother speak like that before. Her mother saw the look on her face and laughed. "I love you both very, very much. All I am saying is that we are here for each other and our love will get us through this."

"Mom, we may have to come home to Colorado for awhile. Would it be ok if I stayed at the house while we are there?" Sam felt a connection with her mom that she had not felt for a very long time. She had a feeling that everything was going to be ok. Her mom squeezed her hand as if for reassurance.

"It is your home too, Sam. It always has been, you just haven't realized that for a long time." They started walking slowly back towards Jessica's room when the doctor motioned that they could go back in.

When they walked in her room, Jessica was in good spirits again and was more alert.

"Is this the same girl that we just saw a few minutes ago? Boy, what did the doctor give you? Whatever it was, I want some," Sam said obnoxiously.

Jessica laughed and when they saw the strange look that their mother was giving them, they both started to laugh together.

"You know, it smells like a garden in here," Jessica said, smiling at her family. "So who are all the flowers from, anyway?" She glanced around the room again, surprised to see so many beautiful floral arrangements all around her room.

Sam walked around the room, reading all of the cards to her. Of course they were mostly from her family and Austin, but there was one arrangement that was from the people at her new office, and that touched Jessica. Sam noticed the look on her sister's face and she told her that her job was still waiting for her.

Jessica took her sister's hand. "Thanks, Sami."

Sam smiled, but did not say anything. She wanted to update her on everything, but the doctor had asked that she not tell her for a couple of days. He wanted to make sure she was totally stabilized first. Sam felt drained from everything that was happening and did not want her sister sensing her stress.

The man Sergeant D'Vincio had sent to keep an eye on them arrived later that day. His name was Rick and he was the biggest man that Sam had ever seen. Sam watched him as he introduced himself. He was well over six feet tall with large, broad shoulders. His arms and chest seemed to be pure muscle and Sam had to resist the urge to reach out and touch his chest. She tried not to laugh as she saw how his powerful body contrasted his small beady eyes and large nose. She realized that she was not paying attention to him and she forced herself to listen to what he was now saying to her.

In order to alleviate suspicion, they were to introduce him as a concerned uncle who had come to see Jessica. The sergeant was pretty sure, however, that Kyle would not try anything while Jessica was in the hospital. There were too many people surrounding them at all times.

It did not take long for Sam to get used to Rick following her around everywhere, although it did bother Austin when he happened to be there. A few days after the accident, for instance, Sam had gone downstairs to the cafeteria and Austin had gone with her. He was acting edgy and irritable and kept glancing back at Rick, who was following closely behind.

"Why do you need this guy, Sam? Why can't I be your bodyguard? I would look a lot less suspicious than Mr. Monster over here. Besides, I probably won't be seeing you again after you leave."

Sam laughed. "Oh, settle down, Austin. He knows what he is doing and that is why I need him. If Kyle tries something, he will take care of it legally. If you were my body guard and Kyle did something, you would probably end up in jail with him." She grabbed his arm. "And quit being so down. You will see me again, I can promise you that."

Austin grumbled but did not say anything.

He watched Sam from the doorway of the cafeteria. He had stayed away from the hospital at first, but his obsession for Sam had overpowered him. He just had to see her and he could not wait any longer. Hitting Sam's sister in the road had caught him off-guard, although it was only an annoyance. He figured she probably deserved it anyway for trying to hide Sam from him.

He had found a place to hide out for a while until he could find a different vehicle and than he decided to risk seeing her. Today was the first time he had come to the hospital, and he watched her closely now. He was curious about the men who were with her. He recognized one from Valentine's Day and wondered who the other was. Was he a relative, from the police, or maybe she was seeing him, too. He did not like the idea of her being with these other men; she belonged to him and only him. He knew that he would have to punish her for not staying faithful to him. The longer he watched her, laughing and throwing her head back while the younger one spoke, the madder Kyle got. He could sneak up behind them and they would never know what hit them. He started to pull his switchblade out of his pant pocket when he noticed the larger man who was with Samantha turn and look in his direction. What is going on here? Kyle did not like the feeling he got from that man and decided that he must be a cop. He turned away and headed for the elevator.

"Don't think you outsmarted me, Samantha," he mumbled as he got onto the elevator. "This is just a temporary setback and I will have you back soon enough."

CHAPTER 55

Jessica had been in the hospital for a week and a half and was recovering wonderfully. Sam had finally decided that it was time to tell her about how they would have to move back to Denver. She doubted that Jess would take it too hard since her new job was out there anyway.

Their mom took Rick outside of the room and Sam smiled warmly at her sister and she walked up to her.

"Hey sis, how are you feeling today?"

Jessica smiled, but Sam could tell by the look in her eyes that she was worn out. "They let me see my face this morning, Sami. Dr. Martin told me that the plastic surgery I am going to need will be a pretty long, drawn out process."

Sam sat next to her sister on the edge of the hospital bed. "Yeah, he had already told me, and we will all be standing by you. Besides, you know doctors. They always tend to give you the worst case scenario."

Jessica smiled and took her sister's hand. "Yeah, I know. I just keep praying that God will give me the strength to get through this."

Sam smiled and then decided that she needed to tell her sister what was going on. "Jess, I need to talk to you about some things. Are you up to it?"

"Let me guess, it must be about Austin. How come he has not been coming around very much, anyway? Did you two get in a fight again?"

"No, not exactly. He is mad because you and I have to leave and go back to Denver." Sam watched the look of surprise on her sister's face.

"What are you talking about? Even though I can't finish my classes right now, you still have a month of school left that you need to finish this semester, not to mention the two years you are still going to need to graduate. How are you supposed to do that and why would you want to go back to Denver now anyway?"

"We both have to go back, Jess. Sergeant D'Vincio found out that Kyle is a very dangerous man and he wants us where he can protect us."

"Is Rick a part of this little scheme? I heard Mom telling a nurse that he was a distant uncle who lived in the area, but I knew better. It seemed kind of strange that some uncle that I have never heard of suddenly is taking an interest in my health. Especially when all he does is follow you around everywhere."

Sam laughed. "Yeah, he is supposed to be looking out for us in case Kyle tries anything here. I guess he will be personally escorting us to the airport, too."

"Wow. I bet Austin isn't taking this very well. No wonder he has been acting so strange."

Sam looked down at her hands. "He doesn't like long distance relationships and from the way he is acting, I don't think that there is much hope for the future."

"I'm sorry, Sam. I don't mind heading back home now, though. I was thinking about doing it anyway. I talked to that manager, Tom Jones, from my new job and as soon as I am ready, he said that I can start to work part-time if I want to. That way I can start at my new job and still finish school out there when I am ready. After I had talked to him I wondered how I was going to tell you that I would be leaving, but you beat me to it. Enough about me, though, how are you dealing with all of this?"

"Jess, you know that this place has become my home." Sam looked down. "I had started to think that Austin and I would eventually even become more than good friends. Remember when he told me that he had feelings for me? Well, although he had never mentioned it again, it has always stuck with me. I guess now he will just find someone else."

"Don't give up on him, Sami. Things will work out."

The girls talked for a short while longer and then the doctor came into the room.

"Hello, girls. How are you feeling today, Jessica?"

"Just fine, doctor. We were just talking about when I might be getting released."

Dr. Martin smiled. "Well, let's look at your chart." He opened her chart and read it over. "You are really doing well, Jessica. I see no reason why we can't have you out of here by the weekend." He glanced over at Sam.

"I told her about going back to Denver," Sam told him.

He nodded. "Ok then, here is what I want you to do, Jessica. You are still going to be off of your feet for a while, so I need you to make arrangements to stay with someone. I also need you to set up a follow-up appointment with a doctor back in Denver for about six weeks from now. I can give you some names if you don't already have a family doctor. Other than that, I will check in on you in a couple of days and then we will take care of your release. Do you have any questions?"

Jessica shook her head. "No, sir."

"Great, then I will see you ladies later." He turned and left the room.

When the weekend arrived, Dr. Martin did as he had promised and released Jessica. Sam, Jessica, and their mother were to leave on a flight back to Denver that evening. Rick took them back to Jessica's house so that they could pack their things for the trip home. Sam tried several times to reach Austin, but he never answered his phone. She finally decided to write him a short letter. When she finished writing it, she read it over again.

"Dear Austin, I know that you have been upset about my leaving, but I would have really liked to have seen you before I left. By the time you read this, I will be on a plane heading back to Denver. I hope that you will not forget about me. I just wanted you to know that I care very deeply for you and I hope that you will write to me. Take care of yourself, Austin. Love, Samantha."

She put the letter in an envelope and had Rick drive her to Austin's house. She ran up to his door, set the letter where he would see it, and then ran back to the car. She had tears running down her cheeks as they drove back to the house. The next thing Sam knew, she was on a plane heading for Denver. As she looked out at the clouds around them, Sam put her hand on the window and, as a single tear fell, she whispered *goodbye*.

PART III
Home Again

CHAPTER 56

After Sam and Jessica got settled in at their mother's house, Sam called Sergeant D'Vincio. When he answered, she told him that they were back in Denver and thanked him for having Rick watch over them.

"I'm glad you got home safely, Samantha."

Sam cleared her throat. "So, what's the next step, Sergeant?"

"Well, first of all, we are going to be working together a lot in the future; I want to make sure that you understand that."

Sam took a deep breath. "Yes, sir, I kind of figured it would have to be that way."

"The only thing I want to do right now is wait until Kyle realizes that you are back home. I am anticipating that it will take a while. Use this time to get organized, but do not make any permanent plans. Once Kyle realizes that you have come back to Denver, I am pretty sure that you mother's house will be the first place he will look. If you hear anything from him, you let me know immediately, do you understand?"

"Yes, sir. You don't think that he will try to come in the house and harm us, do you?"

"From the way he has acted so far, he will call first to see if you are there. After that he might try something, but at this point it is hard to say. I would prefer that you let your mother answer the phone for right now."

"Ok, I will call you if I hear anything."

"I hate to say this, Samantha, but you will hear from him eventually and you need to prepare yourself for when that happens."

Two months passed and Sam had not heard from Kyle. She often wondered where he was and what he must be thinking. She just hoped that his not being able to find her would not fuel the fire that was already burning inside of him. One afternoon Jessica brought the subject up.

"I can't believe that creep Kyle has not tried to reach you here yet. He managed to find you in a small town in Missouri, but he hasn't figured out that you are home yet. Sounds kind of strange to me."

"I know, I have been thinking a lot about that, too. I often wonder if he is back in Missouri or Illinois looking for me. I don't think he will stay out there too much longer though. Especially when he sees your new tenants moving in your house." Sam stretched. "I think I am going to go out and check the mail, I'll be right back."

She patted her sister on the shoulder and walked outside. It was a beautiful summer day and Sam stopped to look at the flowers her mom had planted and to listen to the birds sing. She closed her eyes and felt the sun on her face. She stood there for a moment and then opened her eyes and walked down to the mailbox. She took out the mail and glanced through the letters. Suddenly she stopped and smiled excitedly; there was a letter from Austin. Sam took the mail into the house, set it down on her mother's kitchen counter, and took Austin's letter back to her room. She sat down on her bed and tore the envelope open.

"My darling Sam," she read. "I am so sorry I have waited so long to write to you. I have been going out of my mind trying to decide what to write. How do you express your feelings on a piece of paper?

"I know that I have told you a million times how much I hate long distance relationships, but this is different. I just cannot stop thinking about you. When I am awake, you are all I see and when I am sleeping, it is you that I dream about. I don't know how long I can be away from you, but for now I believe that I belong here.

"I hope you can forgive me for the way I acted before you left. I could kick myself for avoiding you! Now, I would give anything to see you and to touch your beautiful golden hair.

"I guess I probably sound pretty silly, but this whole crazy experience has changed me. I have been doing a lot of thinking and I really feel like I am starting to appreciate things a little differently.

"Again, I hope you accept my apology. Please be careful, Sam, and take good care of yourself and your family. Please also try to keep me up to date on what is happening with the police and that crazy guy Kyle. I will write to you again soon. All my love, Austin."

Sam held the letter against her chest. She had been so sure that she would lose him because of her having to leave, but he was willing to wait for her. She got up, walked to her desk, and pulled out some stationery. She wrote Austin a letter letting him know how happy she was that he still cared about her.

"Times are tough now," she wrote, "but have faith and God will reward us." She finished the letter and ran back into the kitchen where her mother was starting to cook dinner.

"Mom, can I borrow a stamp? I need to mail this letter."

"Sure, honey, there should be some in my purse."

Sam found a stamp and ran back outside to put the letter in the mailbox. She put the flag up and then touched the mailbox tenderly. She smiled to herself and then turned to go back into the house.

CHAPTER 57

It was Thanksgiving morning and Sam still had not heard from Kyle. Jessica was finally up on her feet, although she still had a limp. She had also been going to a cosmetic surgeon and was due to start receiving treatments at the beginning of the year. She came hobbling into the kitchen and announced that she would be going to school in January.

"I'm so happy for you, Jess," Sam said. "You will finally get to graduate."

"Yeah. And my surgery should not get in the way of my classes. I am going to wait until I finish the semester before I go back to work, though. It would just be too much to deal with school, the surgeries, and starting a new job. Luckily my boss is not in a hurry. So what about you, Sami? When are you planning to go back to school, or are you?"

"I am hoping that I can start back next fall."

"Are you going to finish here or go back to Missouri?"

Sam looked at her sister and smiled. "I'll cross that bridge when I get there, sis."

The telephone started to ring and without thinking, Sam ran into the kitchen to answer it. "Hello?"

"Sam? This is Austin. Happy Thanksgiving!"

Sam smiled. "Hello there, stranger. Are you back at the school?"

"Where else would I be?"

Sam laughed. "I wish you could be here."

"I wish I could be there too. Yesterday, I was sitting in the library looking out the window and thinking about you. It reminded me of when we first met. I really miss you, Sami."

"I miss you too, Austin."

Austin cleared his throat. "So, have you heard from you know who?"

"Surprisingly enough, I haven't. I would have though that he would have called by now."

"Well, maybe it didn't occur to him that you had already gone home. He has probably been looking for you out here because he knew that you were going to school here. He probably still thinks that you are out here somewhere."

"Yeah, you are probably right."

They talked for a while and when they finally hung up, Sam felt like she was floating. She started to leave the kitchen when the phone started to ring again.

"Oh, Austin, you just can't say goodbye, can you," Sam said as she ran back to the phone. "Hello," her voice rang out.

"Hello, Samantha. Don't you sound cheery this morning?"

Sam felt as if her heart had stopped. Kyle had finally found her.

"What's wrong, darlin'? Cat got your tongue?" He laughed. "I don't know where you have been hiding out lately, but I always know where to find you for the holidays. Really, Samantha, you are just so predictable. Always running home to Mommy." He started laughing again.

Sam caught her breath. "What do you want, Kyle?" she asked in a calm but cold voice.

"Oh, it's not what I want, it's what I am going to get. And that, my love, is you. Eat, Samantha, and be merry, because soon enough happiness will only be a memory."

Sam slammed down the phone. *How dare he*, she thought to herself. She was surprised at how calm she was and she straightened herself up as Jessica slowly entered the kitchen. She had heard the commotion and had been worried about her sister.

"What's wrong, Sami?"

"He found me, sis. I better call the sergeant." Sam looked at her sister and frowned. "Will you stay here with me while I call him?"

Jessica smiled at her sister. "I'll be right here next to you."

Sam called the police station and asked them to page him immediately. Five minutes later, the phone was ringing. Sam handed the phone to Jessica.

"Hello," she answered. She held the phone back out towards her sister. "It's ok."

Sam took the phone and explained to the sergeant about the brief phone call.

"Samantha, I thought I had told you not to answer the phone." He sighed. "Well, maybe it is better this way; at least we know now that he knows where you are. I am going to send a couple of my men to keep an eye on your house. The way Kyle has been doing things, I would guess that he will make his move sometime during the holidays. He really seems to love the holidays, doesn't he? For now, I want you to write down everything that he says to you. Maybe we will be able to figure out what he is planning to do next."

Sam bit her nail. "I have a small tape recorder that I used for school. Maybe I will be able to get him on tape."

"If you do that, be careful of what you say to him. If we end up being able to use any of that tape in court, what you say could either help you or hurt you. Trying to catch and keep a guy like this can be very tricky, so we have to be careful. Right now all we have is circumstantial evidence and we need something more concrete. See if you can get him to talk about his mother or what happened to your sister. Are you going to be ok, Samantha?"

Sam looked at her sister who smiled back at her. "Yes, sir. I have my family here and they will keep me strong."

"Ok. Call me as soon as you hear from Kyle again."

Sam hung up the phone and took a deep breath. She squeezed her sister's hand. "We are going to get him, Jess. Somehow, we will get him and everything will be ok."

CHAPTER 58

Thanksgiving came and went peacefully, and that December Sam turned twenty-one years old. On the morning of her birthday, Sam stood before the mirror, looking at herself. There were circles under her eyes from all of the nights that she had lain awake in anticipation of Kyle causing problems. She kept waiting for him to call or leave a note somewhere again, and it was driving her crazy waiting. Sam looked at herself again in the mirror.

"Sami girl, for being twenty-one, you sure look to be about forty," she said to her reflection and then she shook her head. She put on some sweats, put her hair up in a ponytail, and headed for the kitchen. Her sister and mother were waiting there for her to wake up.

"Happy birthday, Samantha," they said together.

Sam laughed. "Thanks, but I was hoping that you guys would have forgotten."

"Oh, we remembered," Jessica said. "And we made you breakfast. Well, actually Mom made you breakfast. I was afraid that if I cooked, you would not have eaten it," she said laughing.

Sam hugged them both and sat down at the kitchen table. Her mom carried over the plate and Sam watched her in surprise. "Wow! An omelet, sausage, bacon, toast and even honeydew melon. I need to have more birthdays," she said as she eyed the food hungrily.

"Hold on, we aren't quite ready yet." She walked around the counter and then came back with a candle, which she stuck right in the middle of the omelet. Sam laughed.

"Well, it's too early for cake," Jessica explained.

They talked while she ate and then Sam opened her presents. Her mom had bought her a knit sweater and Jessica's gift to her was a beautiful gold bracelet. Sam was thanking them for the presents when the doorbell rang. Sam got up and went to the door and was greeted by a man holding a large white box.

"Samantha Higgins," the man asked. She nodded and he handed her the box. "Have a nice day, ma'am."

Sam carried the box into the living room and set it on the floor. Jessica

195

and their mother walked in from the kitchen.

"Who was it, Sami?" Jessica asked, noticing the box. "Wow! Who's that from?"

"I don't know." She opened the box and all three of them gasped. There were about three dozen red roses layered inside the box. "They are so beautiful," Sam whispered. She pulled out the card and read it aloud. *To the most beautiful woman I know on her 21st birthday. Love, Austin.* Sam smiled and then she ran into the kitchen to call him. She grabbed the phone and dialed his number, but he did not answer. She hung up and dialed again. While she was trying to reach him, the doorbell rang again.

Sam looked at the phone, frustrated that he was not home. "Austin," she mumbled, "where are you?"

"I'm right behind you."

Sam jumped and turned around to see Austin standing in the kitchen doorway, smiling at her. "Oh, my God, you're here!" She said as she dropped the phone and ran to him. "Oh, my God, you're here," she said again, but with a panicky tone as she looked down at her sweats and realizing that she had no makeup on and her hair was a mess.

He laughed and grabbed her and hugged her tight. "I'm actually only here for the day. I wanted to take you out for your birthday, but then I have to get back and study for finals."

"You scared me half to death standing behind me like that," she said with a smile as she tapped him lightly on his arm. Then she looked up at him. "Thank you for the beautiful flowers. I can't believe that you flew all the way out here just to spend the day with me. You are incredible, Mr. Sinclair, do you know that?"

Austin smiled and gently touched Sam's face. "And you are beautiful, Ms. Higgins. Man, have I missed you."

Sam blushed, and then they slowly walked out to join Sam's family. They talked for about an hour and Austin pulled lightly on Sam's ponytail.

"You better go get changed so we can get going. I have our entire day filled."

Sam smiled and then she remembered that she still had not put on any makeup yet. "Why didn't someone remind me that I look like I just woke up?" she said as she blushed again and rushed out of the room. She heard everyone laughing as she headed down the hall.

"Ok, Austin is wearing jeans so I have to wear that pair of jeans that Jessie says looks good on me. Where is it?" She mumbled as she searched her closet. She decided to wear the new sweater that her mom had bought her for her birthday as well. She put on some makeup and light perfume and fixed her hair. She checked herself one last time in the mirror and smiled at her reflection.

"Ok, now you look more like twenty-one." She grabbed her purse and went back to the living room. When they walked outside, Sam was surprised to see a limousine parked in front of the house. She looked up at Austin in surprise and he smiled.

"Only the best for you, my darling."

"Oh, Austin, you should have told me. Here I was taking my time getting ready and there was a limo waiting for us. I'm sorry."

Austin laughed. "Don't worry. I anticipated that we would be here visiting for a while so I had the driver leave and then come back."

Sam was relieved. He helped her into the car and then told the driver to head downtown.

"It is still pretty early. Do you want to walk around for a while?"

Sam smiled as she rested her head against him. "I would love to. It seems like forever since I have been downtown. It is so pretty in the winter time."

After about twenty minutes, the driver dropped them off and Austin talked to him about the time and place they would meet him later. He walked up to Sam and looked up at the sky. "I hope it doesn't snow. Are you warm enough?"

Sam zipped up her jacket and put her gloves on. "I'm ok. We'll warm up when we start walking. Besides, it is still early. Maybe it will warm up more as the day goes on."

Austin zipped up his own coat and then he took one of Sam's hands in his own. She looked up at him warmly and they started walking. They laughed and talked as they walked along the outdoor mall. Sam would stop and look in the shop windows and point out things that she liked. It was overcast and they could still see the decorative lights that hung along the businesses and trees.

"This is so beautiful, isn't it?" Sam mused as they strolled along the sidewalk.

Austin smiled and squeezed her hand. They walked a little further and then they came up to a horse drawn carriage.

"Oh, I have always wanted to ride in one of these," Sam said as she watched the beautiful horse. The horse lifted its front leg slightly and Austin pulled Sam close to him.

"Your wish is my command," he said into her hair as he hugged her close.

She laughed. "You are bad," she said. She felt so comfortable with him at that moment and she loved the feeling of being close to him. She felt something stir inside of her and slowly pulled away. He helped her up onto the carriage and handed the driver some money. When he sat back next to Sam he pulled her close to her again.

"Oh look," he said suddenly sitting forward. "Champagne."

Sam's face froze when she saw the bottle. She could picture Kyle popping the cork on the champagne bottle after he had viciously raped her. She tried to push the nightmare back into the darkness of her mind but found herself pulling away from Austin.

"What's wrong, Sam? Are you alright?" he asked as he watched the look on her face.

Sam tried to smile. "Nothing, Austin. I am just surprised by everything you have done. You really are wonderful."

Austin could see the clouds in her eyes, and could tell by the tone of her voice that he had lost the moment. He set the bottle back where it was and leaned back. He turned his face away from her and sighed deeply. After a few tense moments, Sam straightened her shoulders and reached over to take Austin's hand. He looked down at their hands and then back up at her and she smiled.

"I know I can't get rid of the bad memories overnight, but eventually I will. In the meantime, I have new and wonderful memories in the making right now. I really do appreciate all of this. This is the best birthday I could ever have imagined. Although just having you here would have been enough," she said and she knew in her heart that she meant every word.

Sam could feel the cool air on her cheeks as they rode around downtown and suddenly the sun started to slightly peak out from behind the clouds. There was still some snow on the ground and it glistened in the sunlight. *It's like a winter wonderland,* Sam thought as she rested her head on Austin's shoulder.

After the carriage ride, Austin bought her lunch at an underground café called Hidden Venus. As they walked into the restaurant Sam had to adjust her eyes to the dim lighting inside. As they were led to a table Sam looked around at the other people who were eating. It was a cozy atmosphere and almost romantic.

When they sat down Austin was quiet as he watched the soft glow of the lights on Sam's hair. She was looking down at her menu and then glanced up to see Austin watching her and she blushed. He smiled and then before he could say anything a waiter appeared. Austin gave him their order and then he sat back against his seat watching Sam. There was soft music playing and Austin asked Sam if she would like to dance.

Sam looked around embarrassed. "But no one is dancing."

"So?" he said as he stood up and held out his hand for her. She giggled nervously and then she took his hand. When he pulled her close to him she was almost afraid of the feelings she had inside of her. She glanced up at Austin for a moment and he smiled tenderly at her. She leaned her head against his chest and closed her eyes, trying to forget about her fears. After a short time she slowly pulled away from him and their eyes locked. She thought for a moment that he was going to kiss her, but instead he smiled again and led her back to her seat.

After their lunch, he surprised her by taking her ice skating in the park. She laughed as she watched Austin trying to skate around while she put her skates on. It came as no surprise to Sam when he finally admitted to her that he had never really learned how to ice skate. They both had to hold each other up most of the time and they laughed so hard that they finally had to sit down.

"Somehow I don't think we should have done this right after lunch," Sam said as she laughed again. "I have laughed so hard my stomach hurts."

Austin laughed and sat down next to her. "I really like it here, Sam. The atmosphere is a lot better than back in LA. I don't know if I would have felt as comfortable doing this out there." He laughed again. "Next time I may have to take lessons, though."

Sam laughed. "I haven't gone ice skating since I was a child. My mom put me in lessons, but I didn't stay in it very long. I guess you could probably tell that, though, right?"

Austin laughed and squeezed her hand. "We better head back or we might miss our ride home."

Sam was quiet as they walked back to where the limousine was waiting. Austin noticed how quiet she was and when they got to the car he looked at her seriously. "What's wrong, Sam? Didn't you have a good birthday?"

Sam smiled up at Austin. "That's why I'm so depressed. I had such a wonderful time that I wish it didn't have to end."

Austin smiled and squeezed her hand again. They got back in the car and when they reached her mother's house, Sam asked him if he would like to come in.

Austin took her hand. "Unfortunately I have to get back to the airport. My time is up on this limo, and I am about to miss my plane."

"I could drive you to the airport," she said with hope in her eyes.

Austin looked into her eyes and softly touched her cheek. He smiled and then led her up to her front door. When they reached the door, Sam turned to look up at him and saw Kyle smiling back at her. She jumped back and shook her head as she tried to shake away the image she had seen. When she opened her eyes she saw Austin looking at her in surprise.

"Sami, what's wrong?"

She took a deep breath and tried to smile. "Nothing, Austin. I'm sorry. I guess I just got a cold chill for a moment." She knew that he did not have time to press the issue and she quickly thanked him for giving her such a wonderful birthday.

Austin watched her for a moment and then he leaned down and gently brushed his lips against hers. Although it took her by surprise, she did not push him away. They hugged tightly and then she waved as he walked back to the car. She was shivering slightly as she watched the limo go around the corner and disappear. Sam touched her lips and thought about all of the confusing feelings she was experiencing.

She tried to pull herself together and looked in the direction that the limo had just driven off to. She smiled softly and then turned and walked back into the house.

CHAPTER 59

As Christmas neared, Sergeant D'Vincio was convinced that Kyle was waiting until then to make his move. He almost seemed obsessed with finding Kyle and Sam was not sure whether to be grateful or worried. As the holiday approached, the sergeant was starting to make the necessary arrangements to protect Sam's family. The week before Christmas there were so many people coming in and out of the house that it was hard for Sam and her family to have their traditional celebration. The tree had gotten knocked down twice and the men kept eating everything that Sam and her family baked.

"Is this really necessary?" Sam's mom whispered in annoyance to Sam as she stepped out of the way of a man hurrying by. "I mean, it's not like Kyle is a killer or something."

"We don't know that, Mom. What if he killed his own mother? What would stop him from killing me or you guys? He ran Jessie down and didn't even blink. I think this is great that Sergeant D'Vincio is so adamant about finding him." Even as Sam said the words, she wondered why he really was doing so much for her.

On Christmas Eve the sergeant was sitting in their kitchen, hooking up a tracer to the phone line, when Sam walked in. She sat down and watched him for a moment.

"Shouldn't you be with your family for the holiday?" she asked him.

He stopped what he was doing and looked over at Sam. "I'm divorced and my daughter is spending Christmas with her mother this year. Right now my place is here, trying to catch this guy so that you and your family can get on with your lives. But thanks for your concern."

Sam winked at the tone in his voice. She decided to be bold and ask him what was going on. "If you don't mind my asking, why have you taken such an interest in catching Kyle now? At first you barely had any interest at all. I mean, come on. You don't spend every Christmas living in people's homes trying to catch every bad guy that comes along, do you?"

He took a deep breath. He pulled out his wallet and handed Sam a picture of a young girl. "That's my daughter, Theresa," he explained softly. "She is around your age and she was also attacked. We never found the scum that hurt her and I have never forgiven myself for it. Neither did my wife. She eventually left me. I think that they both expected that, because of who I am, that I could find the guy and take care of the situation. Instead, my daughter has lived in fear because the guy who hurt her is still living out of the streets." He shrugged. "I guess you can say that by catching Kyle, I am hoping that I can at least be at peace with myself that I helped someone out there. Besides," he said seriously again. "This is my job." He glanced down at his watch. "And now I better get back to it" He took his wallet back and immediately turned back to what he was doing.

Sam was touched at his honesty and smiled politely as she walked out of the kitchen. She did not know what to say to him about his daughter and her instincts told her that it would probably be best if she did not say anything at all to him about it. He was handling things within himself the best way he knew how and he seemed to have enough to worry about at the moment, anyway.

Sam wandered into the living room where her mother and Jessica were picking up broken ornaments from the floor.

"This is turning out to be a crazy Christmas this year. So much for traditions," Sam said as she sat down on the couch.

Sam's mother smiled and walked over to her. She sat down and took Sam's hand.

"This is all pretty crazy, isn't it? Hopefully it will all be over soon. Besides, sometimes traditions have to be temporarily broken. I almost got lost in all of this, too. But you know what? We can't forget what the true meaning of Christmas really is."

Sam hugged her mother. "Thanks, Mom. You always know what to say to make things better than what they seem."

Sergeant D'Vincio came out of the kitchen. "We are done hooking everything up. I will be the only one staying here tonight, and then the rest of my team will be joining me again in the morning. Would you mind if I stayed on your couch tonight?"

"Of course, Sergeant, as long as you understand that you will be joining us tonight when we sing carols and drink eggnog," Sam's mother said smiling. Jessica and Sam laughed at the surprised look on his face,

"Oh, I don't know. I mean, I don't want to intrude. Well, I mean we are already intruding, but…"

Sam laughed again. "We would be honored if you would join us for Christmas," she said smiling.

He smiled and his eyes lit up. "Well, that definitely beats being alone tonight. Thank you."

That night they all laughed and sang Christmas carols. They had decided to open their gifts that night, instead of waiting until Christmas morning when the police would be in and out of the house.

As Sam handed out the gifts, she handed a small box to the sergeant and he looked at her in surprise.

Sam smiled at him. "We wanted to show you how much we appreciate what you are trying to do for us. It's just a little something to say thank you," she explained.

He opened the box and smiled. "A money clip. Thank you, guys."

"Wait, read what we had inscribed," Jessica said laughing.

"Cool cop?" He read with a funny look on his face. Then he laughed. "You guys are too much." Then he pulled out a small wad of bills out of his pocket and slid them into the clip. He looked at it thoughtfully and then slid it into his pocket.

The rest of the night, they all tried to forget about the mounting tension as they anticipated Kyle's attempt to contact Sam. Christmas morning, however, everyone awoke tense and nervous. The sergeant's people started to arrive at seven o'clock and Sam made sure there was plenty of coffee. Once everything was set up, it got strangely silent. No one spoke as everyone sat and waited for something to happen.

At two o'clock in the afternoon the phone rang, causing them to jump. Sergeant D'Vincio gave Sam the signal and she answered the phone. She immediately relaxed.

"It's ok, Sergeant, it's my friend Austin," she explained, blushing.

"Keep it short, Samantha," he reminded her.

She talked to him for a few minutes and explained what was going on. Although Austin was worried, he felt reassured knowing that the police were there with her.

"This cop sure seems to have taken an interest in you, Sam. Are you sure it is only because of Kyle?" Austin asked her, sounding worried.

Sam laughed. "He has a personal interest in this case, Austin, but not because of me. His family was hurt by someone like Kyle. He is a good guy, don't worry," Sam said quietly in the phone.

"It is reassuring that you are being looked after. I wish I could be there, too. My mom flew out here for a couple of days on her way to New York. I didn't realize how much I have missed her."

The sergeant motioned for Sam to hang up. "I have to go, Austin. I will try to call you later when things calm down around here. Merry Christmas, Austin. I really miss you."

"I miss you, too. Call me later!"

The time continued to pass slowly and Kyle still had not called or come by the house. At eleven o'clock Christmas evening, Sergeant D'Vincio finally stood up and told everyone to pack up the equipment. He walked over to Sam and put his hand on her shoulder.

"Just because he did not do anything today, don't think that it's over. I don't know why he hasn't made his move yet, but as crazy as he is, I am sure he will still try to get a hold of you. Make sure and call me when he does, ok?"

Sam nodded and then sat back and watched him and his team pack up all of their equipment. It was one o'clock in the morning by the time everyone left. Sam turned to her mother and shook her head.

"I'm sorry, Mom. Your house was turned upside down and our Christmas was a total mess, and all for nothing."

Sam's mom stretched. "Honey, I would rather the house be a mess than that crazy man come after you again."

They said good night and headed for their rooms. Jessica had already gone to bed hours before. When Sam climbed into her bed, she looked up at the ceiling and sighed. It had been a long day, but she knew that the danger was not over yet.

CHAPTER 60

It was a few days after Christmas and Jessica had gone to see an old friend who was in town for the holidays. Sam was helping her mother clean the house when the phone rang. Sam went into the kitchen to answer it.

"Hello," she said.

"Did you miss me, baby?" It was Kyle.

Sam was not surprised by his call. "What do you want now, Kyle?"

"Oh, don't we sound annoyed." He laughed. "I like how you had all of the police in your house on Christmas."

Sam felt as if her heart had stopped.

"You didn't really think I would be stupid enough to fall for your little trap, did you?" He laughed again. "You are just so predictable, Samantha. I bet you had those police convinced that I would be showing up, too. I hope you feel bad for taking all of those people away from their families on Christmas, and all for nothing."

"Leave me alone, Kyle. Don't ever call me again," Sam said in a shaky voice.

Kyle laughed. "I'm afraid I just can't do that, darling. You see, you belong to me, or have you forgotten? You can call your little police friends, but it won't do you any good."

Sam slammed the phone down and then, with shaky hands, she dialed the sergeant. He had given her a different phone number so that she could reach him directly any time. When he answered, she told him about the conversation. She could hear him sigh.

"Sam, I think it would be a good idea if we get you out of your mother's house. As long as you are living there, you are putting your mother and sister in danger, too. If we get you in a place of your own, then Kyle will only concentrate on you. I have a new idea on how we might be able to get him, but before we go into that, we need to find you a different place to stay. Let me make all of the arrangements and I will call you back shortly."

Sam hung up the phone and then told her mother what was going on. Sam started to cry and her mother immediately came to her and held her. "Shhh. Don't cry, Samantha, everything will be ok. It will all be over soon."

"You know, Mom, it's not so much what he is saying to me that bothers me so much, but that he just won't stop. Granted, he was right that I felt horrible about having all of those police here on Christmas. It just seems like every time I start to relax, there he is again. It just gets me so unnerved, you know?"

"He knows that he is getting to you, Samantha, and you can't give him that satisfaction. Right now he feels like he has total control because he knows how to get to you."

"I know you're right, but I can't get myself to not get upset." She shook her head in frustration.

Sergeant D'Vincio called back and within an hour he was at their front door with a truck. "I have a safe place lined up for you to stay," he explained to her. "Let's get your things and get you over there right away. I don't want to take the chance that Kyle is watching you already." He turned to Sam's mother. "I am having one of my men watching the house for a few days. If Kyle calls again, let him know that Samantha is not living here anymore. We will take care of it from there."

Sam packed up a few of her things and handed them to the sergeant, who put them into the back of the truck. Once everything that she would need was in the truck, Sam went to her mother and hugged her. "I love you, Mom. Tell Jessica what happened, and I will try to call you guys as soon as I can." They hugged again and then Sam got into the truck. As they started to pull away from the house, Sam waved goodbye to her mother, hoping that everything really would be over soon.

CHAPTER 61

Sam was quiet as Sergeant D'Vincio drove her to what was to be her new home for awhile. He stopped the truck in front of a small apartment building.

"We use this place sometimes when we need a safe place to hide someone or for cases like this, where we want to entrap someone. It should work for now," he told her as they got out of the truck. He gathered some of her things and led her to one of the apartment doors.

"Here we are, Samantha." He pulled some keys out of his pants pocket and opened the door.

Sam walked in and quietly looked around. There was a bedroom, bathroom, living room and kitchen and each of the rooms were very small. She sat down on the couch and watched as he carried in the last of her things.

He took a deep breath, "Ok, that's the last of it." He sat down next to Sam and looked seriously into her eyes. "This place has a lot of hidden security devices. There are cameras at the front entrance, in the main hallway, and here in your living room."

Sam looked up where he was pointing and saw a plant hanging from the ceiling. She guessed correctly that the camera was hidden behind the plant.

"We also have listening devices set up throughout the entire apartment. Although we continuously monitor the outside camera, we only check the inside devices from time to time. We want to give you as much privacy as possible, but we still need to keep an eye on you. The character that we are dealing with is very dangerous and very smart."

"Do you think he will find me here?" Sam asked quietly.

"I don't want to wait to find out. My plan is to purposely lead him to you. If we can get him on camera either threatening you or trying to harm you in any way, we'll at least have a case against him there. Plus, we might be able to shed some light on what happened to his mother." Sergeant D'Vincio watched her face for a moment. "Don't worry," he added. "We won't let him hurt you."

"I know. I just want this to be over with."

He stood up and turned towards the door. "I better get going. Are you going to be ok?"

Sam nodded. "Yes, sir, I'll be fine."

"Ok then, I'll call you tomorrow to tell you what our next step will be."

Sam stood up and walked him back to the front door. When he left, Sam turned and looked around the apartment again. She shook her head and started to put her things away. She felt like a robot whose life was being run by someone else.

This is getting old, she thought to herself.

Sam lay awake most of the night, just staring up at the ceiling. When the phone rang the next morning, it felt to Sam like she had just fallen asleep. She reached over and grabbed the phone. "Hello?"

"Sam? It's Sergeant D'Vincio. Get dressed and I will be there to pick you up for breakfast in about an hour." He hung up the phone and Sam moaned.

She got up out of bed and moved her weary body into the bathroom to take a shower. She had just put on some sweats when she heard knocking at the front door.

"Hi, sarge," she said as she opened the door.

"Good morning. Are you ready for breakfast?"

"Uh huh." She grabbed her purse and followed him out to his car.

He drove her to a café that was about a block from her apartment. He grabbed a file out of the glove box and they went in and sat down. After they ordered their breakfast, the sergeant looked at Sam with a serious look on his face.

"Samantha, you may not like what I am about to ask you to do."

"If it will put Kyle behind bars, I will do anything."

He cleared his throat and opened the file in front of him. "As I recall, when we first talked, there was a friend of yours that you felt had betrayed you, is that correct?"

"Yes, you are talking about Laura, but what does that..."

He held up a hand to stop her from talking. "I am about to tell you. This friend of yours, Laura, had slept with Kyle and then she, in a sense, became captivated by him as well, right?" She nodded. "Ok, then based on Kyle's past actions, I'll bet that he is staying close to her just in case you decide to call her again."

Sam shook her head. "But why would I possibly want to call her again after what she did to me?"

"You have to think about this the way Kyle would. You were friends with her long before you ever met Kyle. You two shared a special bond. In reality, that bond was broken when she betrayed you, but Kyle will probably think that you will someday start to miss her. I want to take advantage of that possibility."

Sam nodded as she started to understand what he was implying. "In other words, you want me to call her and pretend that I have forgiven her and that I miss her and that I want to get chummy with her again?"

"Maybe not that extreme, but you have the right idea. For starters, I want you to give her the phone number to your new apartment and I am trusting that she will in turn give it to Kyle."

"I'm sure she will," Sam said sarcastically.

He smiled. "Do you think that you can handle it?"

Sam smiled and gave him a determined look. "Let's do it," she said.

CHAPTER 62

Sam stared at the phone nervously and again went over what she was going to say to Laura. She hated the thought of even talking to her on the phone, but she knew that this was something that she had to do and that she would have to sound convincing.

Sergeant D'Vincio had thought it would be best if he left her alone to make the call and Sam was grateful. She knew that she would be nervous enough just being by herself. She picked up the phone and dialed Laura's number. It was kind of funny how, after all this time, she still had the number memorized.

The phone rang several times and Sam was about to hang up when Laura answered.

"Hello," she said rudely. She also sounded out of breath.

Sam could tell by how annoyed Laura sounded that she must have interrupted her old friend's exercise workout. She smiled as she remembered just how mad Laura used to get when the phone rang while she was exercising.

"Hello, Laura, it's Sam." Sam waited for Laura to catch her breath. "It's been a long time, hasn't it?"

Laura did not say anything for a moment, although Sam could still hear her breathing hard. When she finally did speak, she sounded surprised.

"Sami? Is that really you? I didn't think I was ever going to hear from you again."

Sam lowered her voice and tried to sound sincere. "I have been thinking about you a lot lately. We have been friends for so long that I don't think that we should let someone like Kyle get in the way of our friendship. I really just want to put the past behind us, if you can do that, too. I miss what we had; we were so close."

Laura cleared her voice. "Yeah, we were really close once. I'm glad that you decided not to let my relationship with Kyle get in the way of what we had."

Sam shook her head. It made her sick to think of Laura sleeping with Kyle. Sam knew that she should have responded to what Laura had said, but

210

she just could not get herself to speak. Instead, Laura continued to talk.

"I heard that you have been moving around a lot. So where are you living now?"

Sam took a deep breath. This was not as easy as she had thought it would be.

"Sam? Are you still there?"

Sami tried to think quickly. "Oh, I'm sorry. I was just thinking about old times. You wanted to know where I was living, right? Well, I'm still living in the city, although I have a place of my own now." Sam remembered that the sergeant had wanted her to stress that she was alone, and Laura took the bait.

"Oh? You're living alone now? No boyfriends or roommates?"

"No, why do you ask, Laura?"

Laura cleared her voice and tried unsuccessfully to sound nonchalant. "Oh, no reason. I just thought you might get lonely being by yourself."

"No, not at all. I see you are still living at home with your mom, though."

"Yeah, well, it beats paying bills. My mom is still out of town most of the time so it works out pretty well."

"So, are you still seeing Kyle, or are you dating anyone else special?" Sam asked the question, hoping that Laura would be honest with her. From what Laura had already told her, Sam was pretty sure that they were still seeing each other, but Sergeant D'Vincio had wanted her to know for sure.

Laura, however, did not seem to know how to answer the question. "Well, I, um, I don't know. I'm not really serious with anyone right now."

Sam shook her head. It was as if Laura was afraid to admit that she was still seeing Kyle. *I wonder why,* she thought to herself. Sam decided to play on her friend's uneasiness.

"What? Is this the Laura I used to know? Isn't this the Laura that could not survive without at least one man hanging all over her?"

Laura was quiet for a moment, but then she cleared her voice and spoke very quietly. "I guess I am just not the Laura you used to know."

Suddenly Sam felt sorry for her. *What if Kyle has the same type of hold on Laura that he had once had on me,* she thought to herself.

Sam was sincerely worried. "Seriously, Laura, are you ok?"

"Really Sam, don't worry about me. So anyway, can I have your telephone number? You know, so I can call you now and then."

"Yes, Laura, you can have my telephone number." *So you can give it to Kyle and I can get on with my life.* Sam gave her the telephone number and they spoke for a few more minutes.

When Sam hung up she felt depressed. She was disappointed that her old friend had not done something more with her life, not to mention her still being involved with Kyle. Sam started thinking about her own life. She thought about her education and wondered if she would ever get her degree. School, of course, reminded her of Austin and when she thought about him, she always smiled. After what had happened back in Missouri, she felt somehow closer to Austin. Sam picked up the phone again and started to dial his number. Before she had finished dialing, she hung the phone back up again. She was in too much of a sentimental mood to call him and she also remembered that the phones were being bugged. That was all she needed – a bunch of cops eating pizza and laughing while they listened to her get all emotional on the phone. Instead of making the call, she stood up and went into the kitchen to make herself a cup of hot tea.

She was sitting at the small kitchen table lost in her thoughts when the phone rang. She went into the living room, half expecting the call to be from Kyle.

"Hello," she answered.

"Samantha, it's Sergeant D'Vincio again. Are you alright?"

Sam relaxed and then she sat back down on the couch. She wondered if he had been listening in on the phone call. "Yes, sir, I'm ok."

"Well, how did it go? What do you think?"

"Well, let's just say it pretty much went the way you expected it would. She grabbed on to the fact that I am living alone and she wanted my phone number. When I asked her if she had a boyfriend or if she was still seeing Kyle, she stuttered and never really answered me directly. From the way she talked, though, I'm pretty sure that they are still involved."

"Hmm. Ok, so now we see if Kyle calls. Keep me informed, and Samantha, you did well."

Sam hung up the phone and sat back. She looked up at the hidden camera and then back at the phone again. She sighed loudly.

"Ok, Kyle, hurry up and call me so I can get on with my life."

CHAPTER 63

Several days passed and Sam continued to stay by the phone. One cold evening, Sam had fallen asleep on the couch, when suddenly the phone rang, startling her. She quickly grabbed the phone, not quite awake yet.

"Hello," she mumbled.

"Hello again, Samantha." Kyle's voice rang out loudly and Sam instantly came alert. She instinctively glanced at the hidden camera.

"How did you find me this time?" Sam tried to sound scared and unsuspicious.

"Oh, I have my ways."

Yeah, right, Sam thought to herself.

She knew that she had to keep him on the line for a while so the police would be able to trace the call.

"So, what do you want from me now, Kyle?"

"You surprised me, leaving your family the way you did. You were smart though, because this really is just between you and me."

Sam's eyes lit up with fire and hatred. "How can you tell me that this is just between you and me? In case you forgot, you put my sister in the hospital."

Kyle laughed. "Gee, Sam, I don't know what you are talking about. Accuse me all you want; you know you don't have any proof."

"Oh, that's what you…"

Kyle interrupted Sam. "Sorry, babe, time's up, got to run. Don't worry, I'll be talking to you very soon." He laughed and hung up.

Sam slammed the phone down. She was furious and she was shaking all over. The phone rang again almost instantly and she quickly grabbed it.

"Samantha, it's ok, it's me," Sergeant D'Vincio quickly reassured her.

"I hope you got a trace on that bastard. Please excuse my language, but, oh, does he get my blood boiling."

"Well, take a deep breath. Unfortunately he was playing it safe and hung up just before we could get a trace on him. At least our suspicions were confirmed about Laura still being connected to Kyle."

"Yeah, great. So now what?"

"Now we sit still and wait for his next move."

Sam shook her head and hung up. She was starting to get tired of all of the games everyone seemed to be playing. There were always "next moves" that she was waiting on and none of them ever seemed to bring them any closer to ending this charade.

The next day Laura called and when she spoke, her voice sounded shaky and nervous.

"Hello, Sami? How are you doing?

"Oh, just fine, and you?" Sam knew that she probably sounded somewhat sarcastic, but she really did not care anymore.

"Fine. Look, um, can you meet me at the park over by where we used to, um, you know, go to school?"

"When?"

"Tomorrow, say about two o'clock?"

"You got it, Laura."

"Hey, and Sami? No police." She hung up and left Sam staring at the phone.

CHAPTER 64

Sam shook nervously as the female officer hooked the wire underneath her sweater. She watched Sergeant D'Vincio, who was standing by the front door talking to another officer, and she took a few deep breaths to calm herself down. Sam pulled her sweater down over the wire and turned back to look at the sergeant expectantly. He caught her eye, and then came over and put his hand on her shoulder.

"Are you going to be ok?"

Sam kept shifting her weight. "Yeah, I'm just a nervous wreck."

He smiled reassuringly. "You will be ok. Remember that my men will be all around you. If he shows up and tries anything, nothing will happen to you."

Sam smiled nervously. "I keep trying to convince myself that he can't hurt me now."

"It's time to go," an officer yelled from the kitchen.

"Alright, Samantha," the sergeant said as he looked into her eyes. "You know what to do. We brought your pickup here – you will be driving in your truck and we will be following behind."

Sam walked out to her truck. Her mind was racing with a thousand thoughts; *what if he is hiding and shoots at me? What if he grabs me before anyone can do anything?* Sam tried to calm herself down. The sergeant had told her that he was convinced that Kyle had an entirely different reason for this meeting in the park, and that he was too smart to try anything. Sam hoped that he was right.

Sam drove through the familiar neighborhood where she had grown up. When she reached the park, she parked her car and slowly walked over to the swings. She ran her fingers along one of the swing's chains as she looked around and wondered which of the people around her where undercover police. There were joggers, people walking their dogs, and even a homeless person digging through the trash. She laughed to herself. In the movies, the homeless person was always the undercover cop.

"Sami?"

Sam turned around and saw Laura standing behind her. She gasped as she looked at her old friend. Laura had a black eye and a cut over her lip and Sam could imagine what other injuries she probably had as well.

"Here, Sami." Laura handed her an envelope and started to turn away.

"Laura, wait." Laura stopped, but did not look back at Sam. "Don't walk away from me, I can help you."

Laura slowly turned to look at her old friend. "Don't you think that you have done enough? You just don't understand."

Sam smiled kindly. "But I do. Did you forget that he beat me for a year and a half? I got away from him and so can you."

Laura shook her head and looked around. "He is here somewhere, watching us. I can't take the chance."

Sam shuddered at the thought of Kyle watching them, hidden and unseen. "Laura, I can't beat him alone, but together we can stop him. Don't you see that? Please don't walk away. There are people who can help you, too."

Tears were rolling down Laura's cheeks. "I really wish..." She looked emotionally at Sam and then she turned and started to run off in the opposite direction.

"Laura!" Sam screamed after her, but her friend never stopped and never looked back again.

Sam looked down at the envelope that Laura had handed to her. She tore it open and read it softly aloud, for the sake of the officers who had her wired.

"Hello again, Samantha," she read, "I was not sure if you would really come, but I knew that if you did, it would not be alone.

"I know the real reason why you called Laura, and it was not to reconcile an old friendship. I am really disappointed in you, Samantha. Do you think that I am stupid?

"Did you know that I am here at the park right now, watching you, and I guarantee that your police friends will not find me. I am sure that as I watch you, I am hating you even more than before.

"Knowing you the way I do, I am sure you were probably expecting me to jump out of the bushes shooting, but what I have in store for you is not that simple.

"I must admit that at first you were making the chase interesting, but the game is getting boring. It is just not challenging enough. Don't you see that all you are doing is prolonging the inevitable?

"Don't think you can ever outrun me either, for I will always find you. See you soon, Samantha. Kyle."

Sam crumpled the letter and stuffed it into her pocket. She knew that Sergeant D'Vincio would be furious that she had done that, but at this point, she did not care. She ran back to her truck and quickly left the parking lot. The sergeant had told her to drive around for a while, just in case Kyle decided to follow her, and she was paranoid enough to follow his instructions before heading home.

He watched the confrontation between Laura and Sam and was furious to see Laura staying to talk to her. Laura would have to be punished for disobeying him. He watched Sam read the letter and then run to her car. He smiled. He knew that it would be a waste of time to follow her, and besides, he had more important things to take care of at the moment. He had accomplished what he had wanted to and now it was time to take care of a very, very bad little girl.

She had only been back at her apartment for ten minutes when the sergeant was knocking on her door. When he came in, she handed him the crumpled letter and then she sat down on the couch. He sat down next to her and silently read over the letter.

Sam turned to look at him. "You know, sarge, I really thought that things were going to be easier than this."

He stood up and smiled. "Life is never that easy, Samantha. I need to take this letter to the station. Are you going to be ok?"

Sam shrugged. "Yeah, sure."

"I'll check on you later." He walked out, leaving Samantha to dwell on her own thoughts.

CHAPTER 65

The day after Sam's meeting in the park, she got a disturbing call from Sergeant D'Vincio.

"I need you to come down to the station right away," he had told her.

"What is it? What's wrong?"

"Just please come down here, I will explain it all to you when you get here."

Sam got to the police station as quickly as she could and hurried to the sergeant's office. She was breathing hard as she knocked on his office door.

"Come in," she heard him call out.

Sam opened the door and immediately noticed his face change when he saw that it was her. He motioned for her to sit down.

"Alright, Sergeant," Sam said nervously. "What is going on?"

"Sam, I need you to go to the hospital with me."

"The hospital?" Suddenly Sam panicked. "Is my family alright?"

"It's not your family, Samantha." He looked down for a moment and when he looked back up at her, she did not like the look in his eyes. "Earlier this morning the body of a young girl was found behind a trash dumpster downtown. We are pretty sure it is your friend Laura. Her mother is out of town and we have been unable to reach her – Sam, we need you to identify her body."

Sam froze. "Oh God, no. What happened?" She closed her eyes as tears started to roll down her cheeks and her hands started to shake.

"You don't need to worry about that right now…"

"Just tell me what happened. I have to know," she screamed.

He took a deep breath. "Apparently she was beaten to death."

"No." Sam dropped her face into her hands and started sobbing uncontrollably. Sergeant D'Vincio got up and walked around his desk. He put his hand on her shoulder and tried to comfort her. This was one part of his job that he hated the most.

Sam looked up at him. "It's not fair, sarge. How can one man go around and destroy so many lives so easily?"

"I don't know, Sam. My job is to try and catch them so justice can be served. I have never been able to understand why they do what they do."

Sam stood up. "Yeah, well the way I see it, if you had been doing your job, maybe my friend wouldn't be dead."

He looked away and Sam saw the look of pain cross his face. Sam sighed. She knew that she had no reason to talk to him like that.

"I'm sorry, Sergeant. I know that you are doing the best you can. I am just really frustrated right now. Why don't we just go to the hospital and get this over with."

They walked quietly out to a waiting patrol car and neither of them spoke during the short ride to the hospital. As she followed him down the hospital corridor, a thought occurred to her.

"Sergeant, you and I know that Kyle did this to her. Were there any witnesses or any evidence at all that could lead to his arrest?"

He shook his head. "Not at this point, but forensics is working on it." He stopped in front of a door and motioned for her to go ahead of him. When she walked in, a horrible smell surrounded her and she thought she was going to be sick. She covered her nose and mouth with her hand and looked pleadingly at the sergeant. He handed her a rag that she gratefully held over her face. She turned back around and saw tables lined up with bodies covered in sheets. She felt sick again and was afraid to go any further. She started to take a step back when the sergeant gently grabbed her arm.

"You are the only one who can do this right now, Samantha. We need you."

Sam swallowed hard and walked to the table that he led her to. She nodded her head and an attendant lifted up the sheet. Sam gasped. It was Laura and she was so badly beaten that Sam almost did not recognize her. She looked away and the sergeant nodded to the attendant who immediately dropped the sheet back down. He took Sam's arm and led her back into the hallway.

"I am really sorry I had to put you through this, Samantha. This just gives me that much more reason to get this guy. I have some more ideas on what..."

Sam was shaking her head. "No. No more ideas. No more plans. I can't do this anymore. If Kyle had his way it would be me on that table instead of Laura. I can't let any more people get hurt – or killed for that matter. I should have called the police back when he was first abusing me because maybe then I would have had a case, but not now. Now all I have is a life of torment, a sister who has had to go through months of plastic surgery, and a friend who will never get a chance to get married or have children. Don't you see? I need to get my life back together again. I'm tired of trying this and trying that, and for what? All that happens is Kyle calls and laughs about how predictable I am or how the game is not challenging enough for him. That is all this is to him; a game. Well, I quit. Please, just take me back to my car."

Sergeant D'Vincio nodded, understanding that she was just upset after having to identify her friend's body. He took her back to the station where she silently went back to her truck and drove away. As he watched her leave, he decided that he would give her a few days and then he would call her about his new plan. She never gave him the chance.

Sam went directly from the police station to a moving van company where she rented a small van. She went back to the apartment and packed everything into it. The phone rang constantly while she worked, but she never answered it. She just did not care anymore. If it was Kyle, he would just laugh at her, and if it was Sergeant D'Vincio, he would just urge her to help him get Kyle. She just could not do it anymore.

After most of her belongings were in the truck, Sam made a few phone calls. She finally found an apartment complex that had a unit available and she made her way over to her new home.

Once she got all of her things into the new apartment, Sam relaxed. She felt a freedom that she had not felt for a long time.

She looked around and thought about how much she had changed. She was a totally different person than she used to be. She sighed as she thought about how crazy she and Laura had been.

"Boy, Laura, we sure used to get drunk," Sam said out loud as she laughed. "Do you remember the time that your mom caught us and kicked me out of your house?" Sam looked down at her hands as tears started to fall down her cheeks. "I'm sure going to miss you, Laura. Why did he do this to you?"

Sam grabbed a box of her things and opened it up. On the top there were some pictures in a small bag. She pulled them out and found an old picture of her and Laura. She held the picture close to her chest and cried for the loss of her old friend and for the things that had happened that never should have.

CHAPTER 66

Two days after she had moved in to her new apartment, Sam's phone got hooked up. She had avoided calling her family to tell them about Laura for several reasons. The main reason being, of course, that she did not want to face Sergeant D'Vincio once he realized that she had disappeared without telling him that she was leaving. But she also needed some quiet time to herself so that she could try to deal with the loss of her friend.

It took a couple of days for the reality of what happened to finally sink in and when it did, she called her mother. Both her mother and sister were shocked to find out about Laura, and they both said that they would be by her side at the funeral, which was to be that following weekend. Sam also called Austin and told him what was going on. He was also very supportive and, although he could not be there for her, he let her know how much he cared. Sam did not tell him that she had decided not to continue pursuing Kyle, fearful of hearing the same disappointment that everyone else was showing.

The day of Laura's funeral, Sam was an emotional wreck. She could not stand still and, as she paced around her living room, she realized how much she dreaded going to the funeral parlor. She knew that before she could handle going to the funeral, she first had to face Laura' mother. She drove over to her house and sat outside in her car for a moment. She finally walked up to the front door and rang the doorbell. When Laura's mother answered the door, her eyes were swollen and red and she looked at Sam with so much pain it tore at Sam's heart. She stepped aside to let Sam in and Sam quietly walked past her. They walked into the living room and sat down on different chairs.

"I know that you probably hate me right now," Sam said with tears starting to flow down her cheeks, "but I have grown up a lot and I am so, so sorry for all of the pain that I caused you over the years. Laura was my best friend and like a sister to me. Somewhere along the line things got really messed up, and I had to tell you that I'm sorry that I couldn't fix it." Sam was crying so hard that she could hardly talk.

Lorraine Steiner looked over at Sam as tears ran down her own cheeks. "You know what Laura said to me the last time I saw her? She said 'Mom, why did you always have to be out of town working? You have no idea who I am anymore or what I am going through.' You know what, Sam? She was right. I spent so much time traveling around with my job, thinking that the more money I made the better off Laura would be, but I lost my little girl. I saw her at the morgue, you know. I didn't even recognize her."

Sam quietly watched her as she continued. "I'm sorry, too, that I wasn't there for you girls. There is so much that I might have been able to change had I just been here more."

Sam walked over to her and Laura's mom cried in her friend's arms. She cried for the daughter she never really knew and for all of the lost years that were now gone forever. They talked for a short time and Sam felt a huge weight off of her shoulders for having been forgiven for leading Laura down the path she had led her. Before Sam left, Lorraine asked if Sam would say a few words about Laura at the funeral. Sam went back to her apartment and tried to put aside all of the feelings she had towards the end and tried to only remember the good times that they had growing up together. After several futile tries, she ended up writing a short poem – one which she hoped she would have the strength to read.

Sam started to pace back and forth in her living room, trying to figure out how she was going to handle going to the funeral. She jumped when her doorbell rang and when she opened the door and saw her mother and sister, she just fell into her mother's arms. They stood in the doorway for a moment and then they finally went into the living room.

It had been almost a month since she had seen her family and she now realized just how much she had missed them.

"I'm so glad you guys are here."

Jessica reached over and took Sam's hand. "You have been through so much, little sister."

Her mother sat down and looked over at Sam seriously. "Honey, I know that you don't like talking about this and maybe right now is not the best time, but I wish that you would think about what you are doing. I mean, look at everything that Kyle has done; he has put your sister through hell and there is not a day that goes by that we are not afraid that he will be back. And now, today, we are having to go to the funeral of someone so young." She shook her head. "I understand the frustration that you feel, but I think you should keep with it. He will keep running the streets until someone like you does something about it."

Sam looked at her in frustration. "You know what, Mom? First I don't do the right thing. I just sit and let the jerk do whatever he wants to me. Then I finally get the nerve to do what I thought was the right thing, and my friend ends up dead. I don't even know what the 'right thing to do' is anymore. All I know is that too many people have gotten hurt or killed and I am over it." She paused and shrugged her shoulders. "The problem is that none of our efforts have gone anywhere. Now I really don't want to talk about it anymore."

Sam's mother smiled apologetically. "I'm sorry, honey. I know you have enough things to worry about right now."

Sam's mom drove them to the funeral. There was a small gathering of people, most of whom Sam knew. Laura's mother was standing at the front and Sam tried to comfort her. Sam was relieved to know that Laura's mother did not know about Kyle or what had been going on. She questioned Sam about the changes she had been starting to see in Laura, but Sam just told her that they had not seen each other in quite some time. Sam felt it was easier that way. If the police were ever to tie Kyle to Laura's death, maybe the truth would come out then.

Just before the service started, Sam turned and looked around at the small crowd of people who were seated behind them. She saw Sergeant D'Vincio standing in the back row and when he caught her looking at him he nodded. She turned back and grabbed tightly to her mother and sister's hands. Seeing him there made her wonder if Kyle was there too, hiding somewhere as he watched Sam grieve. She shook her head and tried to concentrate on the service.

The pastor of a local church gave a wonderful sermon that gave Sam a sense of peace inside believing that her friend was now in a better place. Laura's mother and grandmother each gave a heartwarming and tearful speech about how wonderful Laura had been and how much they would miss her.

Suddenly it was Sam's turn. She took a deep breath and approached the podium at the front of the room. When she turned around and saw all of the faces watching her, she froze. She slowly looked around until she was looking into Lorraine Steiner's eyes. She could see her long time friend staring back at her through her mother's eyes. Sam looked down at her hands for a moment and then calmly looked back up.

"Laura and I had been friends for a long time," she began. "We grew up together. Unfortunately sometimes when we get older we tend to lose track of those who have meant the most to us in life. Although Laura and I were away from each other for a while, I will never forget the special friendship and bond that we shared. When we were younger, Laura and I used to write poems for each other." Sam smiled and then blushed slightly. "I've written a short poem for her that I would like to share with you now." Sam cleared her throat.

She closed her eyes and pictured Laura's face in her mind. When she opened her eyes, she spoke the words that she had written from her heart.

Wish upon a silver moon,
A single heart in time,
Such a young and innocent,
Dear young friend of mine.
A single cross with our love,
Upon a mountain high,
In the clouds soar memories,
To never say goodbye.

By the time she finished her poem, Sam had tears flowing down her cheeks. When she glanced at Laura's mother, she saw that she too had tears, but that she was smiling at Sam.

Sam walked back to her seat and then one of Laura's aunts sang "Amazing Grace." Sam closed her eyes again and silently asked God to take care of her friend.

After the funeral, everyone went to Laura's house. Sam felt uncomfortable being there after everything that had happened, but she stayed, out of respect. The entire time Sam noticed Sergeant D'Vincio watching her, although he always kept his distance. Just before Sam and her family were ready to leave, she decided to approach him, but he had disappeared. She shrugged and left with her family.

CHAPTER 67

Sam slowly started to pull her life back together. She had found a job that was within walking distance of her apartment and, realizing that summer was approaching, she had also called a few of the area colleges to get registration information. She had decided that she wanted to go back to school the following fall semester. Although she desperately missed Austin and the small college in Missouri, she felt if would be best if she just stayed in Denver.

Sam and Austin talked to each other on the phone or wrote letters constantly. As much as she loved to hear from him, she was sure that he must have had another girlfriend back in Missouri by now. It was something that they often argued about.

"Don't you realize how much you mean to me, Sam?" he had said to her on the phone one morning.

Sam shook her head in frustration, which she always did when they had this conversation. "I know you care, Austin, but no one in their right mind would sit and wait for someone that may never be available."

"But you are available and I know that once you get the past settled, you will be ready to start your life over again. Until that time comes, I will be waiting. I have done a lot of changing, Sami, especially after you left. Something like this makes a person grow up and mature, you know? Besides," he said obnoxiously, "I like Colorado. I may just move there sometime."

Sam ignored his last comment. She was not in a joking mood. "Austin, you do not know how long it will take for me to, as you put it, get my past settled. As long as Kyle is running around a free man, I don't know if I can. I am so tired of always looking over my shoulder, why would I want to drag someone else that I care about into it, too?"

Austin lowered his voice. "Sam, honey, you know that you do not have to look over your shoulder anymore. All you have to do is say the word and I will be there to protect and love you."

Sam smiled as she cradled the phone against her ear. "You are so sweet, Austin. I do want us to have a future someday, but I want it to be when I can be with you because I love you, not because I need you."

"Sam, when two people are in love, they should be able to rely on each other, to feel like they need one another, not just love one another."

"You know that is not the need I am talking about."

Austin sighed. It was a never ending battle with her and he often wondered if he would ever win.

Sam wondered what he was thinking. "You got quiet all of a sudden," she said, hoping he would open up to her again.

"Oh, Sam, I just keep wondering when we are going to stop this argument and move forward with our lives."

"Now you know why I am so sure that you have a new girlfriend."

Austin pulled the phone away from his ear and looked at it as if he was seeing Sam. "I give up," he mumbled.

Sam laughed, "I heard that."

Austin laughed despite his frustration. "Girl, you are going to drive me insane. By the time you get off of the crazy wagon you're on, you will be visiting me in the nut-house."

They talked for a little while longer and, as it always did, their conversation ended pleasantly. Every time she talked to him, she always felt a lot of conflicting emotions. Of course she was always worried that he would finally have had enough and want to get on with his life, although he always seemed pretty determined to not give up. She was also very confused about how she felt about him. She knew she cared very deeply for him, but she was afraid to admit that she might be in love with him. Despite all of her many fears, she knew that he was a very special man; one who she really did hope would not give up on her.

After talking to Austin, Sam realized that she still had a lot of unanswered questions in her mind and that she needed to confront Sergeant D'Vincio about them. Although she had not discussed them with anyone up to this point, she knew that she had to find out the answers. She picked up the phone and held it for a moment. She took a deep breath as she called the sergeant's number. When he answered, he did not sound surprised to hear from her.

"Hello, Samantha. How have you been?"

"Fine, Sergeant. I'm sorry it took me so long to call you. I guess I owe you an apology for running off the way I did." The sergeant did not say anything, so she continued. "There was so much unfinished business, if you want to call it that, when I left. There are some things that keep nagging me and I was wondering if I could ask you about them."

"What kind of things?"

Sam took another deep breath. "Well, for one, did anyone ever question

Kyle about his mother's death?"

Sergeant D'Vincio coughed on the other line before he spoke. "Yes, we finally did question him about his mother. In fact, we asked him about it when we questioned him about Laura's death. Of course he denied knowing anything about either situation. He claimed that he and Laura were just friends and that he did not keep track of what went on in her life and he also denied having gone to visit his mother."

"What? But he told me that he had gone out to see her."

"That is what you are saying and I believe you, but in court that won't hold up as evidence. Apparently his mother lived in a very remote area and very few people knew her. In fact, when officers questioned those people who had known her, none of them even knew that she had a son and no one had noticed anyone visiting her at the time of her death. If he had indeed gone out there, he did it in such a way that he would not be seen."

Sam shook her head. "What about Laura? I'm sure that there were people that noticed her and Kyle spending a lot of time together. And didn't you see the bruises on her face that day I met her in the park?"

"Samantha, you never told me that you had seen bruises on her face and from where we stood, we could not see her face clearly. As far as Laura's friends and family were concerned, her mother was out of town all of the time and did not even know anything about Kyle, and Laura had disassociated herself from all of her other friends. There is absolutely no plausible evidence that links Kyle to either situation. Besides, you know as well as I do that unless Laura had admitted to someone that Kyle had hit her, there is no way that we can legally point a finger at him."

When Sam hung up the phone, she had an emptiness inside of her that left her feeling numb. Kyle had literally gotten away with murder and there was nothing anyone seemed to be able to do about it.

CHAPTER 68

Sam was cleaning her apartment on a sunny spring day and listening to some music when the phone rang. She danced her way over to the phone and picked it up.

"Hello," she said.

"Samantha, it's Sergeant Joe D'Vincio. How are you?"

She immediately tensed up. "Hold on a second, sarge." Sam set the phone down and ran over to her stereo to turn down the music. She came back to the phone and picked it back up.

"Sorry about that. I am doing ok, although I have a little spring fever. How about you?" She hoped that he did not pick up the nervousness in her voice.

"I am ok. Look, the reason I am calling is that I need you to come down to the station this afternoon."

Sam remembered the last time he had asked her to come down to the station, and once again she felt as if her heart had stopped. "What happened? What's wrong? Please tell me it's not someone from my family. I don't think I can handle that again."

"No, nothing like that. I'll explain everything when you get here. What time can you be here?"

Sam looked at her watch. It was almost noon. "How about three-thirty this afternoon? I have some things I need to take care of first."

"Perfect. I'll see you then."

Sam hung up the phone and wondered why he would want her to come down to the station. She was about to get back to her cleaning when the phone rang again. She grabbed it, wondering if Sergeant D'Vincio had forgotten to tell her something.

"Hello," she answered again nervously.

"Boy, don't we sound cheery." It was Austin.

Sam laughed. "Sorry. I just got a strange call from the sergeant and I was trying to figure out what might be going on."

Austin sounded worried. "What did he say?"

"He just asked me to come down to the station."

228

"Is your family alright?"

"Yeah, he said it was something different than that. I just hope that whatever it is, that it's good. I don't know if it was my imagination or what, but there was something odd in the tone of his voice. I don't know how to explain it, but he just sounded different than he usually does."

"Well, please let me know as soon as you can, ok?"

Sam smiled. "You got it. Hey listen, I don't mean to sound rude, but I need to get some things done before I meet him this afternoon. Can I call you tonight?"

"Sure. What time are you meeting Sergeant D'Vincio?"

"Three-thirty, why?"

"Never mind. I will talk to you tonight."

Sam hung up the phone and rushed to finish her cleaning. She ran some errands and then spent some time trying to prepare herself for the upcoming meeting. At three o'clock she left to go to the police station. She got more and more nervous as she let her imagination go wild. She must have thought about a million different things that he might be telling her; all of which were horrible, to say the least.

When she got to his office, she knocked on the door. He opened the door and smiled when he saw her standing there.

"You look nice, Samantha."

"Thanks. So don't keep me in suspense, what is going on?"

He motioned for her to come into his office and sit down. He went back to his desk and looked at Sam pensively for a moment.

"Sam, we have arrested Kyle."

Sam sat up in her seat. "What? How? What did you arrest him for? Was it for Laura's murder?"

His face got serious as he explained what Kyle had done. "Apparently he had viciously raped and beaten a fifteen-year-old girl, leaving her for dead."

"Oh, my gosh," Sam said, shocked.

"Well, the girl did not die and she identified Kyle. We had our artist do up a picture of him, and it matched what we had on file. As soon as she got out of the hospital, she identified him in a lineup. Sure enough, she identified Kyle."

"That poor girl. Do you want me to talk to her, maybe try to comfort her?"

"No, Samantha, not right now. She is getting some very good help professionally. The reason I called you in here was so that you could also identify him in a police lineup."

Sam shook her head in confusion. "Why? I don't understand."

"Let me put it this way. If the man you pick out turns out to be the same man that this young girl picked out, we can use your testimony in court."

Sam looked up at the sergeant, not sure how to react.

"Samantha, I want you to understand that you probably would not get anywhere if you tried to press charges at this point, but you could make this girl's case against him even stronger. You could be, in a sense, a character witness that works against him. In other words, Samantha, your testimony, along with the indisputable proof we will present, could very well be what leads the jury to find Kyle guilty beyond any reasonable doubt, as well as for the judge to give him a longer and tougher sentence."

Sam looked down at her hands. The thought of seeing Kyle again after all of this time frightened her. She also knew that, for Laura's sake, she had to do what was right. She set up a time for the next day to view the lineup.

There were so many roses and they were leaning towards her, just out of her reach. She reached out for them but stopped. There was blood dripping from the thorns. Suddenly Kyle was there. He was laughing and he opened his hand and Laura was lying in his palm crying out to Sam. She tried to run to her but her feet were stuck. When she looked down she was falling and below her there was a bed of blood with chains all around it. She screamed and screamed. Suddenly Sam sat straight up in her bed. She was sweating and out of breath and it took her a moment to realize that she had only been dreaming.

At three in the morning Sam finally called Austin. She was so upset about the upcoming lineup that it was making her throw up. Austin calmed her down as best as he could and then she finally was able to get a couple hours of somewhat restless sleep.

The next morning Sam went to the police station. She was sweating and could not stop chewing on her nails. When she first entered the room it was so dark that she could barely see her hand in front of her face. Suddenly she heard Sergeant D'Vincio call out and a light came on behind a glass wall that was directly in front of her. She watched as a group of men were led out one by one into the small room in front of her. Suddenly she saw him and she froze. Everything around her seemed to be moving in slow motion and her whole body started to shake. It took her a moment to realize that she was actually staring at Kyle, the man who made her life hell for so long. She glared at him with so much hatred she was afraid that she might lunge out at the glass in front of her.

She could hear sergeant D'Vincio's voice from somewhere behind her. "Samantha Higgins, do you see the man who assaulted you?"

"Yes," she said quietly, pointing at Kyle. "That's him." Suddenly as if

Kyle had somehow heard her, he turned and looked straight at her. She gasped. She knew that he could not see her and yet she felt her knees give away from beneath her.

Suddenly she saw flashes of another time of her life; a time that she had long ago locked away to never be disturbed. Kyle was looking at her in such a caring way and she reached out towards him... Suddenly there was fierceness in his face... He was so angry and he was coming at her... *Noooo, don't hit me again*... There was so much darkness and so much pain... Kyle was screaming something at her... He was laughing as he popped the cork on the champagne bottle... Laughing... There were candles all around her and shadows dancing on the walls... Blood, there is so much blood everywhere... *Laura? Is that you Laura? Oh, please don't leave me, Laura... Oh God, help me...* Someone was calling her name in the distance...

"Samantha? Samantha, can you hear me?"

Samantha opened her eyes and saw Sergeant D'Vincio standing above her. She was lying in a fetal position on the floor and she looked up at him and started screaming hysterically.

"Why? Why did he have to do what he did to me, and to my sister, and especially to Laura? Why?" She cried as Sergeant D'Vincio held her and motioned for the other officer in the room to end the lineup.

"Samantha," he said as he pulled her up until she was sitting and looking at him. "There are not going to be any more games. We have Kyle now and we are not about to let him go. You don't have to be afraid anymore. It's finally going to be over this time."

"Yeah, but what if he gets out. What if he pleads insanity and worse yet only gets a couple of years in jail and is back out on the street."

"All you have to worry about is telling the truth about what he did to you and your family and friends. No jury in their right mind would want to see him loose out on the streets, Samantha. For right now, let's just take one day at a time, ok?"

Sam tried to regain control over her fears and emotions and calmly headed out of the lineup room. Seeing Kyle had brought out so many things in her mind that she wondered what she was going to do with her life. The thought that Kyle might someday find her again terrified her. What bothered her even more was that she suddenly realized how vulnerable she was. Who was to say that the next person who crossed her path might not just be another Kyle, waiting to find his next victim?

Sam closed her eyes and tried to clear her mind. Suddenly she jumped as someone put a hand on her shoulder. She turned around and blushed when she realized it was Sergeant D'Vincio.

"I'm sorry if I startled you, Samantha, but I wanted to give you this."

Sam looked down and took the business card out of his hand.

"What is this?"

"It's the name of a good therapist. I think that with her help, you can start to deal with those fears and emotions that you have been keeping bundled up inside of you. I think that she will really be a big help during the trial, too. You think about it, and I will be letting you know when we will be going to court. Take care of yourself, Samantha."

"Thank you for all of your help, and I'm sorry for being kind of rough on you at times."

Sergeant D'Vincio laughed. "Don't worry about it. It comes with the job."

Sam started to turn away but stopped and looked back at him. "Sarge?"

He stopped and turned to look back at her. Sam smiled. "Your family would be proud of you." He tilted his head slightly and smiled. She could see the appreciation in his eyes. He slowly turned and walked away.

Sam breathed in slowly and then also turned away to head out of the building. She was suddenly feeling better than she had in years. She glanced down at the card she held in her hand and then closed her fist tightly and smiled. She knew that once she entered the courtroom she would have to face everything she had been through, but she knew now that she would not have to face it alone. She took a deep breath, opened the main door and was immediately enveloped in a warm breeze. She closed her eyes, feeling the warmth of the sun on her face, and sighed with relief. *It really is finally over,* she thought to herself. For the hundredth time she thought back to when everything had begun four and a half years ago. As always, she wondered about everything she could have done to avoid all of the pain. There were so many things she wished she had done differently. *No,* she thought. *I have to stop this. It's time to move forward now.*

When she opened her eyes again, she gasped with surprise. There, standing at the bottom of the steps, was Austin, smiling up at her. She blushed when she realized that he had been watching her and then she laughed. She had a lot of work ahead of her, but seeing Austin waiting for her now gave her a new hope that everything would be ok. She walked down the steps to join him and deep inside she knew that she would finally be able to let go of the shadows of her past and begin to work on the brightness of her future.

*